Praise for *The Sisterhood of the Travelling Pants*:

'An outstanding and vivid book that will stay with readers for a long time. Readers will hope that Brashares chronicles the sisterhood for volumes to come.'
Publishers Weekly

'Convincingly and honestly written, this is a book that will help girls understand a little more the pains and hardships of teenage life . . . At the same time they'll be keen to know what happens to Lena, Tibby, Bridget and Carmen, as they continue to grow up. Let's hope Ann Brashares is ready to let us in on the story.'
Waterstone's Books Quarterly

'A wonderful story'
USA Today

'A feel-good novel of substance'
Kirkus Reviews

www.kids**at**random**house**.co.uk

Also by Ann Brashares and published by Corgi Books:

The Sisterhood of the Travelling Pants
The Second Summer of the Sisterhood

Girls in
Pants

GIRLS IN PANTS
A CORGI BOOK 978 0 552 55277 6 (from January 2007)
0 552 55277 1

First published in Great Britain by Corgi Books,
an imprint of Random House Children's Books

Originally published in the USA in 2003 by Delacorte Press
an imprint of Random House Children's Books

This edition published 2005

3 5 7 9 10 8 6 4

Papers used by Random House Children's Books are natural, recyclable
products made from wood grown in sustainable forests. The
manufacturing processes conform to the environmental regulations
of the country of origin.

Set in 12/14½ Bembo by
Falcon Oast Graphic Art Ltd.

Corgi Books are published by Random House Children's Books,
61–63 Uxbridge Road, London W5 5SA,
a division of The Random House Group Ltd,
in Australia by Random House Australia (Pty) Ltd,
20 Alfred Street, Milsons Point, Sydney, NSW 2061, Australia,
in New Zealand by Random House New Zealand Ltd,
18 Poland Road, Glenfield, Auckland 10, New Zealand,
and in South Africa by Random House (Pty) Ltd,
Isle of Houghton, Corner Boundary Road & Carse O'Gowrie
Houghton, 2198, South Africa.

THE RANDOM HOUSE GROUP Limited Reg. No. 954009
www.kidsatrandomhouse.co.uk

A CIP catalogue record for this book is available from the British Library.

Printed and bound in Great Britain by
Cox & Wyman Ltd, Reading, Berkshire.

Girls in Pants

Ann Brashares

Corgi Books

For Jacob,
my own worthy boy

Acknowledgements

First and always, I would like to acknowledge and thank Jodi Anderson. I also thank, with great warmth and editorial sisterhood, Wendy Loggia and Beverly Horowitz, and gratefully acknowledge the entire Random House Children's Books group, with special thanks to Marci Senders, Kathy Dunn, Judith Haut, Daisy Kline and Chip Gibson. I wish to thank Leslie Morgenstein, who's been in it from the beginning. And I thank my friend and agent, the incomparable Jennifer Rudolph Walsh.

I lovingly acknowledge my parents, Jane Easton Brashares and William Brashares, and my brothers, Beau, Justin and Ben Brashares. And last and most, my small tribe, Sam, Nathaniel and Susannah.

We, the Sisterhood, hereby instate the following rules to govern the use of the Travelling Pants:

1. You must never wash the Pants.

2. You must never double-cuff the Pants. It's tacky. There will never be a time when this will not be tacky.

3. You must never say the word 'phat' while wearing the Pants. You must also never think I am fat while wearing the Pants.

4. You must never let a boy take off the Pants (although you may take them off yourself in his presence).

5. You must not pick your nose while wearing the Pants. You may, however, scratch casually at your nostril while really kind of picking.

6. Upon our reunion, you must follow the proper procedures for documenting your time in the Pants.
   - On the left leg of the Pants, write the most exciting place you have been while wearing the Pants.
   - On the right leg of the Pants, write the most important thing that has happened to you while wearing the Pants. (For example, 'I hooked up with my second cousin, Ivan, while wearing the Travelling Pants.')

7. You must write to your Sisters throughout the summer, no matter how much fun you are having without them.

8. You must pass the Pants along to your Sisters according to the specifications set down by the Sisterhood. Failure to comply will result in a severe spanking upon our reunion.

9. You must not wear the Pants with a tucked-in shirt and belt. See rule #2.

10. Remember: Pants = love. Love your pals. Love yourself.

In summer, the song

sings itself.

—William Carlos Williams

PROLOGUE

If you are reading this, you may know about us. Or about our Pants, anyway. If you do, you can skip ahead a few pages. If you don't, hang here with me for a minute. I'll try to make it painless.

You may say, I don't want to read a book about pants. And I can understand how you feel. Especially if you're in Britain, where it means underwear. But trust me, these are epic Pants. These Pants have the stunning power to transform four ordinary teenage girls into raving beauties living lives of astonishing adventure, not to mention causing delicious young men to fall constantly at their feet.

OK, I exaggerate. They don't actually do that. But they do hold us together when we're apart. They make us feel secure and loved. They walk us to places we wouldn't otherwise dare to go. They help us know which boys are worthy and which ones are not. They make us better people and better friends. All this, I swear, is true.

And they look good along the way.

Who are we? We are we. We have always been we. Sometimes we are us. (Grammatically, it's just a fact.) It's all thanks to Gilda's gym in Bethesda, Maryland, for offering a prenatal aerobics class roughly eighteen years ago. My mom, Carmen's mom, Lena's mom and Bee's mom bounded and sweated through a long, pregnant summer and then they each gave birth to a baby girl (plus a baby boy, in Bee's mom's case) in September. As far as I can tell, in those first few years our mothers raised us more like a litter of puppies than as actual individual children. It was later that our mothers started to grow apart.

How can I describe the four of us? Let's use the metaphor of cars.

Carmen would be a torqued-up cherry-red gas-guzzler with a V-8 engine and four-wheel drive. She can make a mess of things, but she's a lot of fun, she sticks to the road, and she's got mad acceleration.

Lena would get good gas mileage. Like one of those hybrid cars. She would be easy on the environment and, of course, easy on the eyes. She would have state-of-the-art GPS, but it would be wrong sometimes. She would have air bags.

Bee would have no air bags. She might not have bumpers. She might not even have brakes. She would go a million miles an hour. She would be an ocean-blue Ferrari minus the brakes.

And I, Tibby, would be a . . . bike. No, just kidding. (I *am* old enough to drive, damn it!) Hmmm. What would I be? I would be a muscular Plymouth Duster, dark green, with a picky transmission. OK, maybe that's just what I'd *want* to be. But I'm the one writing this, so I get to decide.

The Pants first came to us at the perfect moment.

That is, when we were splitting up for the first time. It was two summers ago when they first worked their magic, and last summer when they shook up our lives once again. You see, we don't wear the Pants year-round. We let them rest during the year, so they are extra powerful when summer comes. (There was the time this winter when Carmen wore them to her mom's wedding, but that was a special case.)

We thought it was a big deal two years ago, our first summer apart. Now we're facing our last summer together. Tomorrow we graduate from high school. In September we go to college. And it's not like one of those TV shows where all of us magically turn up at the same college. We are going to four different schools in three different cities (but all within four hours of one another – that was our one rule).

Bee is the sloppiest student of us four and she got into every school she applied to. (Can you say all-American?) She chose Brown. Lena decided, against her parents' advice, to go to art school at the Rhode Island School of Design, Carmen is going to Williams just as she always dreamed, and I am starting film school at NYU.

As life changes go, it's really, really big. If you're my dad, you say, 'Hey. You'll see each other at Thanksgiving.' But if you're me, you realize that life as we've known it is over. Our shared childhood is ending. Maybe we'll never live at home again. Maybe we'll never all live in the same place again. We're headed off to start our real lives. To me that is awe-inspiring, but it is also the single scariest thought in the world.

Tomorrow night at Gilda's we'll launch the Pants on their third summer voyage. Tomorrow begins the time of our lives. It's when we'll need our Pants the most.

A fterwards, the

universe will explode

for your pleasure.

– Douglas Adams

'OK, Bee with Greta and Valia and Lena,' Carmen ordered, shepherding a wandering grandmother with her hand. Bee and Lena intertwined their legs, trying to tip each other over, as Carmen clicked her digital camera.

'OK, um. Effie and . . um, Perry. And Katherine and Nicky. With Tibby and Lena and Bee.'

Lena cast her a look. Lena hated pictures. 'Are you getting paid or something?' she asked grumpily.

Carmen pushed her hair off her sweaty neck. The shiny black gown permitted no flow of air. She shook off the mortarboard (who ever thought of that name?) and pressed it under her arm. 'Squeeze together, would you? I'm losing Perry.' Tibby's three-year-old sister, Katherine, bleated angrily as her older brother, Nicky, stomped on her foot.

It wasn't Carmen's fault her friends had large families. But it was graduation, for God's sake. This was a big day. She wasn't going to miss anybody. She didn't have any official brothers or sisters. She had to make the most of her unofficial ones.

'There is no shade,' Valia, Lena's grandmother, noted bitterly.

It was a football field. Carmen briefly imagined the

trouble with an elm or oak planted at the fifty-yard line. The thought of this made her turn towards the raucous bunch of graduating football players, their families and admirers. It was one of the many clumps and cliques spread out over the hot field – a last stand for social order.

Carmen's grandma, Carmen senior (Seniora, as Tibby called her), cast searing looks at Albert, Carmen's father, as though blaming him for the merciless heat. Carmen could practically read her grandmother's mind: if Albert could leave Christina, Carmen's mother, what couldn't that man be capable of?

'Now's the big one, OK, everybody?' It had been a long morning. Carmen knew she was wearing everyone thin. She was irritating herself at this point. But who else looked out for posterity? Huh? 'Last one, I *swear*.'

She arranged the dads and full-grown boys in the back. Even Lena's dad – not because he was tall (Bee had a good three inches on him) but because Carmen was a generally thoughtful person, if she did think so herself.

Grandmothers and mothers took the next row. Valia, Carmen senior, Tibby's ancient great-grandma Felicia, who didn't know where she was, Greta nervously patting her perm. Then there was Ari in her handsome beige suit, Christina constantly looking over her shoulder at her new husband, David, Tibby's mom with the lipstick on her teeth. And there was Albert's wife, Lydia, looking eager but also anxious that she might be taking up an extra square inch of space.

Lastly, Carmen ordered the remaining siblings into

19

place. Effie pulled a dire face about having to kneel on a level with Nicky and Katherine. Tibby coaxed Brian from his spot on the sidelines and arranged him in the back row.

And now it was the Septembers' turn. Sitting in the front, they clutched each other in a mass of hot black polyester, leaving a space in the middle for Carmen. 'OK! Great!' Carmen shouted at them all in encouragement. 'Just hold on one second.'

Carmen nearly wrestled Ms Collings from the dais. Ms. Collings was the teacher who'd sent Carmen out to the hallway the greatest number of times, but she was also the teacher who loved her best.

'We're all set,' Carmen said. 'Here.' She demonstrated to Ms Collings the camera placement she wanted. For a moment Carmen studied the viewfinder. She saw them all, encompassed in the little frame – her beloved friends, her mom, stepmom, stepdad, actual dad, grandma. Her friends' moms, dads, families who felt as close as if they were her own. This was her whole life, right here. Her tribe. Everything that mattered.

And this moment. This was it, somehow. All of them celebrating a day and an accomplishment that belonged to the four of them equally. This was the culmination of a shared life.

Carmen threw herself into her pile of friends. She screamed, out of pure emotion, which got them all screaming. She felt the heave of flesh as every layer of their group seemed to sink into the whole more fully – arms wrapped around shoulders and waists, cheeks pressed together, wrinkly and smooth. Then Carmen burst into tears, knowing that in the picture her eyes would look very puffy indeed.

Granted, Tibby was in a mood. All she could see was change. All anybody talked about was change. She didn't like Bee wearing heels for the second day in a row. She felt peevish about Lena getting three inches trimmed off her hair. Couldn't everybody just leave everything alone for a few minutes?

Tibby was a slow adjuster. In preschool, her teachers had said she had trouble with transitions. Tibby preferred looking backward for information rather than forward. As far as she was concerned, she'd take a nursery school report card over a fortune-teller any day of the week. It was the cheapest and best self-analysis around.

Tibby saw Gilda's through these same eyes. It was changing. Its glory days of the late nineteen eighties were far behind it. It was showing its age. The once-shiny wood floor was scratched and dull. One of the mirror panels was cracked. The mats looked as old as Tibby, and they'd been cleaned much less. Gilda's was trying to get with the times, offering kickboxing and yoga, according to the big chalkboard, but it didn't look to Tibby like that was helping much. What if it went out of business? What a horrible thought. Maybe Tibby should buy a subscription of classes here? No, that would be weird, wouldn't it?

'Tibby, you ready?' Lena was looking at her with concerned eyebrows.

'What if Gilda's closes?' Tibby opened her mouth, and that was what came out.

Carmen, holding the Travelling Pants, Lena, lighting the candles, Bee, fussing with the dimmer switches near the door, all turned to her.

'Look at this place.' Tibby gestured around. 'I mean, who comes here?'

Lena was puzzled. 'I don't know. Somebody. Women. Yoga people.'

'Yoga people?' Carmen asked.

'I don't know,' Lena said again, laughing.

Tibby was the one most capable of emotional detachment, but tonight it all lay right on the surface. Her irrational thoughts about Gilda's made her feel desperate, like its demise could swallow up their whole existence – like a change in the present could wipe out the past. The past felt fragile to her. But the past was set, right? It couldn't be changed. Why did she feel such a need to protect it?

'I think it's Pants time,' Carmen said. The snacks were out. The candles were lit. The egregiously bad dance music played.

Tibby wasn't sure she wanted it to be Pants time yet. She was having enough trouble maintaining control. She was scared of them noticing what all this meant.

Too late. Out of Carmen's arms came the artifacts of their ritual. The Pants, slowly unfolding from their winter compression, seeming to gain strength as they mixed with the special air of Gilda's. Carmen laid them on the ground, and on top of them the manifesto, written on that first night two years before, describing the rules of wearing them. Silently they formed their

22

circle, studying the inscriptions and embroidery that chronicled their summer lives.

'Tonight we say goodbye to high school, and bye to Bee for a while,' Carmen said in her ceremonial voice. 'We say hello to summer, and hello to the Travelling Pants.'

Her voice grew less ceremonial. 'Tonight we are not worrying about goodbye to each other. We're saving that for the beach at the end of the summer. That's the deal, right?'

Tibby felt like kissing Carmen. Brave as she was, even Carmen was daunted by the implications of looking ahead. 'That's the deal,' Tibby agreed heartily.

The last weekend of the summer had already become sacred in their minds. Sacred and feared. The Morgans owned a house right on the beach in Rehoboth. They had offered it to Carmen for that final weekend, in part, Carmen suspected, because they had gotten an au pair from Denmark and felt guilty about not hiring Carmen to babysit this summer as she had done the summer before.

The four of them had promised each other in the spring that it would be their weekend. The four of them and nobody else. They all depended upon it. The future was unfurling fast, but whatever happened this summer, that weekend stood between them and the great unknown.

They all looked ahead to college in different ways, Tibby knew. They all had different amounts to lose. Bee, in her lonely house, had nothing. Carmen did; she dreaded saying goodbye to her mother. Tibby feared leaving the familiarity of her chaos. Lena flipped and flopped – one day she was afraid to cut ties, and the next she was dying to get away.

The thing they feared equally and powerfully was saying goodbye to one another.

After drawing for the Pants (Tibby won), reviewing the rules (unnecessary, but still part of tradition), and taking a brief hiatus to chew down some Gummi Worms, it was at last time for the vow. Like they had the summer before, they said it together.

'To honour the Pants and the Sisterhood
And this moment and this summer and the rest of our
    lives
Together and apart.'

Only this time, Tibby felt the tears fall when they said 'the rest of our lives'. Because in the past that had always seemed like a distant road, and tonight, she knew in her heart, they were already on it.

Somebody already

broke my heart.

— Sade

That night Tibby had a dream about taxidermy. In it, her crazy great-grandma Felicia had had the Travelling Pants stuffed as her graduation gift. 'It's just what you wanted!' Felicia shouted at her.

The stuffing job looked totally professional. The Pants were mounted on a polished marble pedestal and inhabited by fake legs to look as if they were jauntily midstep. As animated as they looked, you had to notice that there was no body or head or even any feet. They were connected to the marble base by a brass pipe sticking out of one pant leg.

'But they can't go anywhere,' Tibby pointed out timidly.

'That's the point!' Felicia thundered. 'It's just what you wanted!'

'I did?' Tibby asked, confused and guilty for having maybe wanted it. She found herself wondering if they were too heavy to be circulated among their various dorm rooms.

Now we really won't have to worry about washing them, she consoled herself in her dream-reality.

When Tibby awoke, Katherine was at her side. Katherine's head as she stood there loomed one inch from Tibby's as she lay down. 'Brian's visiting.'

Katherine loved trying out words. She was happy with herself that she'd said *visiting* as opposed to just *here*.

Tibby groggily sat up. 'What time is it?'

Katherine moved herself in front of Tibby's clock radio and studied it hopefully.

'God, it's almost eleven,' Tibby answered herself.

She was about to head directly down the stairs, but then she decided to brush her teeth first. When she arrived in the kitchen, Brian was at the table setting up dominoes with Nicky.

'Let's try to set up a few at once,' Brian counselled patiently, arranging them in a snaking row.

Nicky only wanted to knock them over.

'Hey,' Tibby said.

'Hey.'

'Did you eat breakfast?' she asked.

'Uh-huh. Yeah.' He seemed a bit nervous for some reason, the way his shoulders were rising towards his ears.

'What's up?' she asked him. She went to the refrigerator to inspect.

'Just, uh . . . Can I talk to you for a second?'

She closed the refrigerator and stood up straighter. She looked at him. 'Sure.'

'In . . . there?' He gestured toward the living room.

Tibby's eyebrows nearly joined over her nose. 'In there?'

Nobody ever did anything in the living room in her house. Loretta ventured in once a week to clear out the cobwebs. And every few months her parents had a party and acted like they relaxed on those perfect sofas all the time.

Mystified, she followed him. They posed on the sofa like cocktail party guests.

'So . . . what?' she asked him, a sprout of worry in her chest. It was slightly funny how they were sitting next to each other and both facing forward.

He rubbed both palms against the denim covering his thighs.

Tibby pulled her legs up onto the sofa so she could turn to him. 'Everything OK?'

'I wanted to ask you something.'

'OK. Ask.'

'You know the thing tonight?'

'Uh . . . you mean the senior party?'

'Will you go with me?'

Her eyebrows compressed even further. 'We're all going. Right? Lena . . . Bee . . .'

He waved a hand to acknowledge all that. 'But will you go with me?'

She was utterly perplexed. 'You mean like a date?' She blurted it out because it sounded so ridiculous.

'Kind of. Yeah.'

Suddenly, it seemed mean to snort or laugh at the preposterousness of this concept. She tilted her head. He was very brave to keep looking at her eyes the way he did.

She clasped her hands. It dawned on her that she was wearing a tank top and her pyjama bottoms. Tibby spent an unusual amount of time in her pyjamas, so it wasn't like Brian hadn't seen her in them hundreds of times.

But here, in this stage-set living room, under the glare of this weird question, it only accentuated the weirdness.

'A kind of date?' she asked slowly.

'Kind of.'

She wouldn't hurt his feelings. She just wouldn't. It didn't matter where this would lead them. She nodded. 'OK.'

She felt raw sitting with him on the sofa. When he leaned towards her she had absolutely no idea what was going to happen. His body moved in slow motion, and she seemed to see herself and Brian from some distant spot in the room. He possessed a new kind of confidence, a deliberateness. She was both terrified and eerily calm.

So she sat still, looking into his eyes as he reached towards her face. He didn't kiss her or anything like that. But what he did felt just as shockingly intimate. The first three fingers of his right hand landed lightly on her warm face and smoothed out the rumple of consternation in the centre of her forehead.

'OK,' he said.

One day in the early spring when Lena stayed home sick from school, she watched a young woman on a daytime talk show who'd written a book about being adopted. This woman had never met or been contacted by her birth mother, and yet she spent her whole life wishing and hoping her birth mother would find her. She talked about how she didn't want to move from the home where her parents had first adopted her. She didn't like to take long trips. She always left explicit forwarding instructions when she moved. She made sure her phone was listed under her own name. She left her little trail of breadcrumbs. She wanted to make sure she could be found.

Since then, Lena had thought about this woman many times, and she wasn't sure why. She didn't dwell on it. Minds worked in weird ways. Like how Lena always thought of Ritz crackers when she shaved her legs. Who knew why? And did it even matter?

But now, as she lay on her bed, filling out forms for school in September, Lena thought about the woman on the talk show again. She filled out a room-mate questionnaire and she kept flashing on the woman's sad grey eyes. She filled out the dorm preference sheet and she saw the woman's twitching lower lip.

And as Lena lay back on her bed and put her hands over her face, it finally dawned on her. This woman reminded Lena of herself.

Without even realizing it, Lena had subtly resisted the idea of going away this summer. Even a week away from home made her feel slightly unglued. The thought of moving to another city in September, thrilling as it was, was also a source of agony.

Lena wanted to leave home. For one thing, she was ready. For another thing, since her dad had forced Valia, his widowed mother, to leave her beautiful Greek island and relocate to suburban Maryland, the Kaligaris house had been full of tension.

Lena looked forward to RISD. She wanted to be an artist, she was almost sure of it. Her art class this summer was the single joy in her life, apart from her friends.

And yet. And yet Lena didn't want to go. And the reason was that she didn't want to leave the place where Kostos could find her. And on a deeper level, she didn't want to put more distance – in time or in space – between now and the time when he'd loved her. She didn't want to become a different girl from the one whom he had loved.

The phone rang and Lena snatched it up before Valia could get it and yell at the innocent caller.

'Hello?'

'Hi, it's me.'

'Carma. Hi. What are you doing?'

'Getting dressed. I had another waxing fiasco. What are you wearing?'

Lena cast her eye at the clock. She was supposed to meet everybody at the senior party in half an hour. She was bringing Effie as her date, because she had no other date and because Effie was spocking on some senior guy or other.

Lena then cast her glance on her open closet. She had no excitement in getting dressed. Her wardrobe had two categories: the clothing she had worn with Kostos – filled with memories – and the clothing she hadn't – empty. She didn't want either.

'I don't know. I didn't pick yet.'

'Lenny, it's a big night,' Carmen cajoled. 'Get dressed. Wear something great. Put on make-up. Do you need me to come over?'

'No. I'm all right.' She didn't feel like setting Carmen loose in her closet.

'Don't wear that khaki skirt,' Carmen warned.

'I'm not,' Lena said defensively, even though it was exactly what she had planned to wear.

Unfortunately, Lena's wardrobe represented her life. It was binary, like a computer with its universe of zeros and ones. Lena had two settings: 1. Thinking about Kostos. 2. Avoiding thinking about Kostos.

Lena deeply empathized with the adopted woman on the talk show. Lena too had been abandoned by the person she thought loved her best of all. And without meaning to or wanting to, she harboured a passive, unquenchable hope that someday he would come for her.

Where there is great

love, there are always

wishes.

– Willa Cather

'Brian! Brian's here!' Katherine threw open the front door and shouted the news to the top of the house.

Brian clearly longed for a real live date. He presented flowers to Tibby and a box of chocolates to Alice for the family. It was as though he'd read about dating in a manual somewhere. Nonetheless, he didn't seem to mind that his real live date was wearing jeans while he was wearing a suit jacket and tie.

'You look beautiful,' he said, taking in the look of her, from the Travelling Pants, to the filmy iris blouse that showed what cleavage she had to its best possible effect, to the antique rhinestone clip in her hair, to the kohl shading along her upper eyelids. She really had tried to look pretty.

One thing about Brian was, he understood the Pants. Just like Bailey, two summers before, had understood them implicitly. The Pants, in a way, were like the ultimate litmus test, separating the worthy from the unworthy. And no matter how he looked, Brian was the most worthy guy she'd ever known.

Few people in the course of history had ever transformed, even just physically, as much as Brian had since the afternoon two years before when Tibby and Bailey first filmed him at the 7-Eleven.

It was great and all. A supreme dork with a golden heart whom you befriend because you love him grows to six feet two, gets his dental hygiene together, accidentally breaks his hideous glasses, and morphs into a virtual heart-throb before your eyes. It was like dumbly buying a share of stock at one dollar and watching it soar to one hundred. Tibby still observed in stupefaction how girls whispered and flirted around Brian these days.

But on the other hand, it seemed to Tibby like another example of destiny's strange sense of humour. The single safest guy in Tibby's life had turned imposing. He didn't impose on purpose, she knew. He didn't desire her to be mean to her. He didn't plant these feelings in her heart to make her sad. But desire was there, his and hers, and as a consequence, it wasn't a safe relationship any more.

'Brian, Brian, Brian!' Katherine and Nicky were literally dancing around him. Brian had earned their love the hard way, not by being their peevish older sister, but by playing every endless, tedious game they could devise and listening carefully to every hare-brained thing they could think of to say. They were a lot more demonstrative than his real live date, come to think of it.

Brian's innocence gave him a funny kind of confidence. It was hard to explain. He didn't care that he had walked all the way to her house because he had no car. He wasn't self-conscious that their date car was her car. Once outside, he gallantly opened the door for her. On the driver's side. He didn't care, so it didn't matter.

Inside the car, it was private. So dark and private. He touched his hand to the inside of her elbow. She got scared, and fumbled the key into the ignition.

They were growing up. That was a fact she had to face. He had grown from a kid to nearly a man. He was eighteen years old. He wanted Tibby in a different way than he used to. He looked at her differently. He wasn't pushy or gross, but his eyes did linger on her breasts. When he put his hand on her, she could tell he was feeling the curve of her waist. And when he looked at her like that, she felt different too. It was natural, right?

In the school parking lot he reached for her hand. Hers was clammy.

What about friendship, though? What about the ease between them? Where was that going to go? And if they let it go, could they ever get it back?

That was the thing about this summer. With everything that was happening, she wondered, was there any going back?

The auditorium was dark and the DJ was loud and grating like at every school social function, but this was their last one, and for that reason, Tibby couldn't bring herself to hate it quite as much.

Brian held her hand fast. He was declaring their couplehood. Ironically, he did her more credit than himself. This spring his social star had certainly risen past hers. Not that he noticed or cared. In spite of her beautiful friends, Tibby was identified more with the disaffected artist types. Bee was a glamour jock. Carmen had turned into quite the babe, the target of a lot of underclassman fantasies, though she'd never curried favour with the ruling set. Lena flew under the social radar. And Brian, oddly, had become a darling of the social whirl – even they needed new blood occasionally – getting invitations none of the rest of them got. Tibby was one of those who sat on the sidelines in dark clothes, making cynical observations with other self-designated misfits who were too cautious to jump into the fray.

Of all the boys in school, only Brian seemed to notice how Tibby's hair had grown out, how her delicate shoulders looked in a tube top, how the Pants made her small behind look especially nice. She loved being noticed like this. And also, she didn't.

Bee and Carmen found them right away. Lena and Effie hadn't arrived yet. Effie was an infamously slow and primping date. Bee was wearing a white halter dress and her hair was brighter than the tea lights. She looked like an extremely fit Marilyn Monroe. Carmen wore a siren-red slip dress, to which the boys were already flocking. As stunning as they looked in their finery, Tibby was still grateful it was she who had drawn for the Pants.

Bridget and Carmen hustled Tibby off to the bathroom in their time-honoured way. The cavernous girls' bathroom was always the most happening spot at a school party. 'You both look unbelievable,' Tibby said along the way.

'You, Tibby, are luscious,' Carmen responded. 'Brian looked like his heart was going to break when we took you away.'

An army of gussied girls were perfecting make-up, smoking, and gossiping in front of the mirrors.

Bee took out her lip gloss. She put some on and shared it around.

'Hey, Bee?' Carmen said.

'Yeah?'

'If you ever meet a guy and you fall in love with him, but because of some weird genetic mutation he doesn't seem to return the feeling?'

Bee always went patiently along with Carmen's counterfactuals. 'Yeah?'

'Wear that dress.'

Bee laughed. 'OK.'

Lena arrived a few minutes later, dressed down as usual, in an olive-green cargo skirt and a black shirt.

'Lenny, did you have to wear the ponytail?' Carmen asked fake-irritably.

'What do you mean?' she asked.

'Come on, it's our last high school party,' Bee said.

Together, they put some mascara and lip gloss on her and coaxed the elastic out of her hair.

Looking at their faces in the mirror, Tibby felt as though she might cry. This was the place where they'd spent the majority of school events these last four years. They had had more fun here, together, than any place else. This, on some level, was their real high school experience.

Carmen caught her look. 'It's sad, I know.'

'Let's get back out there,' Tibby said. She didn't want to feel these things right now.

Back in the auditorium, they dispersed. Brian was

waiting eagerly. 'Do you want to dance?' he asked Tibby.

Was she allowed to say no? Was a real live date allowed to say no? As he took her hand and led her to the floor, the fast song changed into a slow one. Was that better or worse? She couldn't decide.

It would have taken her an hour to figure out how to get her arms around Brian, but he went right for it. He closed in and held her tight.

So here it was. This was a first. She had, admittedly, thought a lot about Brian's body and how it would feel. Friendship seemed to fuzz at the edges as this new thing happened.

He was so much taller than her now, her head barely reached his chest. His hands were on her waist, her hips, her back. Slowly touching the places he'd looked at for so long. She felt a lightness in her lower abdomen, a wobbliness in her legs.

This was going too fast. It was getting away from her. She couldn't do it.

Her cheeks were deeply flushed as she pulled away. 'Can we go?' she asked.

'Where?' he asked.

'I'm not sure.' She took his hand and led him out of the auditorium and towards the parking lot.

She suddenly had her idea. She'd get them back to basics.

He followed her into the car without complaint. In silence she drove to the seminal 7-Eleven on River Road.

He realized what she was up to. He smiled and

39

shrugged at her under the pulsing lights of the store. He went obligingly towards Dragon Master and fished around in his pockets for change. Even as she watched him she knew he would play their old game to please her, but his life was outside of the screen now.

'Never mind,' she said. She was skittish. Her legs were jumpy. A drop of sweat rolled down her spine. She couldn't figure out where to be. She was on the run.

They got back into the car. She drove to a small neighbourhood park equidistant from their houses. It was another of their places.

They got out of the car and sat on a picnic table. It was quiet and dark. She was just going to have to stay still and let it catch her. She knew it.

She hopped off the table. She stood in front of him. With her standing and him sitting, their faces were at the same level. She put her clammy hands on his knees. He scooted towards her, to the very edge of table, and pulled her into his arms. He held her like that for a long time while her heart slammed out a beat.

When she looked up he kissed her first on the forehead and then on the lips. It was such a kiss. Full of pent-up desire and no uncertainties at all, he put his hands under her hair, supporting the back of her head. He paused the kiss for only a moment to say something in her ear. 'I love you' was what he said.

It was beautiful to her, unlike anything she had ever felt before. It brought tears to her eyes and still more warm blood to her face.

Tibby felt the odd sensation of a wind blowing

through her mind, alternately hot and sultry, then cold and bracing. And when the wind subsided, she realized that the friendship, as it had been, was gone.

S omeday somebody's

going to ask you

a question that you

should say yes to.

– Old 97's

Carmen was on a supremely important mission: She needed to steal her mother's fake eyelashes and she needed to do it now.

She'd gotten up early to say goodbye to Bee one last time before Bee left for camp in Pennsylvania. She'd eaten breakfast with her mom, and spent a few minutes feeling guilty about not having a job as she watched Christina trundle off to work. She'd written a long e-mail to her friend and stepbrother, Paul.

Then she'd started to feel sad about saying goodbye to Bee and it reminded her of goodbyes generally. So Carmen turned to the most recent issue of *CosmoGIRL!* for solace, as she often did in moments like these. And *voilà*, she was swept away by the imperative need to copy the innovative use of fake eyelashes on page 23. Sometimes it paid to be shallow.

It was so different for Carmen these days, walking into her mother's room. The reason was obvious: it wasn't her mother's room any more. It was her mom and David's room. A woman's room was so different than a woman's room together with a man. It was utterly different when the woman was your mother and the man was her spanking-new husband, whom you'd met less than a year before.

44

Carmen wasn't grateful for her parents' divorce. There were so many things she'd lost. But it took David's presence now to show her what remarkable access and role-defying closeness she'd shared with her mother for all those years when it had been just the two of them.

When her father had first left, a lot of the usual boundaries had come down. She'd slept in her mother's bed almost every night for a year. Was it for Carmen's sake? Or for Christina's? Once there was no dad coming home after a hard day of work, 'we girls', as her mother called them, had eaten Eggo waffles or scrambled eggs for dinner many nights. Carmen had considered it a treat, not having to saw through some hunk of flank steak and stomach the obligatory vegetables.

Carmen used to feel an easy ownership of this room. Now she trod uncertainly. She used to flop at will on her mother's bed. It was a different bed now. Not literally a different bed, but in every other way different. She steered wide around it now.

It wasn't just that the room contained a lot of male stuff. David wasn't a slob or anything. He was always conscious that this apartment had been Christina and Carmen's long before he joined up. He commanded one closet, three bookshelves and a new bureau from Pottery Barn. He didn't even have pictures yet. The room now testified not so much to him but to *them* – their intimacy, the things they whispered to each other when they were falling asleep. Even when they weren't present, Carmen felt like she was invading it.

The bathroom used to bloom with female stuff –

creams, lotions, make-up, tampons and perfume. Now, in deference to *them*, Christina kept it all mostly stowed in the cabinet. Even seeing David's shaving cream can lined up next to Christina's nail-polish remover made Carmen feel like she'd just crawled between them in bed.

The false eyelashes weren't in the medicine cabinet, Carmen quickly discovered. When you lived with your daughter, you left things like that in easy view. When you lived with your brand-new husband, you hid the evidence.

Carmen already knew that most of the stuff Christina didn't want David to see, she stored in the cabinet above the toilet. Yes, this was the right department, Carmen realized as soon as she'd jiggled open the sticky door. There was wart remover, there was moustache bleach, there was bikini wax and hair-straightening balm and a box of Nice 'n' Easy in Deep Mahogany. Carmen snaked her hand towards the back, knocking over appetite suppressants and a pack of laxatives. A plastic bottle was set rolling by the falling laxatives. Carmen watched in displeasure as it fell off the shelf and . . . *splash*, into the toilet. Damn.

She watched it bobbing in the toilet water. She could see it contained some kind of vitamins. She really hoped the cap was watertight.

While she delayed reaching her hand into the toilet – who hurried to do a thing like that? – she absently wondered why her mother kept vitamins in the cabinet of shame. David was all about vitamins. He ate them for breakfast. He talked about various herbal supplements like they were his best friends. What kind of vitamins would Christina keep from her dashing nutrition-man?

Carmen's curiosity was always her best motivator. She stuck her hand in the toilet and plucked out the bottle, tossing it directly into the sink and running hot water over it. She added some liquid soap. Once the bottle and her hand were sufficiently clean, she turned it over to satisfy her questioning mind.

Her head grew chill and fuzzy. The fuzz invaded her chest and expanded in her lower abdomen. The front of the label communicated precisely why this bottle lived between the laxatives and the Preparation H. But it wasn't David her mom was trying to hide them from. At least, that was what Carmen powerfully suspected.

They were prenatal vitamins. The kind you took when you were having a baby. And Christina was almost certainly hiding them from Carmen.

Tibby squinted in the morning sunlight. She was groggy and disoriented, her lips were swollen and her eyes felt puffy. She felt like she had a hangover, but not because she'd had any alcohol.

It was one of those mornings when you come to terms with a strange new reality. You ask yourself, Did I dream that? Did I actually do that? Did he really say that? Reality comes back in bits and pieces, and you experience the novelty of it all over again. You wonder, Will this day and this night and tomorrow and all the rest of the days be different because of what happened last night? And in Tibby's case, she knew the answer.

She put her fingers on her lips. Could you get a hangover from kissing?

Was Brian awake yet? She pictured him in his bed. She pictured him in her bed. She got the shivery feeling in the bottom of her stomach, so she stopped picturing him in her bed. Was he regretting anything? Was she regretting anything?

What would they say when they saw each other again?

Would he just drop by during pancakes the way he often did? Would he plant a wet one on her lips and wait to see if anyone noticed?

She stood up and looked at herself in the mirror. Did she look as different as she felt? Hmmm. Same black watch plaid pyjama bottoms hanging down around her hips. Same undersized white tank top baring several inches of belly. Maybe not.

Her room was a big, cluttered mess. There was nothing new about that, but she did notice it in a new way as she looked around. Had she ever thrown out anything in her life?

There were layers and layers of Tibby detritus both on the walls and on the floor. You could do an archaeological dig in this room and probably unearth her Fisher-Price farm if you tried hard enough. What was the matter with her?

It was dusty and stuffy and it bothered her. It was always dusty and stuffy. It didn't always bother her. In an uncharacteristic move, she walked over to the window and forced it open. It was hard going, because she had not opened this room to actual air in as long as she could remember. The paint stuck a bit as she wrenched up the sash. Oh.

The air came in and it did feel good. It was nice, open like this. The breeze blew around some of the papers on her desk, but she didn't mind.

She heard her mother downstairs in the kitchen. She thought of telling her about Brian. A part of her really wanted her mom to know. Alice would be excited. She would make a big deal about it. She loved Brian. She would love the idea of her daughter telling her about a juicy milestone like this one. It was her mother-daughter fantasy – the very thing Tibby so often denied her.

As Tibby left her room she registered the sound of the rustling leaves of the apple tree, so little heard here, and she liked it.

Tibby watched her mother in her usual morning flurry. Would she be able to slow down for Tibby's news? Tibby tried to formulate the opening sentence. 'Brian and I . . . Me and Brian . . .'

Tibby opened her mouth, but Alice got there first.

'Tibby, I need you to stay with Katherine this morning.' Alice already sounded mad and Tibby hadn't even refused yet.

Tibby's words dried up.

Alice wouldn't look in Tibby's eyes, indicating that she felt guilty somewhere down deep, but the guilt only made her less patient. 'Loretta has to take her sister to the doctor and she can't be back till after lunch.' Alice snatched the juice boxes from the shelf and shoved one at Nicky. 'Or that's what she says, anyway,' she added ungenerously.

'Why does her sister have to go to the doctor?' Nicky asked.

'Sweetie, she has some kind of infection, I don't know.' Alice gestured the whole issue away with a sweep of her arm, as if it might or might not be true, but she couldn't spend any more time thinking about it.

Alice was flinging things into and out of her purse. 'I have to take Nicky to camp and then go to the office.'

'I'm not doing it,' Tibby said. Not only had she lost all desire to tell her mother about Brian, she never wanted to tell her mother about anything she cared about ever.

Alice gave her a look. 'Excuse me?'

'I'm not the babysitter. I'm sick of you dumping the job on me every time it's convenient.'

'You're living in this house, and that means you have to help out, just like everybody else.'

Tibby rolled her eyes. This fight was nasty, but it had taken place so many times they might as well have been following lines of a script.

Katherine stirred her Cheerios around in her bowl. She slopped some of the milk onto the kitchen table.

Tibby always felt distantly guilty for refusing to babysit Katherine in Katherine's presence, but she managed to get over it.

'I can't wait to go to college,' Tibby muttered, as though to herself, but not really. The statement was untrue, and she said it only to make her mother unhappy.

Half an hour later, Tibby sat on the back deck with a pile of papers and brochures from NYU, while Katherine careened around the backyard. The fight with her mom had shaken all the magic right out of her. She was back on the ground, looking down at the bugs rather than up at the sky.

Eventually Katherine's appetite for independent play ran out. She appeared in Tibby's face.

'You want to climb the tree and pick apples?' This currently represented Katherine's greatest fantasy.

'Katherine, no. Anyway, why do you want those apples so bad? They're not good. They're not ripe yet. And even if they were ripe, they'd be hard and sour.' Tibby had fallen into that shameful parent-ennui where you said no before you even listened to what the kid wanted.

'Did you ever eat one?' Katherine asked.

Tibby hadn't ever eaten one, but she didn't feel like getting argued to the ropes by a three-year-old. 'I'm telling you, they're gross. If they were good, wouldn't we all be eating them instead of buying apples from the bin at the A&P?'

Katherine seemed to find this kind of logic depressing. 'I still want to try one.'

Tibby sat there, watching Katherine sizing up the apple tree. She was too small to reach even the lowest branch, but she was undeterred. She backed up ten or so yards from the trunk of the tree, ran as fast as she could, and jumped. Her attempt was so meagre and ineffective it was almost heartbreaking.

Katherine backed up for another go. She backed up farther this time for optimum speed. She ran with her arms bent tight at her elbows in a caricature of sprinting. It was so cute, objectively speaking, that one part of Tibby longed to get it on camera.

But at the same time, Tibby was annoyed. She indulged herself in pettiness. She did not want to babysit. She was annoyed with her mother. If she were to let herself be absorbed into Katherine's world, it would be almost like enjoying babysitting. Which she didn't.

So Tibby watched. Katherine was inexhaustible. Why did she want the damn apples so much? Tibby couldn't imagine the nature of her desire.

But Tibby could remember being small and wanting to jump, running and jumping just like Katherine, and imagining you were going to practically take flight – thinking you could jump so much higher than you really could.

The first thing Bridget did when she got to soccer camp was find Diana. They'd spoken on the phone and exchanged many e-mails, but Bridget hadn't seen Diana in two years – not since the day they'd left Baja. And of all the things and people she'd encountered there, Diana stood out as her single happy memory.

When she found her in their cabin, she screamed and hugged Diana so hard she lifted her off the ground.

'God.' Diana examined Bee's face. She stepped back. 'You look great. You grew?'

'You shrunk?' Bee asked back.

'Ha.'

Bridget tossed her gigantic duffel bag onto her bunk. She wasn't big on folding or sorting. She used to pack in Hefty bags, but Carmen made her stop.

She hugged Diana again and admired her. Diana had kept her hair straightened two summers ago, but now she'd let it collect into long, pretty dreads. It looked unbelievably glamorous to Bee. 'Look how you are! You are stunning and fabulous! Do you love Cornell?'

Diana hugged back. 'Yeah, except I live and breathe soccer. You'll see how it is.'

'You had time to find Michael, though, right? Did you bring a picture?'

Bridget exclaimed and swore appreciatively at the picture of Diana's good-looking soccer-playing boy-friend and also at the pictures of her hilariously hammy younger sisters.

'So who else is here?' Bridget asked, gesturing at the second set of bunk beds in the cramped cabin.

'Two assistant coaches.' Diana got a vague look on her face.

'You met them?' Bridget asked.

'At lunch. Katie and Something,' she said. She closed one eye, trying to remember. 'Allison. I think. Katie and Allison.'

Bridget sensed an issue. 'And they are . . .?'

'Fine. Great.'

'Fine and great? Katie and Allison are fine and great?'

Diana smiled. Vaguely.

'So what's the problem?'

'What problem?'

'Why do you look like that?'

'Like what?' Diana asked, glancing downward.

Bee felt impatient. Diana was an honest person. Why wasn't she being honest now?

Diana pulled a hair elastic off her wrist and stretched

53

it between her index finger and thumb. 'You haven't . . . met the other coaches yet. Have you?'

Diana's words came slow, and Bee's came very fast. 'No. Have you?'

'Uh. Not all of them. But I saw . . .' Something about Diana's hair elastic was so fascinating her words trailed off in her deep contemplation of it.

'Who?' Bee shot out.

'You probably already—'

'Who?'

'I'm pretty sure you—'

Bridget huffed in exasperation. She grabbed the arm that wore Diana's wristwatch and held it up so she could read it. 'We have a staff meeting in eight minutes. I'm going to go find out who you're talking about.'

I don't have to be

careful, I've got a gun!

– Homer Simpson

Carmen was sitting at the table in the small kitchen of the apartment later that day, clutching the bottle of prenatal vitamins.

In this time of thinking, certain facts aligned themselves in Carmen's mind. Her mother had gained weight in the past couple of months. Carmen had put it down to happiness, but now she felt silly for not being more observant. Christina's wardrobe had subtly but certainly shifted towards the roomier stuff in her closet. Had she stopped drinking wine? Carmen tried to think. Had she gone for a lot of doctor's appointments?

Carmen had once overheard her mom joking with her aunt about how it was easy to hide stuff from teenagers because they were so self-absorbed. She felt the sting of it now, though she'd laughed it off then.

She heard a key in the lock of the front door – her mother, arriving home from work at the usual time. Carmen stayed sitting, knowing her mother would appear in the kitchen moments after she'd put her bags down. Carmen hadn't planned an ambush, exactly, but it came off a lot like one.

'Hi, *nena*, love.' Christina's whole body looked tired as she entered the kitchen. She'd always eschewed the practice of wearing sneakers with her suit to and from work, but recently she'd caved on her dignity. Now Carmen understood why.

Wordlessly Carmen held up the bottle.

Wordlessly Christina stared at it, and slowly its significance registered. Her eyes widened, and her expression changed from confusion to surprise to dread to exhaustion and back again.

Carmen decided to skip to the crux of the matter. 'How far are you?' she asked in a moderated, matter-of-fact tone, though her heart was pounding. She knew it was true, but still she wanted her mother to deny it.

Christina seemed to stiffen her spine to mount a vivid defence. She seemed to consider several possible angles. And then, before Carmen's eyes, she deflated again. Her dark red blouse appeared to crumple. 'Five months.'

'You're kidding.' Well, there it was. 'When were you planning to tell me?' Carmen's voice was flatly accusatory.

'Carmen. Darling.' Christina sat down across from her. She wanted to reach for Carmen's hand, but Carmen was sitting on one, and the other was strangling the neck of the vitamin bottle. Christina withdrew her attempt. She was quiet for a few moments, collecting her breath. 'Just let me explain, OK? It's complicated.'

Carmen offered something between a shrug and a nod.

'David and I have talked and thought a lot about having a baby. He hasn't had that joy in his life, as I have. We didn't know if it would be possible. But we agreed, life is too short not to try for something you want.'

Carmen hated the 'life is too short' rationalization.

57

She thought it was one of the lamer excuses in the history of excuse-making. Whenever you did something because 'life is too short not to', you could be sure life would be just long enough to punish you for it.

'At the very least we thought it would take me a year or two to conceive, if I did at all,' Christina went on. 'We never dreamed it would happen so fast. I'm almost forty-one years old.'

Carmen cocked her head sceptically. With half her mind she was calculating whether they'd conceived this baby before or after their wedding. It was a close call.

'I didn't even guess I was pregnant until I was almost three months along. I just couldn't believe it. And then I needed to think about how to talk to you. The timing was not what I had wished. It's very . . . complicated.'

Complicated. What a totally unsatisfying word. It was a politician's word.

'There were your exams, your senior paper. Then graduation crept up on us,' Christina continued, holding up her hands plaintively. 'I didn't want any of your special things to get overshadowed by this news.'

'Were you going to tell me before it was born?'

Reasonably, Christina looked hurt. 'I was going to tell you this weekend.'

'Do you know what kind it is?'

'You mean a boy or a girl?'

Carmen nodded.

'No. We want to wait to find out when the baby is born.'

Carmen nodded again, knowing as she did that this baby would be a girl. It just had to be.

'So I guess it's due around . . .' Carmen had already calculated the baby would have to be born near her own birthday, but she left the space open for her mother to fill.

'Around the end of September,' Christina supplied slowly, the look of dread intensifying.

Carmen knew, intellectually, that this was happy news on a lot of levels. Christina had a whole new life ahead of her. From about seventh grade onwards, Carmen had feared the day she'd leave for college. She imagined she'd be leaving her single mother alone to defrost food and eat by herself night after night. Instead, this September, she'd be leaving a happy couple bursting with a new baby.

And besides, Carmen was finally getting the sibling she had always professed to want. If she were a big and good person, she would be able to feel and appreciate this happiness. She would be able to congratulate and even hug her mother. But she wasn't a big or good person. She'd dashed too many such opportunities not to know the truth about herself.

'It's kind of convenient, in a way,' Carmen stated, sounding robotic, like she didn't much care. 'Because you can just use my room for the nursery, right? I'll be going just before the baby comes. Good planning.'

The corners of Christina's mouth quivered. 'It wasn't good planning. It wasn't planned like this.'

'And you can even combine birthday parties. What a funny coincidence.'

59

'Carmen, I don't think it's funny.' Christina's gaze was earnest and unwavering. 'I think it's serious, and I know you must have a lot of complicated feelings about it.'

Carmen looked away. She knew she was being spooky. She could tell by the worry in her mother's eyes. Carmen was well known to whine and complain and lash out destructively. Christina's posture, much like that of a person girded for the arrival of a hurricane, indicated that she was ready for just such a lashing.

Carmen didn't want to give her mother anything, not even that.

Yes, Carmen did have feelings, and they were damming up behind her face, generating a mammoth pressure somewhere around the back of her eyes. Carmen was afraid her face might explode if she had too many more of those feelings just now.

Silently she handed her mother her vitamins and stood to leave. Earlier she'd debated telling her mother that they'd fallen in the toilet, but as she strode out of the room she figured she would just let her mother go ahead and eat them.

Carmen hated herself right now, but she hated her mother a little bit more.

Oh, Carma,

I, of all people, won't dare congratulate you or anything. I swear I won't remind you how you always said you wanted a brother or sister, like all those *%&#$-all people did to me. I feel your pain. I mean, couldn't they have just gotten a dog?

I hope the Oreos provide comfort for at least an

hour—just eat the box and think later. I got the kind with extra stuff in the middle, because I love you extra.

Tibby

The air in the dining hall of the Prynne Valley Soccer Academy was charged in a peculiar way. Bridget felt goose-bumpy and alert. She had an idea, but she didn't want to have that idea – to give it words or a picture. Or maybe she did want to have that idea but didn't want to *want* the idea. Maybe that was it.

The room was knotty pine from floor to ceiling. Wide planks for the walls, medium for the floor, skinny for the ceiling. It was filling up slowly with coaches, trainers, administrators and blah blah blah. The campers wouldn't arrive until tomorrow. Every stranger looked like someone she knew. Her intensity made her invisible; she was seeing so hard she forgot about being seen.

'Bee?'

Diana's voice was behind her, but she didn't turn. Diana was a real friend, but she wasn't telling Bee what she needed to know. So Bee would find it out for herself.

There was a long table to one side. On it were sodas and an industrial-sized coffee-maker and a few plates of store-bought cookies. Oatmeal with bits of raisin.

Was it dread or hope that made her chest pound? Her toes clutched so hard inside her clogs they were falling asleep.

She sensed the presence of a significant body just off

her left shoulder. She wasn't sure with which sense she sensed it. He was too far away to touch him or to feel his body heat. He was too far behind her for her to see him. Until she turned, that is.

Her eyes seemed to go in and out of focus. Was it him? Of course it was him! Was it him?

'Bridget?'

It was unquestionably him. His eyes were dark under dark, arching eyebrows. He was older and taller and different and also the same. Was he surprised? Was he happy? Was he sorry?

Her hand went protectively to her face.

He made a gesture as if to hug her, but he couldn't seem to bridge the strange air between them.

The time came for her to say something, and then it passed. She stared at him in silence. Socially, she never cared much about covering her tracks.

'How are you?' he asked her. She remembered that he was earnest. It was something she'd liked about him.

'I'm – I'm surprised,' she said honestly. 'I didn't realize you would be here.'

'I knew you would be.' He cleared his throat. 'Here, I mean.'

'You did?'

'They mailed out the staff list a couple weeks ago.'

'Oh.' Bridget cursed herself for not reading her mail more thoroughly. She hated forms (*Mother's maiden name . . . Mother's profession . . .*), and between this camp and Brown, she'd had far too many of them.

So he'd known. She hadn't. What if she had known? Would she have willingly tossed herself into a summer full of Eric Richman, breaker of hearts and minds?

It was amazing, in a way, that he occupied space like a regular human being. He was so monumental to her. For these two years he'd represented not only himself but all the complicated things she'd felt about herself.

He was looking at her carefully. He smiled when her eyes caught his. 'So, from what I hear, you haven't gotten any worse.'

She looked at his mouth moving, but she had no idea what he was talking about. She did not disguise this.

'At soccer,' he clarified.

She'd forgotten they were at soccer camp. She'd forgotten she played soccer.

'I'm all right,' she said. She wasn't even sure what she was talking about. But she said it again, because she liked the ring of it. 'I'm all right.'

Your chances of

getting hit by lightning

go up if you stand under

a tree, shake your fist at

the sky, and say 'Storms

suck!'

– Johnny Carson

The only adult person in Carmen's life who hadn't smilingly congratulated her about her upcoming baby sibling was Valia Kaligaris, Lena's grandmother. Now, as Carmen sat at the counter in Lena's family's glossy kitchen and Valia sat at the breakfast table, Carmen felt grateful for that.

Granted, Valia wasn't up for chatting these days. As Carmen waited for Lena to come back from the restaurant, Valia glowered at the Cheerios box and then trudged, still in her purple bathrobe, to the darkened den, where she turned on the TV so loud Carmen could hear every word even though it was two rooms away. It was a soap opera. Apparently Dirk had abandoned Raven at the altar the very day before her identical twin sister, Robin, went missing. Hmmmm.

Carmen could privately ridicule it because it wasn't *her* soap opera. *Her* soap opera (to which she had become progressively addicted since she'd been accepted to Williams early decision in January and stopped doing her homework) was called *Brawn and Beauty* and it would never have a plot line as dumb as this one. Carmen's addiction centred on one actor (hailing from the Brawn side of things) named Ryan Hennessey. He was absolutely, explosively gorgeous, and her one true love, no matter how much her friends made fun of her for it. He was a *good* actor. Seriously, he was. He'd done some sort of Shakespeare thing before he'd gotten the soap gig. At least, that was what Carmen had read in *Soap Opera Digest* while she was waiting with Tibby to pay for the Diet Coke at the A&P the night before.

The Kaligarises' front door opened and closed, and Lena appeared with her mother a minute later.

'Hey, Carma.' Lena looked sweaty from her shift at the Elite. Ari was in her work clothes.

'Hi. How's work?'

Lena rolled her eyes.

'At least you have a job,' Carmen pointed out.

'How's the search going?' Ari asked, pulling a pitcher of water from the fridge and filling a glass. 'Anybody?' She held up the pitcher.

'No, thanks.' If Carmen had wanted something, she would have gotten it for herself. The Septembers had broken down that barrier at each other's houses before it had even gone up. 'The search is . . . uh, slow. I'm kind of, uh, not that much in the mood for babysitting this summer.' Carmen realized that if she didn't rush onward, she could be questioned on this topic. 'But I saw this ad at the A&P to take care of an old lady five afternoons a week. She's kind of blind, I guess, so the job would mostly be reading to her. I called the number and left a message.'

Ari put her glass down a little too forcefully on the granite counter. Lena turned to look at her mom. 'You know,' Ari said, her eyes animated, 'that's strange. I've been thinking about that same thing for Valia. I've been thinking how much she needs some companionship to help her with her errands and correspondence and maybe take her to her doctor's appointments. I don't dare take another afternoon off work this month.'

Carmen nodded.

'I was hoping Lena or Effie could pitch in, but they both got jobs early this summer.'

Carmen kept her expression brightly neutral, so as not to appear to indict Lena.

Ari put her glass in the sink with a definitive motion. 'How much were they offering to pay on the sign you saw?' She was getting quite enthusiastic now.

'Eight an hour.'

'How about I'll pay you eight fifty if you'll look after Valia thirty or so hours a week? We could make up the schedule together.'

Carmen considered, looking down at her chipped red nail polish. In this minute she could go from having no job, no purpose in life, to having one. The money was decent. It would be a little weird to have Ari paying her. But then, it was more comfortable for Ari to hire Carmen than to hire a stranger. Carmen would frankly rather hang out in Lena's airy, spacious house than in what would likely be a stuffy, old-lady apartment.

'Well . . .' Carmen tapped her index finger on the counter. 'OK. Why not?'

'Fantastic,' Ari said.

Carmen hadn't looked across the counter at Lena before this moment. So she hadn't seen how Lena had positioned herself with her back to her mother and was facing Carmen, frantically wide-eyed, mouthing the

68

word *no* and drawing her index finger across her neck, until it was too late.

Lena waited to explode until she'd gotten Carmen up to her room and shut the door.

'Are you insane?'

'Lenny, jeez. What's the problem?'

'Why do you think Effie and I set up jobs in mid-April? Jobs we both fully hate, by the way.'

'Because . . . you're well organized?'

Lena shook her head stormily.

'Because . . . you are ungrateful and uncaring grand-daughters of your recently widowed and helpless grandmother?'

'Because Valia is a nightmare!' Lena practically shouted.

It was a good thing Valia's hearing wasn't so good, Carmen thought.

'I mean, she's an amazing and wonderful woman,' Lena backtracked, looking more serious. 'She really is. And we love her. But she's awful right now! And I'm not saying I blame her for it. She's miserable about Bapi. She's miserable that she's in the States living with us. She hates my dad for making her come. She hates everything about this country. She wishes she were in her own home surrounded by her friends. She is furious at every-body, can't you tell that?'

Carmen was now feeling stupid and a bit defensive. 'Maybe she is. But maybe I can handle it.'

Lena shook her head. 'Trust me. You and Valia are not a good combination right now.'

Carmen narrowed her eyes. 'And what's that supposed to mean?'

69

* * *

Now, and for a long time, the best way Bridget knew to settle her mind was to run. Sometimes she felt that the meditative state of the long, quiet miles helped her think. Sometimes she felt that the pure exhaustion helped her not think.

Sometimes she believed that she was running towards some sort of resolution, and other times she knew she was just plain running away. Still, it was what she did.

This late-evening run took her up and down country roads fringed by scrubby, June-green trees. The sinking sun poked an occasional sparkling ray straight into her eyes. When she got bored of the cars honking at her (was she posing a hazard in the fading light, or was it her hair?), she leaped off the road. Another girl might have been scared to run through unfamiliar woods as darkness fell, but Bee wasn't. She knew she could out-run virtually any human being who might find her. And the bears in these parts weren't man-eaters, she was pretty sure.

It was exhilarating, if anything. The forest was young and sparse, cut through every which way by paths. She followed a deep, wide bed where she imagined a river had once lain. She pictured herself striving in this same place when the river flowed. She ran until her thoughts shortened and no longer formed lines. They flashed and blipped. She didn't follow them around the corner. She simply felt things without any hows or whys. This was how she settled herself.

Now the sun was entirely gone and Bridget knew the light would soon disappear too. The light that stayed on after the sun always felt to her like an empty promise. Ahead of her, on the dirt bed, something caught her eye. It jostled her breath out of its rhythm and sent her brain spinning. It was less than twenty yards away, and it disturbed her. She slowed her pace to keep the distance from disappearing so fast. She wanted to run wide around it, but she wanted to face it too. She was back in hows and whys.

It was a bird, she thought. A pigeon, maybe. It was clearly dead and bent into a wrong set of angles. Its head seemed to stick up from the ground in a pitiful pose. She was nearly upon it. She wouldn't stop. She would keep going. She would avert her eyes. No, she couldn't avert her eyes.

It wasn't until she was literally over the bird that she realized, in a burst, that it wasn't a bird at all. It was a mitten. It was a lost, greyish mitten with the thumb sticking up and looking very much like the head of a bird.

She was instantly flooded by relief and reassessment. Her mind and body fell back into calm alignment.

But as she ran and ran and the sky turned a dark, bruised blue, she felt sad. And, strangely, even though the twisted body in her path had been a mitten, she found herself remembering it as a bird.

If Lena's mother's car had not overheated it wouldn't have happened. The whole summer would have gone differently.

But her mother's car did overheat, on Thursday afternoon, so Lena borrowed her father's car on Friday and dropped him at work on her way to drawing class. It was easily on the way. In fact, as she drove away from her father, who was already sweating through his white shirt, she considered absently that it was only a short walk from his office building to her class. But at the time, it didn't signify anything.

By midmorning she was deeply immersed in her drawing. At Annik's instruction, the model, Andrew, took five-minute poses. For the first few poses Lena felt so harried she could barely get a gesture out of the tip of her charcoal. But then those five minutes began to stretch out for her. The intensity of hurrying stayed, but the consciousness of time dropped away. Just as her awareness of the model's nakedness had completely bewitched her during the first few days and subsequently floated off. (In hindsight she felt ashamed of her juvenile, red-faced self. To the seasoned artists in the class, Andrew's nudity was about as sexually charged as Lena's coffee cup.)

Lena now observed Andrew's body in extreme detail, staring without a vestige of shyness at the hollow inside his hip and the sharp ridge of his shin. When she passed deeply into this creative state, she didn't really have thoughts any more. The muscles that controlled her arm bypassed her thinking brain, linking directly to her autonomic system. The usual Lena was just along for the ride.

She jumped when the timer rang out for the long break. A shiver radiated from her shoulders. She hated coming up to the surface like this. She didn't want to hear Phyllis's newspaper rustling and Charlie's heels slapping around in his sandals. She didn't want Andrew pulling on his robe. Not for the reasons you might think. No, really. (Though the truth was, she did regain the awkward mindfulness of Andrew's bare skin in that second when he'd pull on the green kimono and again in that second when he'd take it off.) She just wanted to draw. She just wanted to stay in that place where she understood things without thinking about them.

As Lena stared wistfully at her empty coffee cup, she recognized – almost abstractly – her happiness. Leave it to her to detect happiness rather than actually feel it. Maybe it wasn't happiness, precisely. Maybe it was more like . . . peace. At the end of the previous summer her peace had been sliced up like roast beef. The tumult had brought with it a certain strange exuberance, a feeling of living more extravagantly than ever before. But it had also sucked.

She thought back to the end of that summer, when she had first met Paul Rodman, Carmen's stepbrother. Her response to him had taken her by surprise. She had never experienced such an instant physical attraction to anybody – not even Kostos. In Paul's presence, that first time, she had spun these out-of-character fantasies about what she could mean to him, and he to her. But after he left, she retreated, as was her wont. Her romantic side went back into hiding, and after some time, her timid side took over, timidly, again.

Now when she thought about him she felt ashamed. He was one of the many things she'd been hiding from this year. He was one of the people she'd been avoiding.

In February, she had first heard from Carmen that

Paul's father was sick. She felt awful about it. She had thought about Paul. She had worried for him. But she hadn't called him, or written, as she'd meant to. She had learned since, from Carmen, that Paul's father was sicker and would likely not be getting better. She didn't know what to say to Paul.

She was afraid of his sadness. She was afraid to elicit his feelings. She was also afraid not to. She was afraid she would bring it up, and there would fall that most inept failure between them: total silence.

It wasn't until this class, this feeling, that she had regained a sense of balance. The time she spent with her charcoal and her fingers and her broad pads of paper and Andrew and Annik and these deep, stabilizing stretches of meditation – it all felt like too big a gift to be received. She would have to work to receive it.

Her heart soared at the sound of the timer indicating the break was over. Back to work. It was amazing how much she could hate and love the very same sound.

And so began the fateful pose.

For starters, it was unfortunate that the door opened in the middle of the pose, when Lena was least able to process what was happening. It was unfortunate that the person who walked through the door was Lena's father. It was also unfortunate that the door was located near the model stand and that Andrew was oriented in such a way that the first thing you saw, upon bursting through the door in the middle of a pose (which you really weren't supposed to do), was a very up-close look between Andrew's legs. It was particularly unfortunate that Lena didn't recognize all of these unfortunate things in time to soften her father's experience, but instead unwittingly treated her father to a long stretch of her unabashed fixation upon the glories of Andrew.

When her father started talking, overloud, she came to. He was looming over her. It was a rude transition. It took her a moment to find any words.

'Dad, you are—'

'Dad, you didn't—'

'Dad, come on. Let me just—'

She started a lot of other sentences too. The next thing she knew, he had his hand clamped around her arm and was steering her back through the door, turning her forcibly away from Andrew.

Annik appeared in the hall with amazing speed. 'What's going on here?' she asked calmly.

'We are leaving,' Mr Kaligaris blustered.

'You are?' she asked Lena.

'I'm not,' Lena said faintly.

Mr Kaligaris exclaimed three or four things in Greek before he turned to English. 'I will not have my daughter in this . . . in this *class* where you have . . . in this *place* where she is—'

Lena could tell her father wouldn't use the necessary descriptive words in her earshot. When it came down to it, her father was a deeply conservative and old-fashioned man. He'd grown even more so since Bapi's death. But long before that, he'd been way stricter than any of her friends' fathers. He never let boys up to the first floor of their house. Not even her lobotomized cousins.

Annik stayed cool. 'Mr Kaligaris, might it help if you

and Lena and I sat down for a few minutes and discussed what we are trying to do in this class? You must know that virtually every art programme offers—'

'No, it would not,' Mr Kaligaris broke in. 'My daughter is not taking this class. She will not be coming back.'

He pulled Lena through the hall and out onto the sidewalk. He was muttering something about an unexpected meeting and coming to find her to get the car back, and *look what he finds*!

Lena didn't manage to pull away until she was standing in the harsh sunshine, dazed and off balance once again.

It's like, how much

more black could this

be?

And the answer is none.

None more black.

– This Is Spinal Tap

Now bad could it be?

That was what Carmen asked herself as she fixed Valia a cup of tea first thing when she arrived at the Kaligaris house early Monday afternoon and brought it into the den, where Valia was watching television.

'Awful.' Valia nearly spat when she tried the tea. 'Vhat did you put in this?'

'Well, tea.' Carmen was being patient. 'And honey.'

'I said sugar.'

'The sugar bowl was empty.'

'Sugar and honey is not the same. American honey you cannot eat.'

'You can if you want,' Carmen began, but realized this was not a diplomatic avenue. 'Here, I'll try again.' She took the teacup back into the kitchen. She located the box of Domino granulated white sugar on the high shelf in the pantry. She refilled the sugar bowl.

While she waited for the water to boil a second time, her mind travelled to September. From a chilly distance she imagined her mom very pregnant. She imagined a baby shower. She imagined her room, filled with expectations for somebody else.

When she used to think about September, she

imagined herself arriving at college, meeting her room-mate for the first time, unpacking her stuff. Now she could only seem to picture what would be going on in her absence, and in those pictures, it was as though she were dead. Or as though she were the one who hadn't yet been born.

She used to be able to look forward to college. She had dreamed of Williams for so long. It was one of the best colleges in the country. The place her dad had gone. As agonizing as it was to leave her friends, college was something she'd really wanted. Why couldn't she want it any more?

She was angry. She wasn't angry at the baby, exactly. How could she be? She wasn't angry at her mother. Well, she sort of was, but that wasn't the real root of it. She was angry that she couldn't picture her own life any more. She was angry that her mother and this baby had somehow stolen her future and plunged her back into the past.

The pressure was building up behind her eyes again. Reflexively she snatched the phone from the wall.

'Hey, it's me,' she said when Tibby answered.

'You OK?' Tibby asked. It was so nice how a person who loved you could pick up on your mood in three small words.

Carmen could hear Nicky shouting about something in the background. 'I guess. How 'bout you?'

'Nicky, could you do that in the other room?' Tibby called, away from the phone. 'How's Valia?' she asked into the phone.

'She's—'

79

Suddenly a beeping sound overwhelmed the connection. 'Tibby?'

Beep beep. Beeeeeep.

'Hello?'

'Sounds like a modem.' Tibby had to shout over the noise. 'It must be from your end.'

Carmen hung up the phone and went into the den. Sure enough, Valia had moved from the TV to the desk and was steering the computer's mouse like a race car. Carmen watched in surprise as Valia expertly negotiated her way through a series of menus into a rapid instant messaging conversation. Presumably with somebody in Greece, considering that Carmen couldn't read a single letter. She was used to the look of the Greek letters from all her years in the Kaligaris household, but she couldn't tell you what sounds any of them made.

Carmen was supposed to help Valia with her correspondence. And here she had been picturing crumply airmail paper and blue envelopes.

'*Vhat?*' Valia turned round somewhat belligerently, obviously feeling Carmen's eyes on the back of her uncoiffed head.

'Nothing. Wow. You really know what you're doing.' Carmen decided to be mature and not mention how Valia was hogging up the phone line when she really wanted to talk to Tibby.

Instead, she sat down in one of the comfortable TV chairs, mindlessly picked up the remote, and started flipping channels. *Brawn and Beauty* would be starting in seven minutes. She settled back into the chair, resting her heavy head. How bad could it be, spending the summer watching her favourite soap and getting paid while Valia burned up the lines IMing her Greek friends?

'Not that channel.' Valia had turned from the computer, her hands still poised over the keyboard.

'What do you mean?'

'I like channel seven. *The Vorld Apart.*'

'But you're not even watching. You're on the computer.' Carmen could hear her own voice rising.

'I like to listen,' Valia proclaimed.

'But I like to *watch*,' Carmen said tartly.

'Who's the vun getting paid?'

Ouch. Carmen felt as though Valia had bit her. She felt the flush rising in her cheeks. 'Well, could you get off the computer, then? You're hogging up the phone line,' Carmen snapped in a manner that was not very mature.

Tibberon: How's it going with the ancient Greek?
Carmabelle: Ahem. Not bad. Not not bad. Not good. If you see what
                    I mean.

'Just tell me every, every single thing. After that you can drink your smoothie.'

Tibby felt her heart rising again. Carmen's enthusiasm was everything she could wish for. She shook her clear plastic cup of frothy pink smoothie so it wouldn't separate.

'Well, first we danced to that—'

Carmen was waving her hands around. 'No, no. Back up. I want the beginning. I want to hear the whole thing, soup to nuts.'

Tibby smiled in spite of herself. She liked sitting out-side under the umbrella at the smoothie place on Old Georgetown Road, feeling the sun bake her calves. She crossed her legs and let her green plastic flip-flop drop onto the hot sidewalk. Truth was, she wanted to tell the whole thing, soup to nuts. It made it real again. 'OK. So back up to my house. Doorbell rings. Katherine opens the door. He's wearing the suit jacket and tie – kind of short in the arms and obviously cheap, but so, so, so, so cute. And he has' – Tibby wished her face weren't turn-ing pink, but she couldn't help it – 'a bunch of flowers. Dyed pink carnations, fairly hideous. You know, like flowers only a boy would buy, but totally perfect.' Tibby needed to stop and breathe or she was going to pass out.

At that moment her cell phone rang faintly from the lower reaches of her straw bag. She pulled it out and squinted to see the number. It was her mother's cell phone.

'Hello?'

Nobody was there at first. She heard background noise. And then she heard her mother saying something to someone else. She sounded strange.

'Hello?'

'Tibby?' Her voice was ragged.

'Are you OK?'

Her mother was crying.

'Mom, are you OK? What's going on?' Tibby felt a frigid load of adrenaline hit her bloodstream.

'Honey, Dad and I—' Alice broke off. Her crying was too thick to make words. She could hear her father's voice in the background, shouting.

Tibby stood up, jamming her foot back into her shoe. 'Mom, please tell me what's going on. You're scaring me.'

Her mom took a few seconds to get her breath. Tibby had never heard her sound like this before. It set her mind swirling and leaping spasmodically with fearful possibilities. She paced around the table.

What? Carmen was mouthing urgently.

'We're at the hospital. Katherine is hurt.' Alice paused to gain control of her breaking voice again. 'She fell out the window.'

Tibby couldn't move or think. Waves of cold rolled through her body. Hot hysteria began to brew under her ribs. 'Is. She. OK?'

'She's conscious, she's—' Her mother's sobs took on a more hopeful tone. 'That's a good sign.'

'Should I come?' Tibby asked.

'No. Please go home and look after Nicky, OK?'

'Yes. I'll go.' Tibby was crying now. Carmen's eyes were tearing and she didn't even know what had happened.

Tibby needed to ask a question that summed up her dread. But she was afraid, so she waited until the connection was dead.

'Which window?'

Lena sat on the back steps of the restaurant during her break. Inside was hot, outside was hot. She was sticky, and her apron was spattered with tomato sauce. It looked vaguely gory. Like maybe a customer had made one nasty comment too many.

She hated this job. She hated the careless food, all hurried and overcooked in vats. She hated the constant pressure to turn tables over. She hated the green vinyl booths and the way the coffee cups rattled in their saucers, filling the saucers with hot coffee, which she inevitably spilled on her apron. She felt embarrassed by the lame painting of the Parthenon frieze that stretched across an entire wall of the dining room. She hated the fake windows and the fake ivy. She was bothered by the fact that her manager, Antonis, the one with the fuzzy grey hair spilling out of his ears, still thought she spoke Greek in spite of several one-sided conversations.

She would happily sit out here in the back alley and smell the garbage if it meant not being in there. She needed time by herself. She was constantly being talked at, complained to, harassed. Even the polite customers were always waving her down, catching her eye, needing her to bring one more thing.

Some people liked being in communication with other people all day long, but Lena was not one of them. Looking back on the relative peace of Basia's clothing store the summer before made it seem like a dream job.

Her father had pressed hard for the restaurant job. He had personally recommended her to the owner of the Elite. It was what his parents had done back in Greece. It was the life he had grown up in. Since his own father's death less than a year before, these things had become more important to him.

For most of his life her dad had rebelled against Bapi and against his upbringing. He had eschewed the restaurant business in favour of law school. He had changed his name from Georgos to George. He made a point of being American, not even teaching his daughters to speak Greek. It seemed sad to Lena that he had waited until his father was dead to start caring about the stuff his father had always wanted him to care about.

'The restaurant business is very practical,' her dad had told her on several occasions, implying that being an artist was not very practical. 'It's a good business,' he'd say, and she was sure it was a good business. For somebody else. She sort of wondered whether he'd ever stopped and considered who she was. Did he really imagine she was going to start a restaurant in the proud Kaligaris tradition? Could he not see how wrong it was for her?

It had been four days since the disaster in her drawing class. She hadn't been back and she was missing it terribly. She could stand this job if she had her drawing to look forward to. She could tolerate Valia's loud misery and her parents' tension at home if she could draw. But without it, she felt like she was sinking.

She could take some other class maybe. There were still openings in metalworking and mixed media and something called Gender Issues in Three-Dimensional Representation, but she knew in her heart she wasn't going to be that kind of artist. Her love of art wasn't particularly philosophical or political. She wasn't an avant-gardist or a rule breaker. She wanted to learn to draw and paint people like Annik could.

Back in April she'd visited Capitol Street to pick up an application for summer classes. There were lots of showy, strange pieces in the gallery when you first walked in, but they didn't mean much to Lena. Then, just as you turned the corner to the office, there was a quiet, simply framed drawing on the wall. It was a figure drawing of a young woman holding her hair back with one hand. It was quiet, but so beautiful it made Lena's throat ache. It gave her chills from her scalp down to the balls of her feet. The drawing not only exhibited technical mastery and intricate detail, but it contained so much grace, so much feeling, it made Lena know what she wanted to achieve in her life.

Lena had squinted down at the messy signature and then compared it to every teacher's name in the brochure. Annik Marchand. Lena walked into the office of the art school with uncharacteristic boldness and signed up for Annik Marchand's figure drawing class on the spot. For that drawing alone, she loved Annik before she'd even met her.

'Break it down,' Antonis called at three-thirty, indicating the end of the lunch shift. Lena put chairs on tables so the busboys could mop the floor. Then she faced the unhappy prospect of going home. She cared deeply for Valia. That's partially why Valia's surliness made Lena so sad.

Instead of taking the bus north, Lena took it south. She got off and walked a block to the Capitol Street School of Art and Design. She didn't intend to go back to class, exactly. She just wanted to stop by and say something to Annik.

The class was just setting up. Even the look and smell of the studio raised Lena's mood. Annik turned, and when she saw it was Lena, she rolled over in her wheelchair. She looked happy and a little surprised.

'Nice to see you,' she said.

'I'm not here to draw,' Lena said.

'Why not?'

'Well . . . the whole thing with my dad.' She waved her arm in the direction of Andrew. 'My dad's pretty tough when he makes a decision. He already got most of his money refunded.' Lena glanced down at her fingers, her nails bitten short. 'I really just came by to say thanks.'

'For what?' Annik asked.

'For your teaching. I wasn't here long, but it's a great class.'

Annik sighed. 'Listen, I've got to help set up. Why don't you stay for a few minutes – until the first break? You're welcome to draw if you want. I've got extra pads and charcoal. Or you can do whatever. Then we'll have a chance to talk for a minute.'

'OK,' Lena said. She didn't really want to leave anyway. She would stay and water the plants if that were her only excuse.

Annik left supplies out on a free easel. It was like leaving drugs out for an addict. It had been Lena's easel; that's why it was free. At first Lena just stood in the back of class and watched people draw. Then her fingers started itching for a piece of charcoal. She ambled over to the easel, just drawing with her eyes at first. She hesitated. Then she picked up the charcoal and she was lost until the bell rang.

Annik came over. 'That's lovely,' she said, studying the three poses of Andrew laid out on the sheet. 'Do you want to go outside and talk for a minute?'

'OK.' Lena expected they'd talk in the hallway, but Annik led her down the hall, up a ramp, and out into the courtyard. Annik rolled up to a bench, and Lena sat down on it. The dogwood trees rustled and a small fountain gushed appealingly in the middle. Various sculptures and found-object works, one involving a stack of car tyres, decorated the perimeter.

'Are you comfortable drawing Andrew?' she asked. Annik's hair was a beautiful red, made only more so by the sunlight. There was orange and gold and chestnut and even pink in it. Annik was fairly young, Lena realized, probably in her late twenties, and her face was delicate and pretty. Lena wondered, absently, if there was a man who loved her.

'Yes,' Lena said. 'I felt a little awkward the first day, but then it went away. I don't think about it any more.'

'That's what I thought,' Annik said. 'How old are you?'

'Seventeen. I'll be eighteen at the end of the summer.'

Annik nodded. 'Can I tell you what I think?'

Lena nodded.

'I think you should take the class.'

'I think I should too. I wish my dad felt that way.'

Annik put her hands on her wheels like she was getting ready to roll away.

Lena wondered, as she had many times before, what had happened to Annik that made her need a wheelchair. Had she always been in a chair or had she grown up on her legs like a regular kid? Had she had an accident or a disease? Lena wondered what of Annik's worked and what didn't. Could she have a baby if she wanted to?

Though Lena wanted to know, she didn't dare ask. She shied away from the intensity that might come from asking such a question. Intimacy came faster when a person wore their pain and poor luck for all to see. And yet, not asking felt like an act of neglect or cowardice. It kept a distance between them that Lena regretted.

Annik rolled back and forth a little, but she didn't go anywhere just yet. 'You do what you need to do,' she said.

Lena wasn't sure whether this meant take the class or listen to your father, but she had a pretty strong suspicion it was the former.

'I'm not sure how I'd pay for it, for one thing,' Lena mused.

'I'm allowed a second monitor,' Annik said. 'You'd need to help set up and clean up every day, including mopping. But you'd get free tuition.'

'I'll do it,' Lena said instantly, not aware of making the decision.

Annik smiled openly. 'I'm so glad.'

'I'm not sure what I'm going to tell my dad,' Lena murmured, half to herself.

'Tell him the truth,' Annik said.

Lena shrugged, knowing that this was the piece of Annik's advice she was not going to take.

There are many things that we would throw away

if we were not afraid that others might pick them up.

– Oscar Wilde

Tibby sat frozen on a chair in the den watching Nicky watch cartoons. Her thoughts came together and broke apart, occasionally punctured by the sadism of *Tom and Jerry*. Her whole body hurt; every bone ached when her mind flashed on Katherine. She let herself think of Katherine for only a second at a time and then she pulled away, because it hurt too much.

Nicky didn't know anything yet. They didn't want to scare him. Whereas Tibby was good and scared, wanting desperately for the phone to ring, but only if it was good news.

Tibby was not raised religious. For the early part of her childhood, her parents were devout atheists, spewing Marx's 'opiate of the masses' rhetoric. Nowadays Tibby wasn't sure what they believed. They didn't talk about it any more.

But Tibby was not them. As far as Tibby was concerned, you couldn't have someone you loved, really loved, die and not believe in some kind of god. It was the only way to look at it. And besides, Bailey herself – as she had lived, not as she had died – had been proof that somebody or something existed beyond the realm of rational things.

And when Tibby thought of Bailey, it made sense,

because a god who was smart enough to want Bailey back as soon as possible was also smart enough to see the beauty of Katherine. Katherine was too good for the world Tibby lived in. Tibby belonged there just fine, but not Katherine. Katherine was brave and generous and passionate. If she weren't on God's dance card, then who would be? Tibby would stand in the corner of heaven, if she ever made it there, but Katherine, like Bailey, would be doing the polka or the bunny hop or maybe the bus stop with God.

Please don't take her yet, Tibby implored. *She's only three and we love her too much to survive without her.*

Tibby was asking selfishly. Because she knew it was her fault. She had opened a window that was always shut. Why had she done that? She knew Katherine wanted to climb the apple tree. She knew that was how Katherine fell out the window. *It wasn't on purpose. Please, God, believe that.*

It was an accident. It was horrible, but not nearly as horrible as the ways in which Tibby had failed her little sister on purpose. Tibby was jealous and resentful. She hurt Katherine's feelings on the pretence that small kids didn't have actual feelings. And yet Tibby knew in her heart they did – possibly the deepest feelings of all.

If Tibby had loved Katherine as she deserved, maybe she wouldn't have fallen out the window. If Tibby had paid attention to her and given her a boost to the branch of the apple tree, then Katherine wouldn't have been climbing out anybody's window. If Tibby hadn't been so preoccupied with Brian, maybe this wouldn't have happened.

Love was the best padding anybody could have. And though irrepressible Katherine deserved it a million times over, Tibby hadn't given it.

I do love her, God. I love her so much. Tibby just wanted a chance to do better.

The phone rang and Tibby threw herself on top of it. 'Tibby?'

It was her dad. She ran the phone into the kitchen so Nicky wouldn't hear. 'Dad?' Her body was shaking.

'Honey, she's doing better. The doctors say she's going to be OK.'

Tibby gave herself full permission to cry now. She wept and sobbed and heaved and shook. Her dad was doing similar things on his end.

'Can I come?' she asked.

'She's still getting X-rays. Her skull is fractured, which is the most serious thing. She also broke her wrist and her collarbone. We're hoping that's the extent of it. She's talking and alert now, but I'd rather you stay home with Nicky for a couple more hours. Bring him over around six when things settle down here, OK?'

'OK. But I want – I want to see her so bad, Daddy . . .' Tibby's voice got swallowed up in tears.

'I know, honey. You will.'

'Tib, it's me, Carma. We've been terrified all day. Lenny made me stop calling your house, and then she called five more times. I'm so glad K's gonna be OK. I'm thinking about you. Please call when you get a second. I love you.' *Beeep.*

'Tibby! It's Bee! God, Lena called me here to tell me about Katherine. I'm still shaking. She's going to get better so fast, though. I know it. Call me? Love you.' *Beeeep.*

'Tib, sorry I kept calling before. It's Lenny. I just couldn't stand waiting. I'm so glad the news is good. I'll come visit tomorrow, OK? Hang in there. We love you.' *Beeeep.*

'And I saw it really close, so I wanted to get it.' Katherine was propped up on pillows in her hospital bed, slightly woozy from medication but still eager to recount her adventure to Tibby and Nicky, who were both sitting cross-legged on the foot of her bed.

Tibby nodded eagerly, trying not to show her agony at each word of the retelling. Her heart ached at the sight of Katherine's bruised, bandaged head, her cast, her sling and multiple cuts and scrapes. It was made almost more heartrending by the fact that Katherine didn't seem to notice.

'I couldn't reach it, so I climbed.' Here she looked remorseful. 'I'm not supposed to climb. But I almost got it, so I climbed more. And then' – she looked to Nicky for this bit – 'I falled.'

Nicky was entranced. Rarely had his sister done anything so interesting. 'On the ground?' he asked breathlessly.

'First I grabbed on the bottom of the window,' she explained. 'I tried to climb back in because my fingers hurt because I was hanging.'

Nicky nodded, eyes wide and unblinking.

'I couldn't climb back in, so I saw the soft bushes and I falled.'

'Oh,' Nicky murmured.

'They aren't very soft because I crushed my skull,' Katherine added conversationally.

'Katherine!' Tibby could not take this. The images were too awful to bear. She turned her head to get hold of herself. When she turned back, she lay across the bed on her stomach and grabbed Katherine's two bare feet. She tried to smile. 'You are so strong and brave, you know?' She turned to Nicky. 'Isn't she?' She knew his was the compliment Katherine would treasure.

'Yes,' Nicky said solemnly.

'But you have to promise you will never do something like that again, right?'

'I promised. I already promised Mommy and Daddy that.'

Tibby held the pair of small feet up to her face, pressing one to each cheek, and closed her eyes. She was overcome by tenderness and relief mixed with guilt and regret. She breathed deeply and willed back the tears. She didn't want Katherine to see any more crying.

'Brian!' Katherine shouted, with remarkable glee for a girl who had in fact crushed her skull less than eight hours earlier.

Tibby looked up. She had already felt so many things today, she couldn't imagine feeling any more.

Brian's face was wrenched, but he kept his expression bright as he came over to hug the non-injured parts of

Katherine. 'You are all in one piece, Kitty Cat,' he said. 'Good job.'

Katherine beamed. 'I falled out Tibby's window.'

Brian cast the briefest of glances at Tibby, but she could read in it his protectiveness of her. 'That's what I heard.'

Tibby wondered how he'd heard. It was so like him just to come over to the hospital.

Tibby let Katherine's feet go as Brian looked at her in his particular way – projecting all the things he was thinking from his eyes to hers. He was worried about Katherine, but he was worried about Tibby, too. He wanted her to feel better, not to feel bad or responsible. He also wanted – or did she imagine this? – to convey to her that what had happened between them had really happened, that he meant what he had said to her.

She wanted something too. Just one little thing: for them to go back to how they were before.

Carmen lay on her bed thinking about Katherine, worrying about Tibby, and generally wondering things. Her mother was sleeping even though they'd finished dinner only an hour before. Once again, David had not made it home in time for dinner.

David was working on a big case. Seeing his schedule up close convinced Carmen that she did not ever want to become a lawyer. At least, not the kind David was. For a few weeks he'd come home by seven most nights for dinner, but in the last month he never came home before eleven, and even at that hour he was fielding calls on his cell phone. A few times he'd left home for the office one morning and hadn't come home until the next morning. Then he'd taken a shower and gone back again. Carmen had always suspected that people who worked that hard secretly didn't *want* to come home, but she knew that wasn't true of David. He was desperate to be home with Christina. He adored her. Carmen could see that he felt genuinely guilty and sad for every dinner he missed. And that was pretty much all of them.

According to Christina, he was working on a 'big deal'. One gigantic company gobbling up a different gigantic company, as Carmen understood it. And all David wanted to do was finish this 'big deal' before the baby came. Which was why he worked twenty hours a day.

Carmen studied her ceiling, dotted with the glowing constellation stickers she'd excitedly arranged there when she was eight. There should be a law disallowing eight-year-olds from decorating their rooms, especially where stickers were involved. Why had her eight-year-old self saddled her seventeen-year-old self with so many dumb decals and see-through unicorn window appliqués? They were impossible to get off.

The truth was, she continued to have a soft spot for the glowing stars, but tonight they made the ceiling seem closer rather than farther away.

Thinking about her eight-year-old self reminded her of her four-year-old self, who was responsible for packing her closet with so many beautified (er, mangled) dolls. And that reminded her of her baby self, who had also inhabited this very room. And that, of course, reminded her of babies again.

She wanted to leave a hole when she left for college.

That was selfish, maybe, but she did. She wanted to step out of the picture of her old life and leave a big, generous cutout waiting for her return. Giving her the *chance*, at least, to come back.

But now it felt like the minute she stepped out of her life, it was going to close up around her as if she'd never been there at all. The picture would re-form almost instantly with a new family in the place of her old one, and she could never come back again. That was how it felt to her. She was scared to disappear. She was scared to lose her place.

The ceiling was pushing down on her. The pressure beneath her eyes was pushing up. She felt like her eyeballs were in a vice. She got out of bed and turned on the light. She wiggled her mouse to wake her sleeping computer. She went online, and without really planning to, she brought up the website for the University of Maryland. Slowly she clicked around inside the site. It was the usual higher-education propaganda. She found herself clicking on the admissions link, and from there to the online application. The university offered rolling admissions. She wondered if they were still rolling. Her hand caused her to click on the print icon.

Her eyes lighted ever so briefly on the stack of booklets and papers from Williams College. Health forms, dorm info, a course guide, a map showing the leafy spot in western Massachusetts where the campus lay, more than seven hours north of home.

She listened to the buzz and spit of her printer and wondered. What if she didn't go away after all? What if she didn't disappear?

Aerodynamically, the bumblebee shouldn't be able to fly, but the bumblebee doesn't know it so it goes on flying anyway.

– Mary Kay Ash

'I took on an extra shift at work,' Lena told her father at dinner when he asked about her day. 'I'm going to do the first dinner shift, from four to seven.' She looked down at her pasta as she said it.

'Excellent,' her father said.

'How is little Katherine doing?' her mother wanted to know. 'Did you get to stop by there today?'

'Yeah.' Lena smiled at the thought of Katherine's excited retelling. The tragedy had become the single most thrilling incident in Katherine's short life. 'She's great. Only she has to wear a hockey helmet till the end of the summer.'

'I wore a hockey helmet,' Effie recalled, scraping her salad fork annoyingly across her plate. 'Didn't I, Mom?'

'For a week,' Ari answered. 'You had a concussion, not a fracture, thank God.'

Lena chewed a piece of bread. What was it about little sisters smashing their heads? Lena had never had so much as one stitch.

'Vhat kind of sauce do you call this?' Valia asked in an overloud voice.

'Pesto,' Lena's mother said with finality.

'It does not taste good.' Valia inspected it with her fork.

They were all quiet and waited for the moment to pass. Even Effie had been ground down into acquiescence.

A while later, Lena stood at the sink doing the dishes. She stiffened when she heard her grandmother pad into the kitchen behind her.

'I did IMs with Rena today.'

'Oh?' Lena did not turn round. She did not like these conversations.

'She tells me Kostos and that voman are not living together now.'

Lena closed her eyes and stood with her hands in the warm suds. She was glad Valia could not see her face.

Valia had many things to be bitter about, and Kostos was one of them. Her greatest dream was to have her handsome, beloved surrogate grandson, Kostos, marry her beautiful granddaughter Lena. She didn't seem to realize that her own hurt and disappointment were magnified a thousand times in Lena herself. If she had, maybe she wouldn't have brought up the news from Oia as often as she did.

The baby expected by Kostos and Mariana, the reason for their hasty marriage and Lena's heartbreak at the end of the previous summer, did not materialize. That was the first thunderclap to arrive, sometime in December. Valia kept Lena roiling on this news for weeks. No one knew exactly why or what happened, but there was endless speculation. Valia was so biased, Lena doubted that any of her information was reliable. For all she knew, there was a bouncing baby Kostos, beloved by all.

Then, as now, Lena both wanted these rumours to be

true and she didn't. The better part of her didn't. It was all she could do to get over Kostos and keep moving on with her life. She couldn't open her mind to any what-ifs or she would be hobbled by them. She didn't want to know about Kostos. Whatever had happened, it was over. But still, *she did want to know.*

Valia's very presence and her connection to Oia was a thorn in Lena's heart, aggravating the wound whenever it seemed to be healing.

'Kostos stays in an apartment in Vothonas, near the airport. He has a job for a house-building company.'

Lena couldn't control her thoughts. She would have if she could.

Had the baby miscarried, so that Mariana owned his sympathy? Or had it been a hoax, so that Kostos despised her? Had Kostos grown to love his wife? Or hate her? Would there be a different baby, if not the first one? These were the regular thoughts she'd had thousands of times. Now she had new ones to add: were Kostos and his wife really separating? Or was he temporarily relocating for a new job, and she would soon join him?

Lena would have considered electroshock therapy if it meant getting rid of these thoughts.

'That's interesting,' she said faintly to the wall. She couldn't let Valia see how these news bulletins affected her.

Valia launched into her opinions, and Lena stopped listening. She finished up the pots and pans as quickly as possible, made a polite excuse and rocketed up to her bedroom. She called Tibby and talked about nothing in particular. She cleaned her clean room.

She got into bed with a book and tried, as she had so many other nights, not to think about Kostos.

'He's a little taller, don't you think?' Bridget's question floated up to the rafters a few feet above her head. Some of it made its way down to Diana in the bottom bunk.

'Uh. Yeah, I guess.'

Bridget tapped her toes against the metal rail at the bottom of her bunk. 'God, he is cute. In my memory, I didn't exaggerate that part of it.'

'Bridget?'

It was the deep, slow, irritated voice of Katie across the cabin.

'Yeah?'

'Will you shut up?'

Bridget laughed. She appreciated bluntness. 'OK.'

She was happy. She couldn't help it. She was happy that Katherine was OK. She was happy that she felt happy instead of miserable at the thought of Eric Richman sleeping in a bed less than one hundred yards away. Bridget tapped her toes some more. She made a rhythm approximating "Walk on the Wild Side". She tried turning onto her stomach. She cleared her throat. 'Can I say one other thing?'

'No,' Katie barked, but her bark belied a certain amusement.

'Please?'

'What is it, Bee?' Diana asked wearily.

She'd had over twenty-four hours to digest the fact that she would be spending the summer with the mythical Eric. She'd seen him twice that day. They'd smiled at each other, though they hadn't spoken. She was getting the same fizzing feeling she'd had when she'd met him the first time. And that was dangerous, maybe. But she was different now. She felt different.

'I'm not sorry he's here,' she informed Diana. 'I think I might be OK about it.'

LennyK162: Talked to Bee finally. Cannot believe about Eric.
Carmabelle: Cannot either. She said she's OK, though.
LennyK162: Do we believe her? Do we go to Pennsylvania and drag her home?
Carmabelle: Let's give it a week.

Today was the day Valia had her doctor's appointment. Her kidneys had apparently been doing something funky, so she was supposed to get something or other checked once every two weeks at the hospital.

It was their first outing, and Carmen welcomed it. Just leaving the house had to be good. Even if they both got squashed by a bulldozer on their first step down the front walk, it would be preferable to another long afternoon spent in the darkened Kaligaris den.

Besides, today was also the day Carmen got to wear the Travelling Pants, and nothing magical was going to happen sitting inside with Valia close enough to squash it.

They'd only been together for one week, and already Carmen and Valia were in a rut. After madly IMing and yelling at the computer – and at Carmen – for a couple of hours (while also listening to the TV), Valia's energy would start to fade. Sometime around three o'clock she would change to a soft chair and her head would start to nod and swerve as sleep tried to claim her. This was around the time that *Brawn and Beauty* came on. Carmen would perch at the edge of her chair, and gingerly, slowly reach for the remote control. Then, waiting long minutes if necessary, she would watch for Valia's wrinkly lids to shut. Then she would wait even longer. Then . . . slowly she would shift down the volume and slowly scroll through the channels. Her heart would be in her throat at this point. Once she got to channel four, she would imagine victory at hand, she would yearn for that first look at Ryan Hennessey's turquoise eyes . . . and then . . .

Valia would shoot straight up in her chair and bellow, 'Zat is not my show!' and Carmen, in pitiful defeat, would turn back to Valia's show. And then the cycle would start again.

So Carmen was shamefully grateful to Valia's misfiring kidneys as she and Valia shut themselves into Carmen's car. She was deaf to Valia's ten-minute harangue about how Carmen didn't hold the steering wheel right.

They were absurdly early for the appointment, thanks to Carmen's eagerness, so Carmen was the picture of flexibility when Valia insisted they stop at the ice-cream shop round the corner from the hospital. Who was Carmen to turn down ice cream?

Valia wanted pistachio. No, she didn't, she wanted butter pecan. No, that would not be good.

'Vhy do they have the cookies in the ice cream?' she demanded to know.

'Vhat do they mean by this . . . *jimmies*?'

'Who vould eat that purple thing?'

Carmen saw the look on the face of the girl behind the counter, and it was familiar. It was a look that she imagined she herself had worn for roughly thirty hours the week before.

Finally, after an excruciating number of questions and unsolicited criticisms, Valia settled on peppermint ice cream, of all things. It was a garish red, and slimy-looking.

Valia took one bite and shoved it towards Carmen. 'I hate it. You eat it.'

'I don't want it.'

'I hate it.' Valia kept pushing it at her.

Carmen was fuming. She hated Valia's nasty peppermint ice cream too. And furthermore, she hated Valia. Valia was a big, fat baby. Carmen hated babies. She hated old people. She hated everyone in between. She hated everyone.

Except him.

He was a guy – maybe her age or a little older – who walked into the store just as Carmen was dodging the slimy red ice cream.

She didn't hate him, though at her rate, perhaps she could learn to. He wasn't Ryan Hennessy or anything, but some quality about him struck her nonetheless. His straight hair was yellowish brown and a little bit unkempt. His eyebrows were almost blond and his freckles made him look kind of jaunty, like he didn't care about anything too much. His eyes, on the other hand, made him look like he did.

She looked at his face for a moment too long. When

she turned her head back, she saw the scoop of ice cream bobbling on Valia's cone, and it was too late to fix it. Sure enough, the scoop plunged to the ground and skidded a foot or so. Valia, incensed, shouted something at Carmen in Greek and then made a show of striding away. But the peppermint ice cream didn't just look slimy. Valia's heel hit the trail of ice cream, and Carmen watched in horror as the old lady went down hard. Carmen's shout and Valia's scream mingled and merged in the air.

Almost instantly Carmen had Valia in her arms. Valia was lighter and drier than she would have imagined. Her eyes were squeezed shut and her face was twisted in pain. Carmen could tell that her right leg had crumpled in the wrong direction. When Valia opened her eyes, Carmen saw the blurry tears in them, and she felt awful. Her own eyes filled with tears.

'Oh, Valia,' Carmen murmured, trying to get a strong hold of her under her arms. 'I am so sorry.' She heard a little sob escape her own mouth.

At once Carmen saw another pair of arms in the mix. It was the guy she did not yet hate. He was helping her lift Valia from the sticky linoleum.

Now the few other patrons gathered around and the counter girl appeared, bouncing nervously from foot to foot.

Valia moaned. 'My leg is hurt,' she said. 'Don't move it. Please.'

'OK,' Carmen said soothingly. 'It's OK.'

'If you'll just rest your arm over my shoulder I can support your leg,' the guy coaxed her. He got himself in

109

position and nodded to Carmen as if to tell her it was time to lift. She complied.

Valia moaned again, but they had her off the floor.

'Valia, the emergency room is right around the corner. We'll take you right there, OK?' Her voice couldn't have been gentler.

Valia nodded. The ferocity had abandoned her features for once, and they settled sort of sweetly into her face, even in spite of her obvious pain.

Ready? the non-hateful guy mouthed to Carmen. Suddenly they were partners.

They began to walk, Carmen murmuring reassuring things into Valia's ear. On the way out of the shop, Carmen's arms were so occupied she couldn't catch the door as it swung behind her. The sharp edge of the metal door frame caught her hard on the back of her arm. Carmen did all she could not to stagger or groan. She pressed her lips together and tried not to release the tears loading up her eyes. She noticed that the guy was looking at her. He glanced at her arm. She didn't see the blood until he did.

She shrugged a little. *It's OK*, she mouthed over Valia's head. She vowed not to let her tears go.

In the emergency room, they eased white-faced Valia carefully into a chair. Then Carmen shifted into a mode of pure efficiency. She talked her way to the front of the line, collecting forms she promised to fill out as soon as Valia was in the hands of a doctor. By some miracle, Carmen discovered that one of the emergency-room doctors spoke Greek, and before long Valia was safely, gratefully in an examining room, the Greek words a palliative in her ear.

Then Carmen remembered about the non-hateful guy. When she returned to the waiting room, he was still there, elbows resting on knees in a plastic emergency-room chair.

'Thank you,' she said immediately and earnestly. 'That was really, really nice of you.'

'Is she OK?' he asked.

'I hope so. There's a doctor who speaks Greek, which made her happy. He seemed to think she might have torn a ligament in a knee, but he didn't think she broke any bones, which is the good news. They're gonna do an X-ray just in case.'

It was funny to have all this to say, to have this whole project in common with a guy whose name she did not know.

She sat down next to him. He produced a damp paper napkin he'd been holding. 'For you.' He pointed to her arm.

'Oh, God. Right.' The blood had stopped flowing and started to dry, but it looked a bit gory nonetheless. She wiped it off with the napkin. 'Thanks.'

'Are you OK?' he asked.

'Totally fine. It's a scratch.' It was more than a scratch, but she liked the feeling of being brave.

She looked at the streaky red napkin. He looked at her.

'So . . . thank you so much. Again,' she said quietly. Carmen wanted to signal to him that he was free to leave, but he didn't appear to want to leave just yet.

He was still looking at her, like he was trying to figure something out.

'I work here,' he offered to the silence.

'Really?'

'Well, volunteer is more accurate. I'm pre-med, so I, you know, want to spend time in the real world of medicine. To see if I'm up to it.'

'I bet you are.' Carmen blushed, surprised that she had let that out of her mouth.

'Thanks,' he said, looking down for the first time.

They were silent for a minute or two. He was wearing brown Pumas. He had the goldish sparkle of whiskers on his face like a real grown-up man. His hair had the extra shiny quality of someone who spent a lot of time in a pool. His shoulders were wide and his torso was strong and lanky – most definitely the build of a swimmer.

'Is she your grandmother?' he asked.

'Oh. Valia? No. She's . . . well, she's my . . . actually, she's my friend Lena's grandmother. I was bringing her here for some tests – I mean, not the emergency room. That wasn't part of the plan.'

'Right.' He smiled. He was looking at her upper arm again.

Shallowly, she felt pleased that she'd injured a part of her body she felt was particularly good to look at.

'Maybe you'll have to come back again. For the tests,' he said.

'I'm sure I'll be back,' she said. 'Valia can't drive here – especially now – and I have a car all to myself right now and . . .'

He nodded. He got up to go. 'Maybe I'll get to see you again. I hope so.'

'Me too,' she said faintly, watching him go. She felt her heart streaming into different parts of her body, places she hadn't felt it beat before.

And yet, as she went back over the conversation, she felt a trace of apprehension. Valia was her friend Lena's grandmother. Carmen was bringing her for tests. Carmen had a car to herself.

Carmen was also getting paid eight fifty an hour. She realized she could have mentioned that, too.

Hit the point once.

Then come back and hit

it again.

Then hit it a third time

– a tremendous whack.

– Winston Churchill

Today was a day during which Bridget would almost certainly look upon the face of Eric Richman, and he would look upon hers. It made getting dressed a different project than usual. Usually she didn't care that much. Or if she did, it was to satisfy her exuberance (like the shiny, shiny pink pants) or her idiosyncracy (like the pilly green turtleneck everyone hated).

This morning, it was more her vanity calling out to be satisfied. Did she want the ponytail high? Nah. Too severe. Braids? Carmen looked saucy when she arranged her hair into two braids on the sides, but Bee's pale hair made her look like Heidi. Anyway, how much did she want to use that particular weapon?

The Hair, as Tibby called it. It had launched a thousand comments. Cars honked and delivery guys whistled; even respectable men looked too long. Hairdressers exclaimed over it as though it were a living miracle. The Hair. Marly's hair, Greta's hair. In fact, it was nothing more than a bunch of dead cells sprouting out of her scalp, but it was her birthright.

Do I want you to notice me? she wondered, leaning so close to the mirror that her eyes formed one large Cyclops eye.

The mirror in the cramped cabin was speckled with

116

grey and only showed the story from mid hip to mid forehead. If she backed up, she'd be sitting in Katie's messy bunk.

She shouldn't care about this so much. She felt an annoying buzzing around her head: expectations, clustering like so many mosquitoes. She did not like those. She refused to have them.

She would just . . . throw on the first pair of shorts she found. And OK, so they were the really nice short blue Adidas ones. And the first top. Well, the second, because that was the white tank with the racing back, and it looked better than the first one. And the hair. She'd just leave it down. She was not setting a trap. She was not! She was just . . . in a hurry. A coach could not be late. She pulled a hair elastic around her wrist just in case.

She loped out of the cabin barefoot, swinging her cleats by the laces. She'd grown so much, she would probably be taller than Eric in her cleats.

Five coaches were already milling around on the centre field. One of them happened to be Eric. Not that her eyes went there first.

Having finally read the camp's handbook in the hour after sunrise when she couldn't sleep, she now knew the deal. The camp was split into girls' and boys' sides. Each side was broken into six teams. They played soccer for four hours every morning. They put the boys and girls together for speed and agility training for an hour after lunch, and then for the other activities – swimming, waterskiing, hiking, rafting, and all kinds of other campish things. After dinner they had a couple of free hours. Usually there was a movie or something.

Now that she'd bothered to look at the roster of coaches, on which Eric Richman's name did indeed appear in twelve-point type and which had sat folded inside an envelope in her room at home for several weeks, unread, Bridget knew she was assigned to coach a boys' team. That was all right. Diana was coaching one on the girls' side, that was the only negative. They would have had fun together.

Bridget sat down in the middle of the field and plucked out the socks she'd balled up in her shoes. She pulled them on and laced up her cleats. She felt the warm sunshine on the top of her head.

It's different now. It's all different, she was telling herself. But she was not sure her self was listening. Eric circled close to her, with the slightly bemused expression he had often worn around her two summers before. She followed him with her eyes.

The campers were gathering. They were supposed to all be between the ages of ten and fourteen, but the boys particularly were so varied it was almost comical. Some looked like little kids. Some looked nearly like grown men.

She saw Manny, assigned to be her trainer, whom she'd met during coaches' meetings the day before. She waved to him and he waved back.

The boys' director blew his whistle. Joe Warshaw. He'd played for the San José Earthquakes, a major claim to fame. Bridget jumped to her feet, shaking out her legs. This was exciting. She'd coached unofficially in Burgess, Alabama, the previous summer. She'd coached at clinics. She'd assisted the JV coach at school a bunch of times. But she'd never coached her own team before.

She knew her reputation preceded her. She'd already heard whispering behind her back at breakfast that morning. She was not only the youngest coach but also the only high school all-American this year.

She spent most of her life in places where her soccer accomplishments didn't matter that much. Her friends weren't athletes. They were as supportive as they could possibly be. All three of them had cried at her awards ceremony. But they didn't understand what it meant – nor did she really want them to. She loved how much they loved her for everything else. Her dad, always pre-occupied, thought being an all-American was basically comparable to making varsity. And her brother had come to a grand total of one of her games. But here it was like being a celebrity. These kids worshipped the things she'd accomplished. And Eric. He, of all people, knew what it meant.

She ended up at Eric's side as the director called out the teams. Not entirely on purpose. He was the only one she knew. (How strangely she knew him.) And it was a perfectly natural place to stand.

It's not like I'm going to do that again, she promised herself.

Sometimes when she thought of Eric, and now more powerfully when she saw him, she felt some achy nostalgia for her old self. For the dauntless, daring soul she used to be. There was something vaguely enchanted about that time. There were certain qualities you possessed carelessly. And you couldn't retrieve them when they were gone. The very act of caring made them impossible to regain.

Not all of that spirit was gone. She still had it, but she had a more tempered version. That time with Eric in Baja had been both the height of that magic and its calamitous end. He had managed to inspire both.

She was a bit more fragile now. Or no. Maybe she was less fragile. Maybe she had come to terms with her injuries and knew how to protect them. She was more self-protective, that was true. But she was a girl without a mother. She had to protect herself.

Bridget had the sense that she was already popular among her constituency. The boys assigned to her made a big thing about it among themselves. As they gathered around her now, some looked boldly admiring and others just looked terrified. She had several capable, well-muscled kids. One of them, a blond, spoke English with an accent. For some reason, the face that drew her belonged to a broad-faced, freckled, sharp-featured kid with long, gangly legs and extremely large feet. He had a great face – all eagerness – but even just standing still made him look unco-ordinated. He was going to be a project, she could tell.

While their teams put on their jerseys (Bridget's team was sky blue), she found herself standing near Eric again. 'You're popular, aren't you? I've never felt like such a letdown,' Eric said, laughing, and she was pleased if he meant what she thought he meant.

'So how's it going?' she asked him coolly. She wanted him to know she was different now. 'You look tan.'

'I just got back from two weeks in Mexico.'

Bridget felt her face strain. What was he trying to say to her? She'd never been the kind of person who'd overthought people's motives, and she didn't feel like starting now.

From his face, he seemed to recognize that he had already shoved them into slightly awkward territory.

She cleared her throat. 'How was it?'

He was uncomfortable. 'We stayed with my grand-mother in Mulege. And then we travelled down to Los Cabos and ended up in Mexico City for a few days.'

Bridget heard one word louder than the others. He was doing that *we* thing. What was we? Who was we? She wasn't going to stand here wondering.

'Who is we?'

He paused. He wasn't looking at her any more. 'We? Oh, uh, me and Kaya. My girlfriend.'

Bridget nodded. His girlfriend. Kaya. 'Wow. Good for you.'

Had he wanted to tell her this? Had he not wanted to tell her?

'See you,' Bridget said numbly, walking away to stake a place for her team to gather. She wished she could have blasted those buzzing, swarming expectations with a can of bug spray.

You had hopes, admit it. She hated dishonesty, especially in herself. *You know you did.*

Lena stared out the window of the bus. It was empty, so she pulled her legs up onto the seat and hugged them, loving the feeling of the Travelling Pants against her skin. It had been a wonderful afternoon of drawing, almost magical. Partly because of wearing the Pants, partly because she felt she was really making progress.

She pictured the last pose of the day – twenty minutes. She loved the long pose best. They had a new model now, Michelle. She had round hips and long, hyper-extending arms. Lena had no thought of assessing the model in terms of beauty. Michelle represented a series of drawing challenges. Lena looked out the window of the bus, but she saw Michelle's elbows.

Lena liked her time on the bus, and the slow walk from the bus stop to her house in the sweet end-of-day light. It gave her a transition between the meditation of her class and the sharpness of home.

This night she was greeted sharply. Her father was yelling before she could put her bag down.

'Where have you been?' He hadn't changed out of his suit yet. He did not look relaxed.

She kept her mouth shut. She had a feeling he knew where she hadn't been.

'I dropped by the restaurant on my way home from work to say hello and you were not there,' he rumbled.

She shook her head. She felt the dull thud starting in her chest. She would wait to find the extent of his knowledge before trying any damage control.

'You don't work the dinner shift, do you?'

She shook her head again.

'You were at that art class, weren't you?'

Was there any point in denying it? There were many stated rules of the Pants, but she realized there was an unstated one too: you couldn't lie in the Pants. At least, she couldn't.

She needed to start breathing again. 'Yeah.'

His faced moved and twitched in anger. His eyes

bulged. That was the thing she always dreaded. She and Effie knew that when his eyes went like that they were in serious trouble. It had happened very rarely throughout their childhood. But in these long months since he'd brought his unwilling mother to live with them, it happened a lot more often.

Lena's mother appeared in the front hall behind him. She was distressed. 'Let's talk about this in a calm way. George, why don't you change before dinner. Lena, get yourself settled.' She had to pull George away like a coach walking a prizefighter back to his corner.

Lena ran upstairs and closed her door. She waited to see if she needed to cry. She endured a couple heaves. A tear soaked into the knee of the Pants. Her cheeks were blazing and her pulse was throbbing all around her body.

Dinner was a quiet, tense affair. Effie was at a friend's house. Valia's complaints – freshened by her knee injury – actually broke the tension rather than added to it, so thick was the air. At least someone was talking.

Afterwards, Lena and her mother and father closed themselves up in the den.

Her father's anger wasn't as hot, but it seemed to have gotten deeper. 'I've done some thinking, Lena.'

She was sitting on her hands.

'I am deeply troubled that you've lied to us.'

Breathe in. Breathe out.

'You know I've never been happy with the idea of art school for you,' he went on. 'It's impractical, it's expensive, and at the end of four years, you'll have no job prospects. You can't seriously think you'll make a living as an artist.'

Lena looked at her mother. She knew Ari was stuck. She didn't disagree with her husband, but she didn't agree with him either.

'After seeing that class, I felt it was wrong for you in other ways too. It's not a good atmosphere for a young girl. Some parents may accept that kind of environment for their daughters, but I can't.' At least he wasn't yelling. 'I've told your mother this already. I can't support your decision. We will not pay for you to go to RISD. We will pay for a regular university, but we won't pay for that.'

Lena was stunned. 'Isn't it a little late for this decision?' Her voice sounded raw.

'You can find a programme, I think. Your grades are good. Some universities are still taking applications. If not, you can apply for next fall and stay home and work to make money.'

I'd rather die, she felt like shouting at him. But she didn't. She said nothing. What could she say? What would matter to him? Certainly not her feelings.

He was punishing her for disobeying him. He was dressing up his punishment in clothing of practicality, pretending he was being a good father, but she knew what it was.

She pulled her hands out from under her. They felt as cold as marble. Her blood had stopped circulating through her body.

She got up slowly and walked out of the room. He wouldn't hear her words. She doubted he'd hear her silence, either.

Patrick: I'm mad.

SpongeBob: What's the

matter, Patrick?

Patrick: I can't see my

forehead.

There was a funny thing about Carmen, and she knew it all too well: she could understand and analyse and predict the exact outcome of her crazy, self-destructive behaviour and then go ahead and do it anyway. It was called premeditation, and it caused people to have to go to jail for their whole lives as opposed to just a few years.

What made a person like that?

As Carmen once again lay in wait for her tired mother, pretending to flip casually through a magazine in the living-room, she was full of guilty premeditation.

She kindly waited to pounce, though, until her mom had taken off her shoes and lain down on the living-room couch. Now that the truth was out about the baby, Christina's stomach was expanding remarkably.

'I got a call from the admissions director of University of Maryland today,' Carmen said conversationally, flipping the pages of the magazine a little too fast.

The truth was, Carmen wasn't excited about the prospect of spending her freshman year at the University of Maryland. It was a decent school, but it wasn't a fantastic one, like Williams. It was huge and anonymous where Williams was small and personal.

What Carmen was excited about, in some perverse way, was telling her mother.

Christina was too tired even to express the extent of her confusion. '*Why?*'

'Because I applied there, and the admissions lady wanted to tell me they were making a special allowance and letting me in.'

Christina tried to sit up a bit. '*Nena*, I have no idea what you are talking about.'

'I'm thinking about going to UM instead of Williams.'

Now Christina sat the whole way up. 'Why in the world would you do that?'

'Because maybe I'm not ready to leave home just now. Maybe I want to stay and help out and be part of the baby's life.' Carmen tossed this off as though she were describing her plans to get a manicure.

'Carmen?' Her mother's look was satisfying. She was definitely and certainly paying attention to Carmen's future and nobody else's at this particular moment.

'What?' Carmen blinked innocently.

Christina inhaled and exhaled yoga style a few times. She settled back onto the cushions and thought awhile before she opened her mouth to talk. 'Darling. In my selfish heart, I want nothing more than for you to stay home. I hate the thought of you leaving. I'll miss you terribly. You know that. I want you to stay with me and David and the baby. In my selfish heart, that is my fantasy.'

Carmen felt tears bulging out of her lids. She'd swung from pure insouciance to tears in under twenty seconds.

Christina's voice was soft as she continued. 'But a good mother doesn't just obey the wishes of her selfish heart. A good mother does what she believes is the best

127

thing for her child. Sometimes they are the same. This time they are different.'

Carmen pawed at her cheeks with the back of her hand. What kind of tears were these, exactly? Tears of joy? Agony? Fear? Confusion? Maybe a few of each?

'How do you know that?' Carmen's voice was full and high with emotion. 'How do you know they aren't the same?'

'Because Williams is the right place for a girl as smart and capable as you, *nena*. You belong there.'

'I belong at home.'

'You'll always belong at home. Going to Williams doesn't mean you won't belong at home.'

'Maybe it will,' Carmen said.

'It won't.'

Carmen shrugged and wiped her eyes again with the back of her hand. 'I feel like it will.'

Lenny,

You sounded so sad on the phone earlier, we thought these might cheer you up. The lady at the candy store said she never knew a person who only liked root beer-flavoured jelly beans, and to be honest, the all-brown bag doesn't look quite as attractive as the tropical fruit mix, for example. But you are you, Lenny, and we love you like that.

XXXXXXXXXXX OOOOOOOOO,

Tib + Carma

Tibby was outside her window. She was looking up at it, clutching the sill with her hands, feeling the emptiness

under her feet. Inside was warm yellow light, and outside, where she was, it was dark. She could feel the apple
tree somewhere behind her, but she couldn't see it. Her
hands hurt, her arms were lifeless. She wanted to get
back into her room so badly. How had she gotten here?
Why had she done it? She couldn't drop down into dark
emptiness, but she couldn't get back inside, either.

'Tibby? Tibby?'

Tibby opened her eyes and took a moment to orient
herself. She was slumped in a movie theatre chair. The
lights were on. The screen in front of her was blank.
Margaret was ever so gently waking her.

'Hi, Margaret. Hi. I fell asleep, didn't I?'

'You did. Don't worry. Your shift is over. I jis took
care of the garbage for you, so that's all sit.'

Tibby looked at her gratefully. 'Thanks so much. I'll
get yours next time, OK?' Groggily she sat up and let the
dream ebb away. She didn't used to fall asleep in movies.
But working in a theatre could do that to you. Once
she'd taken the tickets for the four o'clock show and
made sure everyone was in their seats and vacuumed the
lobby, she was allowed to watch. That was the whole
reason she'd asked for Margaret's help to get her this job.

But now she'd seen *The Actress* fourteen times. The
first three or four were pretty good. But slowly after
that, the suspense drained out of the suspense. The
spontaneity of the love affair shrivelled to nothing. By
the tenth or twelfth time, Tibby could practically see the
gears working in the actors' heads. She could practically
see the cheap manipulations of the camera work. By the
fourteenth time . . . well, she fell asleep.

As a lifelong movie lover, it was sad, in a way, for her to watch the magic of the illusion dry up like a piece of macaroni left overnight in Katherine's booster seat. It made Tibby feel dull and flat. And watching the excitement on the faces of the audience just made her feel worse. She knew that every audience member was taken in by the big swelling climax, with the cellos and violins and gigantic close-ups of earnest, rapturous faces. They felt it was all happening magically and powerfully for them alone. Of course they didn't consider that they were clutched in the fist of this elaborate fraud. It didn't matter.

Tibby had gotten accepted to the film programme at NYU on the strength of the movie she'd made about Bailey the summer before. She was about to spend four years learning how to make films. She'd thought it was what she wanted more than anything. But now Tibby was beginning to wonder.

She imagined, depressingly, what it must feel like to be a wedding officiator or a doctor who delivered babies. You'd watch these people in the middle of their personal wonders, imagining for themselves a pure, unique, once-in-a-lifetime experience. And then an hour or two later you'd watch somebody else do the same thing. What they thought were miracles were your breakfast, lunch and dinner.

It was sad that what you once thought were marvels on the screen were really manipulations. What you thought was art was just some gimmicky formula.

Bridget discussed it with Diana at night after the campers were in bed. They sat on the edge of the lake, tossing rocks into the still water. Bridget outlined her strategy, which was pretty simple. She'd just avoid Eric. She would stay away from him and throw herself into other things – her team, her training, hanging with Diana and making new friends. And besides, she got three weekends off, and so would Eric. Chances were, they'd be off on different weekends. It didn't need to matter so much that she and Eric were working at the same camp. It was a big camp.

At a pre-breakfast meeting the next morning, the directors gave out assignments to the staff. Besides coaching, they each were assigned partners with whom they would preside over afternoon activities and chaperone certain meals, evening events and special weekend trips.

It was long and somewhat boring and Bridget tuned it out, surreptitiously glancing at more of the pictures Diana had brought – more Michael, her room-mates, her soccer team at Cornell – until she heard her name called.

'Vreeland, Bridget. Rafting and kayaking. Two-thirty to five weekdays. And you've got Wednesday breakfast, Monday lunch, Thursday dinner and Sunday night moonlight swim. Weekend trips TBA,' Joe Warshaw read out.

She shrugged happily. It sounded fun. She didn't know the first thing about rafting or kayaking, but she was a quick learner. And she, more than anyone, loved swimming at night under the stars. Joe was flipping pages on his clipboard. 'Vreeland, Bridget, you'll partner with . . .' He was scanning for a name. 'Richman, Eric.' Joe didn't even look up when he read it. He went on to the next assignment.

Bridget hoped she was hallucinating. Diana cast her a panicked look. If Bridget was hallucinating, then so was Diana.

It was so outrageous Bridget almost wanted to laugh. Was this somebody's idea of a joke? Had somebody from Baja phoned ahead to say that Bridget and Eric shared by far the most wrenching history, so be sure to put them together?

She looked up and Eric caught her eye. She was frowning.

'You can change it,' Diana said under her breath. 'Talk to Joe after. He likes you. He'll change it.'

Bridget marched over to Joe after. 'Hey. Can I ask you something?'

'Sure.'

The kitchen staff was beginning to set up for breakfast.

'Can I, uh, change partners? Would that be all right?'

'If you give me a good reason.' He seemed to anticipate what she was going to say, because he started back in before she could open her mouth. 'And I mean a medical or professional reason. I don't mean a personal reason. I don't accept personal reasons.'

'Oh.' She racked her brain for something that sounded medical or professional. Oozing sores? Would those help? Contagious foot fungus? Multiple personalities? She could make a case for that last one.

'Good. Stick with your partner. Everybody always wants to change at first.' He piled up his papers and stood to leave. 'You'll do fine.'

G od is subtle. But not

malicious.

– Albert Einstein

The ferocity was back on Valia's face, and it was more ferocious than ever. They were due in the hospital again, this time for the double whammy of blood testing for Valia's kidneys *and* physical therapy for her knee. She'd refused to get into the car with Carmen, on account of Carmen's allegedly holding the steering wheel wrong. So Carmen was steering Valia down the sidewalk in her wheelchair, much like a mother pushing the stroller of a very grumpy baby.

Ashes to ashes, diapers to diapers, strollers to strollers, gums to gums, Carmen mused as she pushed Valia along. Who said she hadn't gotten a babysitting job this summer?

There was a reason she was breezing along the two-plus miles to the hospital in the very teeth of the mid-July heat, but she did not yet know his name. And anyway, how much better it was to be outside, sharing Valia with the universe rather than having her in a small dark room, all to herself.

With one hand on the wheelchair, Carmen opened her phone with the other hand and pushed the Lena button.

'Hi,' Carmen said when Lena answered. 'Are you done work?'

134

'I have lunch and dinner shifts,' Lena said. 'I'm on break.'

'Oh. Listen—'

Carmen broke off, because Valia had snapped her head round and was scowling, the lines around her mouth deepening. 'I don't vant to hear you talk on the phone,' Valia declared. 'And how you can push with vun hand?'

'You have to go,' Lena said knowingly, sympathetically.

'Oh, yes.' Carmen snapped the phone shut. Ferocity was etching lines on her face too. One of the advantages of a baby over Valia, say, was that not only were babies considerably cuter but also they couldn't talk.

Carmen pushed the last mile with a clenched jaw. At the hospital she went first to the kidney floor, number eight. As Valia barked at other, non-Carmen people who were trying miserably to help her, Carmen got to roam around in the hallway. In forty minutes she saw many faces pass, but not the one she wanted to see.

It wasn't until they reached the knee floor, number three, and Carmen had been prowling that hallway for twenty minutes that she saw the guy whom she did not yet hate poke his head round the corner. When he saw her, the rest of his body came too.

'Hey!' he said, striding towards her and smiling. God, he could wear a pair of jeans. Had he grown even better-looking in the days since she had seen him?

'Hey!' she said back. Her stomach reacted forcefully to the sight of him.

'I realized I forgot to ask you your name last time,' he said. 'I've been wondering for a week.'

'Did you come up with any ideas?' Carmen asked.

He thought. 'Um . . . Florence?'

She shook her head.

'Rapunzel?'

'Nope.'

'Angela?'

She squinched up her nose in displeasure. She had a very fat second cousin named Angela.

'OK, what?' he asked.

'Carmen.'

'Oh. Hmmm. Carmen. OK.' He tilted his head, fitting her to her name.

'What about you?'

'My name is Win.' He said it sort of loud, as though he were expecting an argument.

Carmen narrowed her eyes. 'Win? . . . As opposed to lose?'

'Win as opposed to . . .' He had a slightly pained look on his face. 'Winthrop.'

'Winthrop?' She smiled. Had she known him long enough to tease him?

'I know.' He winced. 'It's a family name. I hated it from the beginning, but I didn't learn to talk till I was two, and by that time it had stuck.'

She laughed. 'Why *do* we let other people name us?'

'Yeah,' he said indignantly. 'Why? Somebody should change that.'

'I remember that skier in the Olympics,' Carmen recalled. 'Her parents let her name herself and I'm pretty sure she chose Peekaboo.'

He nodded sagely. 'Well, yeah, there is that.'

She smiled. *Win*. Huh. Win, Win, Win, Win. She didn't mind at all.

'How's your . . .' He pointed to her arm.

Not coincidentally, she was wearing her most flattering sleeveless shirt, which offered a long view of her tanned, curvy upper arm. Both of her arms, actually.

'It's fine. Practically all better.'

'Good.'

'How's Valia doing? Ligament, right? Anterior cruciate?'

She nodded happily. Carmen's main problem with guys was that she had nothing to say to them. She loved the fact that she and Win (Win, Win, Win) had all these things to talk about even though they didn't know each other.

'Carmen? Caaaaarmen?'

It was the sound that chilled her blood, that dried her bones and made her lunch crawl back up her throat. Carmen tried to keep her face bright. 'That would be Valia. She needs me. I better go.'

'She doesn't sound happy,' Win observed.

'Well . . .' Carmen bit her lip. She didn't want to vent her suffering to Win. It just seemed wrong here. 'Valia's had a rough time.' She dropped her voice to a low volume. 'She lost her husband less than a year ago, and she had to move here from the beautiful island in Greece where she was born and spent her entire life and . . .' Carmen felt genuinely sad for Valia as she described it. 'She's just really . . . sad.'

Win looked solemn. 'That does sound rough.'

'Yeah. I better go,' Carmen said. She wasn't sure she could endure the Valia wail another time.

'She's lucky about one thing, though,' Win called after her.

Carmen turned her head as she walked away, feeling her long hair swing over her shoulder like a girl in a movie.

'What's that?'

'She has you.'

Lena felt too fragile to go back to drawing class for a few days. She knew her father would be watching her closely now. She waited until she felt strong enough for a confrontation before she dared to go back.

She asked Annik if they could talk during the long break, and Annik agreed. This time Lena led the way to the courtyard. Annik had been so pleased when Lena had first told her about RISD. Annik rattled on about all the teachers she knew there. Now, with the change in plans, Lena felt like she had to tell her that, too.

'So he says I can't go. They won't pay for it,' Lena explained numbly.

Annik's mouth narrowed. Her dark eyes widened within their frames of reddish eyelashes. She seemed to hold back. She probably knew it didn't help to trash a person's parent, no matter what he'd done. 'He says you can't go or he won't pay for it?' she asked finally, flatly.

'I guess both. I can't go if they don't pay.'

'Are you sure about that?'

Lena shrugged. 'I hadn't really thought about it.'

'You should. People go to art school who don't have

any money. There are two ways. I'm guessing that you wouldn't qualify for financial aid?'

Lena shook her head. They lived in a big, nice house with a pool. Her father was a successful lawyer. Her mother had a good income.

'Then you'll have to win a merit scholarship,' Annik said.

'How do you do that?' Lena was afraid to be hopeful.

'I could call my friend—' Annik stopped herself. She put her hands together.

Lena counted Annik's rings, nine altogether.

'If I were you,' Annik went on, changing course, 'I'd go on the website or call them up and find out. And if they tell you no, then ask some more questions until you get somebody to tell you yes.'

Lena looked doubtful. 'I'm not really good at that kind of thing.'

Annik looked impatient. Not mad or dismissive, but definitely impatient. 'Do you want to go to art school or stay home?'

'I want to go to art school. I can't stay home.'

'Then figure out how to do it.' Annik put her hand, briefly, on Lena's elbow. 'Lena, I think you could do something good. I think you have talent, possibly a lot of it, and I don't say that lightly. I want you to try. I can see it's what you love. But I can't fight for you. You have to fight for yourself.'

'I do?'

Annik gave Lena an encouraging half smile. 'You do. You've got to take up some space, girl.'

★ ★ ★

So the first strategy wasn't going to work. Not only was Bridget not going to avoid Eric, she was going to see him constantly. Somebody up there was having a sick laugh at her expense.

Bridget took a long run on her break after lunch and tried to formulate plan B.

She and Eric weren't going to be strangers, so they were going to have to be friends. She could do that. She could treat him like a regular guy. Couldn't she?

She could try to forget that he was her first and her only. She could put aside the disastrous effect their brief fling had on her life. She could ignore – she could try really hard to ignore – the mighty attraction she felt to him. She could make herself accept that he did not feel that same attraction for her.

Bridget was breathing hard now, running up a steep hill, curving round and round. The forest cosseted her on either side.

The truth was, she had never felt so overwhelmingly drawn to anyone. In the two years since they'd seen each other, she had questioned this particular magnetism Eric had for her. Was it real? Or was she so caught up in a mania of her own making that summer in Baja that she had imagined it?

Seeing him again this summer answered her question. It was real. She responded to him the same way, even though she was different.

What was it about Eric? He was handsome and talented, yeah. But lots of guys were. She had adored Billy Klein back in Alabama the summer before, and she had even felt attracted to him, but it wasn't like this.

What made you feel that stomach-churning agony for one person and not another? If Bridget were God, she would have made it against the law for you to feel that way about someone without them having to feel it for you right back.

Bridget reached the top of the little mountain. Suddenly the trees fell away, and she could see furrowed hills and steamy valleys on and on. The camp, in which all of this agitation was contained, was small and circular. From this height, it was small enough to put her arms around.

Bridget knew what to do. She couldn't control her basic response to Eric. But she could control her behaviour. She had been tough and single-minded then, and she was now, too. Just as she'd found a way to seduce him back then, she could find a way not to do it now.

She had a weekend at home coming up. She would pull herself together. And when she got back to camp, she would contain herself: she wouldn't flirt, she wouldn't tempt, she wouldn't pine, she wouldn't grieve. She wouldn't even yearn. Well, maybe she'd yearn a little, but she'd keep it to herself.

She began the run downhill, fast and just a little bit out of control.

Yes, they would be friends. They would be pals. He would never know what she really felt.

It was going to be a very long summer.

C an I buy you a drink,

or should I just give you

the money?

– Failed pickup artist

'Come on, Tibby! We're going!'

Tibby was standing in the front door of her house, watching Bee jump up and down on the lawn and shout at her. Her yellow head radiated light in the darkness.

'Where are we going?' Tibby asked flatly.

'It's a surprise. It'll be fun. Come on!'

Tibby walked out onto the summer lawn, feeling the bits of mown grass sticking to her bare feet. 'I don't want a surprise. I don't want to have fun.'

'That's exactly why you need some.'

Carmen was at the wheel of her car, honking the horn and waving out the window. Tibby could see Lena in the front passenger seat.

Bee came close and bent her head towards Tibby's. 'Come on, Tib. Katherine is bouncing back like a little Super Ball. You're allowed to feel OK, you know? I have one night before I go back to Pennsylvania. I'm not spending it without you.'

Tibby ran back to the house to tell her parents she was going. Usually her parents went out on Saturday nights, but since Katherine's accident they stayed close to home. And besides, since they'd fired Loretta, who was going to cover for them?

Tibby trudged to Carmen's car without bothering to get shoes. 'I don't want to go,' she announced to the group, once inside the car.

'You don't even know where we're going,' Lena pointed out.

'I still don't want to go.'

Carmen released the brake and drove off anyway. 'The lucky thing for you, Tibadee, is that your friends don't listen to you.'

Tibby shook her head humourlessly. 'I don't really see how that's lucky.'

'Because we love you too much to let you fester in your room for the rest of the summer,' Carmen clarified. *Fester* was her word of the week.

'Maybe I like to fester,' Tibby said.

'But festering . . . does not like you.' Carmen nodded decisively, as though this were the last word on the subject.

Tibby sat back and let the comfortable nattering swirl around her. Listening to her friends' voices felt like hearing a familiar symphony, with one instrument coming in and layering atop another. The way the cadences linked and harmonized made her feel safe.

Until Carmen pulled into the parking lot of the Rockwood pool.

'Why are we here?'

'We're going swimming,' Bee offered.

'Why don't we just go to Lenny's?' Tibby asked.

'Her parents are home. And Valia is asleep,' Carmen explained.

Enough said. No sane person wanted to wake up

145

Valia, and her bedroom window faced the back of the house.

'Well, this pool is closed.' Tibby felt sour as she said it.

'Just come on, OK?' Bee said.

Tibby followed them over the bridge of the piddling creek that used to seem to her like a roaring waterway connecting parts unknown. It was probably just for sewage. She followed them up the endless steep stairs that used to seem to her like the stairway to heaven. They approached the locked gates, then fanned out to the sides.

Tibby was starting to get an even worse feeling about this.

'This is the place!' Bee called out, pointing up at the one part of the fence not spangled by razor wire. Bee was already climbing by the time they'd gathered at the foot of it. 'Up and over,' she called gaily, making it look as simple as mounting a bike.

'I'm not coming,' Tibby said.

'Why not?' Carmen and Lena both turned to look at her.

This was the kind of stunt she would normally have gone along with. But the thought of climbing the fence made Tibby feel almost physically sick. She couldn't explain all the reasons, but she knew she wasn't doing it.

'I just don't feel like it,' she said.

Bee paused on the other side of the fence. They were all obviously disappointed that they couldn't get Tibby excited about their plan. Bee reversed her climb. Now Tibby felt bad.

'But you guys go ahead,' she said, trying to lighten her voice. 'Seriously, go. I don't mind. Besides, you need someone to stand guard here . . . you know, like, just in case.' It sounded pitiful to Tibby's own ears.

'I wish you'd come. It won't be as fun without you,' Lena said.

'Next time,' Tibby answered, feeling like a big loser.

So there she sat, slumped against the side of the fence—the outside, the wrong side—pretending she was standing guard, while she listened to her friends strip down to their underwear and splash into the water. They were more subdued than they would have been if Tibby had gone along. But still, they were willing to play.

'Carma, I will pay you back, I swear.'

Carmen rolled her eyes. 'Shut up. Why are you saying that? We don't pay each other back. We're not keeping score.'

Tibby actually paused from her insane flurry of activity to look appreciatively at Carmen. 'So I won't pay you back.'

'Thank God.' Carmen took a tube of cherry-flavoured Blistex from the mess of stuff on Tibby's dresser and put some on. 'Eleventh floor, right?'

'Yeah, check in at reception. Ask for Dr Barnes. There's a little kids' lounge in case you have to wait.'

'No problemo. It's my home away from home.' Carmen held up Tibby's soft charcoal T-shirt and considered stealing it.

'Katherine's going to be very happy about this.'

147

Carmen returned the shirt to the mess. 'And it's good practice for me, right?' Her voice had turned sober.

Tibby sensed her mood and touched her wrist. 'I think you already got it down, Carma.'

Carmen led the way to the foot of the stairs, where Katherine was waiting eagerly, her yellow backpack strapped over both shoulders, her hockey helmet tipped at a slightly rakish angle.

'Ya ready, baby?'

Katherine stood up on her kitchen chair, and with no regard for her cast put her arms up in a point like a diver. She jumped to Carmen.

Tibby helped her load Katherine into the baby seat they'd fastened into Carmen's car, and hopped into the co-pilot seat. First Carmen dropped Tibby off at work, and then she drove to the hospital. As they parked, Carmen enjoyed the good spirits of Katherine, chirping away from the back seat, never complaining once about her driving, in contrast to, say, Valia.

As they whooshed through the automatic doors into the giant lobby, Carmen lifted Katherine into her arms. Sweetly, Katherine clung to her like a koala, her hockey helmet wobbling just under Carmen's chin.

'Can I push the button?' she asked in the elevator.

'Yes, eleven. One one.' Carmen steered Katherine's index finger in the right direction.

Her excitement over this made Carmen feel as though she'd just awarded Katherine a lifetime of good fortune. 'Nicky always gets to push,' Katherine explained, pushing several extra times.

Carmen couldn't keep her eyes from scanning the

148

halls. Her heart was beating a lot harder and faster than normal. Of course she was thinking about him. Of course she wanted to see him. But on the other hand, she didn't.

She rested Katherine on the reception counter in pediatrics. 'Katherine Rollins to see Dr Barnes,' she said to the woman behind the desk.

The woman wrote Katherine's name down and located her file. 'Do you want to play in the playroom for a few minutes, sweetie?' she asked Katherine.

'Can she come?' Katherine touched her pointing finger right to Carmen's cheekbone.

'Of course,' the woman said, and gestured them in the right direction.

Carmen couldn't help looking over her shoulder as she walked. A part of her really wanted to see him. A big part.

Well, another time, she thought, entering the confines of the playroom. It was bright and sunny, involving a few other children and lots of toys and miniature furniture. Carmen would have to content herself with standing or sitting on the floor, because there was no way she was fitting into an Elmo chair. And if by some miracle she did fit in, she wouldn't be getting out. She pictured herself walking out of the hospital with a red plastic Elmo chair attached to her butt.

'Hey, you.' She put Katherine down in front of a bead maze and straightened her helmet. 'What do you want to play?'

Katherine danced around, utterly pleased. She brought over a Noah's ark, a xylophone, two puppets

149

and a book. Carmen knew that Katherine was always miffed at how Tibby's friends came over and spent time with Tibby. Now she had Carmen all to herself.

Carmen heard a girl's giggle from behind the big dollhouse set up in the corner. She also saw a few parts of a man popping out – the girl's father, no doubt. Carmen figured she and Katherine could take over the dollhouse once those two vacated. Twin boys were throwing Nerf basketballs at each other. Carmen observed that somebody had taken a few bites out of one of the balls.

'How about this?' Katherine was shaking the animals out of the ark.

They played. There were a lot of singletons in this version of Noah's story, probably due to loss and theft, but Katherine didn't seem to care. Carmen was the hippo, the elephant, the lion and the penguin. It was good, because Carmen had always had a knack for animal sounds and voices. With the penguins, she really got into character. In this case, her penguin was a mafioso, kind of like Marlon Brando in *The Godfather*, only in a penguiny way. Katherine was laughing so hard she stopped making any noise. The people behind the dollhouse were laughing too. The twin boys were circling them eagerly.

Suddenly Carmen realized that the leg extending from one side of the dollhouse had a brown shoe on the end of it. A brown Puma, specifically. She cut off the penguin's soliloquy. Moments later, a face appeared over a miniature gable.

She put both hands over her eyes in complete

humiliation. 'Hi, Win.' Could she have been any louder?

He came entirely out from behind the dollhouse. He was fighting the impulse to smile. No, probably the impulse to laugh. At her.

'Hi, Carmen,' he said. He crawled over to where she was sitting cross-legged on the floor. He pushed the inner part of her elbow and made the arm she was leaning on collapse. 'Can I tell you I've never heard a more entertaining penguin in my life? I didn't even know penguins could talk.'

'Ha ha,' Carmen said, straightening her arm again. She tried to pull herself up and recapture some tiny amount of dignity.

She cleared her throat. 'Win, this is Katherine. Katherine and I are friends. Katherine, this is Win.'

Katherine stood up somewhat importantly. 'Hi,' she said.

Win pointed to her helmet. 'I like your stickers.'

She nodded. 'I crushed my skull.'

Carmen looked aghast. 'You didn't crush your skull, sweetie. You fractured it.'

Katherine waved this off as an uninteresting detail.

'And it's getting better really fast,' Carmen added, possibly for her own sake.

Carmen could tell that Win was fighting to look serious. 'Hey, Maddie.'

A lovely girl with brown skin poked her head over the dollhouse. 'This is Katherine,' he said.

Katherine headed straight for the dollhouse. 'Hey. Can I see that thing?'

'If you don't mess up the living room,' Maddie

allowed. Maddie looked to be about four, enough older than Katherine to be totally seductive.

Win was sitting close to Carmen on the floor. She could feel the heat from his body. She could smell him. He smelled a little salty, like cashews, and a little sweet, like mango shampoo. She felt woozy.

'I'm surprised to see you here,' she said, feeling shy after all her bellowing and swaggering with the plastic animals.

'This is what I do.'

'I mean, I know you work here—' she started.

'No, this is specifically what I do. Nine to two I work in pediatrics, mostly here in the playroom. I play with kids when their parents need to talk to the doctors.'

She raised her eyebrows. 'Really.'

'Yeah. And if you need work, I'd hire you in a split second. You got the place rocking with that penguin.'

She squeezed her eyes shut. 'Stop.'

'Only it doesn't pay very well,' he said.

'How much?' she asked.

'Nothing.'

'That's not so good.'

'It pays better than my job after two. Then I go up to geriatrics to amuse and entertain the old folks. They're always goading me to buy them stuff out of the vending machine. I'm going into debt with that job.'

A nurse appeared at the door of the playroom. 'Katherine Rollins?'

Carmen got up. 'Hey, Katherine. It's our turn.'

Win got up as well. 'Your . . . sister?' he asked.

'No. I'm an only child,' Carmen said. She had no idea

152

why she said that. It was true, yes, but true in such a narrow and ungenerous way it felt more like a lie.

'She's . . . ?'

'My friend Tibby's little sister. She fell out a window a few weeks ago. She's going to be fine, but she has to get checked out a lot to see how she's healing. Tibby was supposed to bring her, but her job added on a shift today, and she's trying to save money for—' Carmen looked up. 'Why am I telling you all this?'

He shrugged, smiling. 'I don't know.'

'Come on, Katherine,' she called. Katherine was having trouble parting with Maddie and the dollhouse.

'You can tell me more, though,' he added. 'I'll listen to anything you want to tell me.'

She heard in his voice, in its particular hopeful tone, that he meant it. She knew he meant it in a real way and not just a charming or flirtatious way. He was sincerely curious about her; he was utterly observant. She could tell that he did want to know her. And on one level this made her as happy as anything she could possibly imagine.

And on another level it made her sad. Because the girl he wanted to know wasn't her. He wasn't seeing her for how she was. He was seeing her as a kind and selfless person who cared about the people around her. He was coming to all the wrong kinds of conclusions.

And worse than that, she was letting him.

Show me a girl with

her feet planted firmly

on the ground and I'll

show you a girl who

can't put her pants on.

– Annik Marchand

'Vreeland! For God's sake, quit sunbathing and help me get some of these things in the water!'

Bridget opened one eye and sat up on the dock. She started laughing. Eric was trying to pull four kayaks into the lake at once, and he wasn't looking so graceful.

'Dude,' she bellowed in a perfect imitation of her cabin-mate Katie's low, sloppy drawl. 'You're late. I can't keep covering for you like this.' Bridget lay back down, resting on her elbows, letting the Travelling Pants soak up some sunshine. She'd already set up all the rafts, oars, life preservers, water shoes, and both double kayaks. She was always early, he was always late. He was always pretending to be put out by the small amount of work she left for him to do.

'I see it's the usual horde of campers,' he said.

It was another joke between them. Three weeks into camp and almost no one came for their activities. Rafting just wasn't as sexy as extreme mountain biking, it would appear. Well, there was a small group of boys who appeared now and then, but according to Eric, they weren't there for the boats.

If it hadn't been a no-flirt zone, Bridget would have batted her eyes and said, 'Well, why *are* they here, do you think?' But she didn't.

'Why are you scaring the campers away?' Bridget asked. The sun made her yawn.

'Because I don't want to work. I want to sit on my ass.'

Bridget smiled at that. She knew how he killed himself on the soccer field. But sitting around was mostly what they did from two-thirty to five. It was shaping up to be a beautiful rhythm — drive yourself and your team relentlessly in the morning and laze about in the sunshine with the guy you loved all afternoon.

She got to her feet. She'd scrupulously worn her least sexy Speedo one-piece for the last few days, but it was dirty. Besides, today was not just any day. It was a Travelling Pants day. She had brought them back with her from her weekend at home, and their presence now lent a particular sweetness to the air even stronger than the wafting smell of honeysuckle. Today she wore them over her best green bikini. Anyway, Eric probably didn't even notice or care. (Did he?) Why did she bother to think about it?

When she got too hot, she carefully peeled off the Pants, folded them and put them on the dock. She shook her hair out of its braid. For her pleasure alone she did a high, arcing dive off the dock and into the lake. She plunged down deep, not stopping herself until she touched the pebbly bottom. She took her time getting back up. She had always had good lung capacity. When she surfaced, Eric was watching for her.

'What? Are you, like, a whale?'

She pretended to be offended as she bobbed there. 'Thanks a lot. Eric, girls don't mostly like to be called whales. Ask your girlfriend if you are unsure.'

'Humans aren't supposed to stay under that long.'

'Speak for yourself.' She swam over to the row of plastic kayaks. 'Hey, you want to try one of these things?'

This was a novel idea. 'Sure. We might as well look like we know what we're doing.'

She pulled a double one loose from the rocky shoreline and into the shallow water. She sat herself down in the front and put her oars into place. He followed her into the water.

As he climbed aboard he made a point of jostling the boat as much as possible, which got her laughing again. He settled in.

'I think you forgot something,' she said.

He looked around. He shrugged.

'A paddle?'

'Oh, that.' He sat back, tipping his face to the sun. 'Are those really so important?' He was trying not to smile.

'I'm not sure it counts as kayaking if you just float around,' she said. But she put her paddle inside the boat and lay back herself. They floated for a while.

Even in just a week, there had been so much downtime spent together that Bridget was relaxed with him. They talked about things. It was weird to be killing time with someone about whom you felt passionate.

She'd plucked up the courage to mention Kaya, casually, at least once or twice every day. She wanted him to know she understood. She wanted him to know she respected that he had a girlfriend and she wouldn't try to get in the way.

He lifted his head. 'Bee,' he said.

'Yeah?'

'Bee!'

She looked up. He sounded sort of urgent.

'What?'

'No, *bee!*'

He pointed, and she suddenly felt a buzzing around her ear. She yelped and swatted it away and it went to her other ear. She hopped up to her feet. The kayak teetered violently.

The bee went from her to him. It flew into his hair. He jumped up to his feet and caused an even greater disturbance.

She screeched, laughing. She rocked the boat, trying to stay on her feet. He shouted and rocked back. She crashed into the water first. She heard his splash soon after. When they came up they were both laughing even harder.

She sputtered and coughed the water out of her nose. 'I think we really look like we know what we're doing.'

Lena approached Annik before class. She was sweaty and sticky from the restaurant, and her feet hurt and her shirt was filthy, but she was pretty pleased with herself nonetheless. 'The woman at the financial aid office at RISD said if I get my portfolio to the committee by the fifteenth of August I could still qualify for scholarship money.'

Annik smiled big. 'Nicely done.'

'I warned them my dad is going to ask for his deposit money back, and I asked her to keep me enrolled anyway. She said I have to come up with a deposit by the end of this month.'

'Can you do it?'

'I just took on three more shifts at my waitressing job. I really hate it, but it pays.'

Annik clapped her on the back. Wheelchairs built up a person's muscles, Lena decided.

'That's what I call fighting,' Annik said appreciatively.

'Qualifying and getting are different, though,' Lena told her. 'There is one full scholarship left to give out, and they have over seventy portfolios already under consideration.'

Annik looked at the ceiling. 'Well. You better do something good, then.'

After class, Annik waited for Lena while she did her mopping. 'Do you have an hour to spare?' she asked.

Lena figured she could call home and make an excuse. 'Sure.' Effie would cover for her if necessary.

'I want to see what you can do with a longer pose. I'll sit for you. I certainly can't stand for you.' Annik seemed to enjoy her own joke.

Lena was timid to laugh. 'Are you sure you want to?' she asked.

'I'd be happy to do it. I'll set up over here.' She rolled over to the windows. 'We've got about an hour left of decent light.'

Lena felt a little self-conscious setting up her easel. It was weird staring straight at your teacher, but once Lena got drawing, she became immersed. She drew without pause for thirty straight minutes. Then Annik stretched

160

her neck a little and Lena worked for thirty more. She'd never done more than a twenty-minute pose, and it was exciting.

Her self-consciousness returned when it was time for Annik to look at her work. Annik looked at the drawing carefully, wheeling a little back and forth. Lena bit her pinky nail and waited.

'Lena?'

'Yeah?' It came out a little squeaky.

'This is not a bad drawing.'

'Thanks.' Lena knew something else was coming.

'But you didn't draw my chair.'

'What do you mean?' Lena felt instantly embarrassed.

'I mean, you took the drawing down to my shoulders. You would certainly see a good bit of the chair at that angle, but you left it out. How come?'

Lena felt her cheeks warm. 'I'm not sure,' she said, almost inaudibly.

'I'm not trying to give you a hard time,' Annik said. 'It's just that the chair is a big part of who I am, you know what I mean? I have all kinds of deep and complicated feelings about it – resentments, of course, too – but it is part of me. I don't picture myself without it. I'm surprised you left it out.'

Lena felt bad. She'd thought maybe it would seem critical of Annik if she drew the chair. She hadn't been sure what to do about it, so without really thinking, she'd avoided it.

'You could make a really fine drawing, Lena. I can tell this is the right approach for you – portraits, long poses. I can see how deeply you respond to gestures and facial

161

expressions. You'll excel at it if you work hard.' Annik said it like she meant it. 'But Lena?'

'Yeah?'

'You've got to draw the chair.'

Tibby had never liked Loretta until Loretta got fired.

The main reason Tibby didn't like her was because Tibby was too old to be in Loretta's jurisdiction, and yet Loretta acted like she was Tibby's babysitter anyway.

And then there was the time Loretta put Tibby's best cashmere sweater in the dryer and shrank it so small even Katherine couldn't wear it. Tibby knew it was petty, but she nursed a long grudge.

In spite of all that, Tibby was appalled when her parents let Loretta go. Appalled and guilty.

'It wasn't her fault.' Tibby defended Loretta to her parents when she heard the news. 'If it was anybody's fault, it was mine for leaving the upstairs window open.'

But her parents stuck by their decision, and Tibby was left feeling horrible for Loretta. In the too many hours she spent in her cluttered room (windows safely shut), Tibby thought a lot about Loretta and missed her.

Tibby had never realized before what an easy spirit Loretta had. She hardly ever took offence at anything. She managed to defuse even the tensest Rollins family episode with her lightness and good humour. She was the master of deflecting and distracting both Nicky and Katherine from whiny behaviour. This was something Tibby now sorely missed, as she listened to her mother square off and feud with Nicky day after day, sending him into paroxysms of loud brattiness. Tibby wondered how her mother had learned so little during these years of Loretta's wise example.

One night Tibby stayed up too late and got overly weepy. She wept bitter tears of sorrow for knowing Loretta didn't have a job any more, for knowing it was her fault that Loretta didn't have a job any more, and also for never having told Loretta how great she was.

The next morning Tibby found Loretta's address in her mother's book. She clipped her hair in the barrettes Loretta had given her two Christmases ago, pulled on her most cheerful yellow shirt, got into her car and set off to the far reaches of Prince George's County. She had nothing but a map of the greater Washington, DC, metropolitan area and a lot of guilt to guide her.

It took her two and a half hours (one and a half spent getting lost), but the look on Loretta's face when she saw Tibby made it worth it. Even if Tibby spent twenty-four hours getting lost on the way home.

'Tibby! ¡M'ija! ¿Cómo estás? ¡Dios te bendiga! ¡Ay, mira que hermosa! ¡Que suerte verte! ¿Cuéntame, cómo te va?' Loretta exploded in Spanish.

Not only did Loretta not appear to harbour any resentment; she hugged Tibby like a long-lost daughter. Loretta's eyes filled with tears as she planted several kisses on Tibby's face.

Tibby was still blinking in surprise when Loretta pulled her into the small house and introduced her to various family members as though they knew all about her. Loretta gestured to the pale woman on the couch in her bathrobe. 'She no get up. She have' – Loretta pounded her chest in demonstration – 'infection.'

163

That was Loretta's sister, Tibby realized. It made Tibby feel even worse.

Tibby sat at the dining-room table with Loretta, who kept patting her hand and asking exactly how Katherine was doing.

'She's getting better so fast. She's great. She misses you, though,' Tibby added quickly. Tibby then presented Loretta a picture of beaming Katherine in her hockey helmet, which Loretta promptly kissed. Loretta wanted to know all about Nicky, and she even wanted to be sure that certain leftovers were not spoiling in the fridge. Loretta cried a lot, both out of sadness and joy, and said many things in Spanish, which Tibby could not understand.

The thing Tibby could understand was that Loretta truly loved Katherine. She loved Nicky. She even loved Tibby, for God knew what reason. How could Tibby's parents fire someone who loved their kids this much? It was wrong.

Loretta insisted that Tibby stay for dinner, so Tibby accepted. Then Loretta and her niece and another sister buzzed around in the kitchen for the next hour preparing a feast, while Tibby sat on the sofa with the sick sister, watching a TV show. Tibby was handed a big glass of orange soda and banned from helping in the kitchen.

Tibby watched the actors motoring away in Spanish and let her mind go. She was moved by Loretta's capacity to love, even when her employment had ended in such a bitter way. Loretta didn't seem concerned that the whole thing was so unfair, that Tibby's parents had lashed out vindictively.

Some people spent their lives wallowing in resentments, and other people, like Loretta, let ill fortune wash right over them.

When the table was revealed to Tibby with a great flourish, she saw how proud Loretta was. In honour of Tibby, Loretta and her niece and sister had made steak.

Tibby tried to keep the look of alarm off her face. She was moved by this gesture. Clearly this wasn't the kind of household where they ate steak every night. And so Tibby chewed the meat with as much vigour as was possible for a girl who had been a vegetarian since she was nine.

Heard melodies are

sweet, but those

unheard

Are sweeter; therefore,

ye soft pipes, play on.

– John Keats

'Let's call her . . . Good Carmen,' Carmen said.

It was Saturday and they had spent most of the morning at the farmers' market. Now Lena and Tibby were both lying on the deck in back of Tibby's house, chins on hands, nodding.

'This guy who works at the hospital, you see, keeps running into this girl, this Good Carmen.' Carmen sat up in her lounge chair and crossed her legs Indian style. She breathed in the pineapple smell of Lena's sunscreen. 'Good Carmen is taking care of Valia. She's being stoic and selfless. She's taking care of Katherine. She's doing it all out of the goodness of her heart. The problem is that this guy thinks Good Carmen is me.'

'Is he cute?' Tibby asked.

Carmen narrowed her eyes. 'Tibby, have you been listening to anything I'm saying?'

'All of it. I just need a little context. What's his name? What's he like? How much do you care what he thinks?'

Carmen considered. 'Well. Hmmm.' Truthfully, even thinking about him was fun. Talking about him was jubilation. 'Is he cute, you ask? I mean, he's no Ryan Hennessey, of course—'

'No, he's not,' Tibby shot back. 'He's real, for one.'

'Yes. He is real. He does have that going for him. And yes, he is cute.' She couldn't keep the smile off her face.

'He's really cute,' Lena said. 'I can tell. Look at you.'

'What's his name?' Tibby asked.

'Win.' She realized she said it in the same slightly argumentative tone he did. She was already taking his side.

'Win?' they both asked.

'Yeah. Short for Winthrop. What can he do? He didn't name himself.'

'I like it,' Lena stated.

Tibby studied Carmen for a long minute. 'Oh, my God. Carma Carmeena Carmabelle. You like this guy, don't you?'

Carmen was blushing.

'This is amazing. This is new,' Tibby continued. 'You do like him.'

'But he doesn't like me. That's the problem. He is a good person. He's pre-med. He volunteers at the hospital all day long. He likes Good Carmen.'

'So why not set him straight?' Lena asked.

'Because he won't like me any more.'

'Why don't you try it?'

'Because I'm scared to. I don't want to ruin it for him. I'd rather he have his idealized version of me than introduce him to the real thing. I like the way he thinks of me – I mean Good Carmen.'

Lena lifted her sunglasses. She was resolute. 'Carmen, that's just sad. Be yourself. If he doesn't like you for yourself, then he ain't worth it.'

'Hallelujah,' said Tibby.

169

Carmen studied them suspiciously. 'What's with you two?'

Bridget sat with her clipboard on her lap at the side of the soccer field, chewing on a piece of grass. She didn't even bother to lace up her cleats these days. She went around barefoot. She even played barefoot. It was unorthodox, she knew, but who really cared?

Eric was pacing a few yards away. He was watching his team doing dribbling exercises. She didn't get that screaming feeling in her cells quite so much now when she saw him. She was getting used to him.

'Blye at forward,' she said to no one in particular. She'd put Lundgren, the Swede, on defence. He was versatile. The European kids always had the best fundamentals. Naughton, her special favourite, she put in the goal. He was completely unco-ordinated, but he had a weird, seemingly dumb magnetism for the ball. At the moment she had her team carrying out an elaborate pattern of sprints. She wanted to get her roster in order before they got back.

Suddenly her clipboard was in shadow. 'Away. No spying,' she ordered without looking up.

Eric stepped back about one foot. 'You're crazy to put Naughton in the goal.'

'I'm crazy to put him anywhere. No spying. No peeking. No Peking. No Beijing.'

'It's friendly advice.'

'All friendly till we beat you soundly.'

'Ooooh. I'm scared.'

She looked up at him finally. He pretended he was

going to step on her feet. She put her hand over her eyes, squinting in the sun. She smiled at him, and a nice thought passed through her mind. *I think we're really friends.*

Eric had joined her and Diana for dinner the past two nights. At first Diana seemed alarmed, but she got used to him. You could get used to almost anything. They spent three hours sitting at a table in the cafeteria discussing the relative merits of each of their teams like the three big soccer dorks they were.

Bridget and Eric hung out now even when they didn't have to. He joined her for her evening runs sometimes. They ate their lunch on the field together (except Mondays, when they pretended to chaperone in the dining hall) and talked strategy. They didn't make a big deal of it or anything.

She could do this. She could. It wasn't that hard. She loved him, maybe so, but she also loved being with him. She could be happy with just that. She didn't need any more.

Finally, finally, at last the strange air of their encounter was dissipating. Her new relationship with him had almost entirely eclipsed the old one. She felt like she could trust herself with him now.

Bridget watched her breathless team streaming back towards her across the field. She stood waiting for them like a proud mama. Naughton was the first one in her face. She frankly suspected he'd cheated a corner or two, because he wasn't all that fast. 'Hey, Naughty, how'd you do?'

'Good.' He was trying to catch his breath.

171

'You all get water,' she ordered the group. 'Then we'll get to work.'

Naughton continued to hang around her, not quite balanced on his bumpy knees, while the others got water. He was always asking her stuff. He was her project, and he knew it. 'You running tonight?' he asked her.

'Probably. Maybe a short one.'

'Can I come?'

This was new. 'Uh . . . I guess. If you have anything left after I finish with you all today.'

He looked eager. 'I'll keep up. Don't worry.'

This made her remember things that had happened two years ago. How she would foist herself upon Eric when he tried to lead runs in Mexico. She would bother him and show off and flirt outrageously. God, had she really done that?

She was still thinking about this as she and Eric walked to the dining hall for lunch a couple of hours later.

He noticed she was quiet, but he didn't bug her.

Joe Warshaw intercepted them at the front of the room. 'Just the two I need,' he said, pulling them off to the side. He sort of winked at Bridget as if to say, 'See, your partner's not so bad, is he?'

Bridget looked down at her toes.

'We've planned a rafting trip this weekend,' Joe explained. 'It's an overnight down the Schuylkill. It's an easy stretch, one portage. We've got eight kids signed up. Esmer was supposed to do it, but he has to take off this weekend, and you two are both on. Do you mind?'

'Does it matter if we mind?' Eric asked. He knew the way of Joe.

Joe smiled brightly. 'No, actually.'

'Well, then,' Eric said.

'I'll tell the kitchen guys to get all the tents and stuff packed into the van. I'll make it easy for you, how's that?'

Eric and Joe talked logistics while Bridget's mind raced around the place. She was going on an overnight camping trip with Eric. Oh, God. She trusted herself to stick to the friendly banter during meals and even lake duty. She had mastered that subtle art. But sleeping close to him in a sleeping bag under the stars? She wasn't sure she trusted herself to be able to do that.

Hey, girlies,

    41 days!!!! Do you know where your bikinis are?

                                              Bee

It came to her in a dream. It really did.

Lena was dreaming about Valia and her mother and Effie and all kinds of incongruent bits and pieces. And in her dream she went into the dining room − or a place that she knew was the dining room even though it looked kind of different. And instead of her family members sitting in the chairs, there were drawings of them − big wide sheets of paper with charcoal drawings propped on the chairs. Lena not only liked these drawings, in her dream, but she knew that she had made them.

And when she woke up, she knew what her portfolio project was going to be. It wasn't so much that she wanted to draw a series of portraits of her family. It was that she knew it was the right thing to do.

She decided to start with her mother, the source of all things. Besides, she knew she could make her mother agree to it. After dinner, she scouted the house for the right place to pose her.

'Sit there.' Lena pointed to the living-room couch, green velvet, with pillows carefully arranged. She studied her mother. No. She didn't really repose in the living room very often.

'Let's try the kitchen,' Lena said, and her mother followed her there. She sat Ari down at the kitchen table. Better. But her mother was never really sitting down.

'Stand, OK?' Lena said. She let her mother gravitate to her own spot at the counter. That made sense. Without thinking, her mother put her chin in her hands, her elbows resting on the granite counter, waiting for Lena to pick.

'Don't move,' Lena said. 'That's good.' She brought a stool opposite her mother and propped her drawing board on her lap. Lena made herself look for a long time before she started. She wanted to see all that was real and also what was there. She didn't want to let herself shy away.

She started. She liked the softness of her mother's skin contrasting with the gleaming granite countertop, the

174

way the skin of her elbows puddled a bit upon it. Her mother eschewed softness, longed for hardness, but softness was what she had.

Lena wanted to capture her mother's worn, slightly bagging knuckles with the hard permanence of her wedding ring pressing as it now did into her mother's cheek. She considered her mother's severely glinting diamond studs, a twentieth-anniversary gift from Lena's father, sitting in her soft, tired earlobes.

Drawing wasn't a passive exercise, Annik liked to say. You had to find the information; you had to go in after it.

Lena pushed herself to look deeper into the tentative set of her mother's eyes, the lines burrowing towards her lips, made more pronounced by the careful, deliberate way she held them.

Ari wanted to support Lena in some way. She would sit for this drawing until every one of her limbs went to sleep. But she needed to stay allied with her husband, too. She'd made too many compromises already this year to pull out. She was an appeaser, maybe, but by now she was accountable herself.

Lena saw these conflicts fighting in each quadrant of her mother's face. She saw the tiny fault lines betraying the feelings that pulled her mother apart. Ari was so placid in some ways, her smooth hair, her plucked brows, her elegant clothes in every soft shade of beige. And in other ways, Lena could see she was waging an internal war.

Lena imagined herself a field marshal, overseeing the hostilities between her mother's eyebrows. Then she

175

imagined herself a cartographer, mapping out each curve and concavity between Ari's cheekbone and her jaw. She imagined herself a blind person, feeling her way around her mother's neck and collarbone with her charcoal. She pictured herself the size of a mite, crawling over the canyonlike hollows of her mother's shoulders.

When Lena brought the drawing in to Annik the next day, Annik was plainly excited. She was near speechless.

'Do you think I got the chair?' Lena asked timidly.

Annik hugged her, knocking Lena's legs into her wheels. 'I really do.'

Should we have stayed

home and thought of

here?

– Elizabeth Bishop

'Hey, Naughty.'

Bridget hadn't told Naughton exactly the time of her run that evening, but he was there nonetheless. She wondered how long he'd been waiting by the road at the foot of the hill. Eric, this evening, had not come.

They ran in silence for quite some time. The air was so heavy you could practically feel the water squishing around in it. Bridget had to hand it to Naughty. The uphill stretch was fairly brutal – she liked to start a run tough – and he kept right with her even when he looked like he was going to die.

He was fourteen. He seemed infinitely younger than her, but she realized with some mortification that he was no more distant from her age than she was from Eric's.

He kept turning his head to look at her. He was nervous.

She paused briefly at the top of the mountain to enjoy the view. It was part of her ritual. The silence was punctuated by Naughton, who was breathing so hard she was afraid he might blow out a lung.

She waited until they were headed downhill to get conversational. 'How's it going?' she asked him.

'G-g-ood.' He worked hard for the word.

He waited until they had finished the four-mile loop and begun walking to unburden his heart. 'Um, Bridget?'

'Yeah?'

'Do you like Bridget or Bee?'

'Either. Both.'

'OK, uh, Bee?'

'Yeah?'

'I wanted to tell you something.'

'OK.'

Silence.

'Uh . . . never mind.' Sweat made his whole face shine.

'OK.'

He couldn't bear to leave it at that. 'I, uh, think you're . . . pretty amazing.'

'I like you, too, Naughty.'

He cleared his throat. 'I think I'm talking about a different kind of like.'

'Like a girlfriend?' She cut to the chase. This could take all night.

He was surprised. 'Yes.'

'I'm your coach, Naughty. You know I can't be your girlfriend.' That hadn't been good enough for her, back in Baja, had it? Why did she think it was good enough for him?

'Do you have a boyfriend?' he asked.

This would have been an easy out, but she didn't feel like lying. 'No. Not really.'

'Maybe after camp?' he proposed. 'I could wait.'

He was so much sweeter and more rational than she

179

had been. Why seal off all hope? 'Maybe someday. Who knows what will happen?'

A few hours later, she was sitting next to Eric on the dock. The sun was setting behind the trees and she was feeling thoughtful.

'Can I apologize to you for something?' she asked him, kicking her bare feet back and forth in the warm air.

'What do you have to apologize for?' he asked lazily. His hair was messed up from drying with the lake water in it. His face was stubbly and relaxed in a way it had never been with her that first summer.

'Two summers ago.'

He winced a little, but he let her go on.

'That kid Jack Naughton wants to be my boyfriend. He's sweet, but it made me think of myself. It made me remember how I behaved to you, and I felt so ashamed.' She cracked a piece of wood off the dock and threw it into the water. She let out a breath. 'I'm sorry I did that. You must have thought I was so ridiculous.'

Eric's face was pained. He was silent for a long time.

She brought her feet up onto the dock and hugged her knees to her chest. She pressed her chin against one brown knee, afraid to look at him. She could feel the weight of her loose hair drying against her back.

They hadn't talked about this before. In all their many hours spent together, they hadn't mentioned the fact that they'd known each other – much less *known* each other. They never talked about 'us'. There wasn't any 'us'.

But now, she was raising the spectre of 'us', wasn't she? Not to reawaken it, she promised herself. That was

180

not it. Her mind supplied a funny version of the famous *Julius Caesar* line: *I come not to praise us, but to bury us.*

Eric rubbed a hand through his hair. 'I didn't think you were ridiculous,' he said at last, a little defensively. 'It was more complicated than that.'

'But it was all my fault. I know it was.'

He looked terribly tired. One side of his mouth was flat and the other pointed down. She could tell he didn't want to talk about this any more.

'I won't bring it up again,' she said softly. Her eyes pricked with tears that she did not want him to see. 'I promise. We can forget it ever happened.'

When he finally talked his voice was so quiet she could barely hear him. 'Do you think I could forget it?' He brushed his hand over his eye. 'Do you really think it was all you? That I didn't want it too?'

Brian was over, so Tibby stayed in her room. Brian came to see Katherine almost every day. He was transforming her arm cast into a masterpiece, drawing a fierce and sprawling dragon with her Magic Markers, adding a little more each time he came.

Brian also came to see Tibby, Tibby suspected, but she did not want to see him. He would catch her every so often skulking to the kitchen to forage for supplies and ask her, by his hollow-eyed looks, why she was avoiding him. And she just kept avoiding him because she didn't have an answer.

Tibby was perched on her bed, having left the door open a few inches so she could hear Brian's voice but not be seen. That was when Carmen arrived. Brian was

181

careful enough to leave her alone, but with Carmen there was no such luck. Carmen walked in and closed the door behind her.

'What are you doing?'

'What do you mean?'

'Why won't you see Brian? The poor guy is dying.'

'He's here to see Katherine,' Tibby said defensively.

Carmen was not a particularly patient person. 'Shut up. He loves Katherine, I know, but he wants to see you.'

'Why can't I just be by myself if I want?' Tibby asked churlishly.

Carmen sighed. She was in one of her tough-love moods. 'Because Brian loves you. And I am pretty sure you feel the same way. So what are you doing? Like it or not, you're going to NYU in a month and a half. You can't just leave it like this.'

Tibby was tired of hearing it. Her mom had been in her room singing the very same tune not twenty-four hours before. 'Why is everybody in such a hurry to shove me and Brian together? Why does he have to be my boyfriend? Are you not a real person if you don't have a boyfriend? Why does everybody have to be in love with somebody?'

'You don't have to be in love with somebody,' Carmen replied. 'But it so happens that you are. And besides, Brian means more to you than just being your boyfriend.' Carmen looked around distastefully at the mess. 'Is this about Katherine?' she asked. 'Because Katherine's getting better fast and you're the one acting broken.'

'It's not about Katherine,' Tibby said, just to get Carmen off her back. 'It's not about anything. And anyway, maybe you're wrong. Maybe I just don't like Brian in that way.'

Carmen sized her up. 'Are you honestly telling me that you don't like Brian in that way?'

Tibby couldn't say no without lying, so she decided to say nothing instead.

'Hi, Dad. It's me.'

'Hey, bun! How good to hear your voice. What's up?'

Carmen and Al talked pretty regularly on Sunday evenings, so a call on a Thursday night did tend to prompt the old 'What's up?'

Carmen had been, in her slightly sick way, excited to tell her mother she would not fulfil her lifelong dream of going to Williams College. It turned out she was not at all excited to tell her father. She'd put this call off a hundred times.

'I . . . um . . . How's Lydia?'

'She's great.' Her dad obviously knew she was stalling.

'How's Krista?'

'I think she's fine.' Al was always more circumspect on this subject. He didn't want to make it seem like Krista was the girl who lived with him while Carmen was the girl he talked to on Sundays. In spite of the fact that this was true.

'Tell her I say hey, OK?'

'Of course. She'll be happy. Now, tell me. Is everything good with you? How's your job?'

'It's . . . fine. Listen, I'm calling because . . . well,

183

because . . .' She had to make herself say it. 'Because I'm thinking a lot about this fall.'

'OK . . .'

'I might not be ready to leave home just now.' She said it so fast it came out like one long word.

'Bun, explain what you mean.'

'With Mom and David, and Mom expecting the baby and everything. It's hard to picture leaving right now.'

'OK . . .'

'I might just stay here this fall. I might even go to U of Maryland. I got accepted there, you know, like, just in case.'

'Oh, I didn't realize that.'

'It happened recently.'

'So. You say you *might* stay home this fall?'

'I think I probably will.' She let out a breath she'd been holding for at least a minute.

'No Williams, then.'

'Maybe not.'

'Maybe not?'

'Probably not.'

'Probably not.'

'Yeah. The thing is, I have to call them at Williams and tell them. I can't just hold the spot if I'm not going to use it, you know?'

'Yes, I'm sure you're right about that.' Her dad didn't sound mad, really. He sounded calm.

'So I'll go ahead and call 'em, I guess.'

She could hear her father switching the phone to his other ear. 'Bun, why don't you let me take care of it, OK? I put down a big deposit already, and I

184

might need to work with them a bit to get it back.'

'Oh, no. Do you think . . . ?' Carmen couldn't stand the thought of her dad getting stiffed for thousands of dollars along with everything else.

'I think it will be fine,' he said. 'You let me handle it, OK?' He was so calm.

Was it possible her mother had gotten to him first? Carmen detected the faint smell of a parental plot. Even divorced parents were capable of such things when they got concerned.

'Thanks, Dad.' Once again, tears jumped into the breach. 'Are you sure you're not disappointed?' Her voice disobeyed her and cracked on the last syllable.

He sighed. 'If you want to go to Williams, I want you to go to Williams. If you want to go to Maryland, I want you to go to Maryland. I want you to be happy, bun.'

How did she get such nice parents? How did such nice parents turn out such a disaster of a daughter?

He wasn't done being nice. 'I love you, Carmen. I trust you to make the right decisions.'

Carmen felt that an anvil had mysteriously replaced her lower intestines. Sometimes trust felt like the worst gift in the world.

It's the same old story. Boy finds girl, boy loses girl, girl finds boy, boy forgets girl, boy remembers girl, girl dies in a tragic blimp accident over the Orange Bowl on New Year's Day.

– The Naked Gun

The rafting went smoothly. This time there were no dive-bombing bees. No splashing or tipping or crashing overboard. Bridget and Eric made a convincing show of knowing what they were doing.

Meanwhile, the campers, eight boys, did plenty of splashing and colliding and smacking each other with their oars. They had a blast while Bridget and Eric were all business.

During the long hours of floating along the hot, quiet river, Bridget had lots of time to regret her last conversation with Eric. It had changed the mood between them. Of course it had. The ease had vanished. They were suddenly considerate and polite. She really hated that.

Tension of all sorts had risen. She felt self-conscious pulling her T-shirt up over her bikini when she got hot, even though everyone else was in bathing suits already. She averted her eyes from Eric's bare chest, even though she'd seen him like that plenty of times before. While she braided her hair, she looked over to see him looking, and they both instantly cast their eyes down.

When the rain began soon after their dinner of bland, camping-style beans and rice, they both looked slightly stricken. There were three tents: two four-person tents for the campers. One two-person tent for the leaders. The two-person tent looked comically small to Bridget as she began to set it up.

She could guess that Eric had bargained on getting to sleep under the sky. So had she. That way, he could be on one side of the campsite and she on the other, and they could avoid this whole conundrum. The wind blew harder and pushed fat drops of rain down on them as if to make its point. They would all be sleeping in tents tonight.

Bridget was usually good at stomping out tension. It was a special talent of hers. She would march around boldly, crushing it underfoot, not paying it any mind. But this time, it was tricky. It wound its stalks around her ankles and held her fast.

She didn't know where to go to change out of her bathing suit. She didn't want him to see her brushing her teeth or her hair. Obviously she didn't want him to spot her peeing in the woods. She didn't want to walk into him wearing just his boxers, or worse. She felt nervous about the thought of him watching her climb into her sleeping bag in her nightshirt.

When she thought of her recklessness with him two summers before, she recoiled. How could she have done that? She didn't even know him then.

Maybe that was exactly how she had done that.

Eric gave her a good long time by herself in the tent before he politely asked if he could come in. He was so polite, he was soaked.

Lying in her sleeping bag, her hair bundled under her neck, she turned her back to him, like she wasn't

189

noticing him getting into his own sleeping bag not two feet away. She wished they could laugh about this, but she couldn't find a way.

There they were lying in a tiny orange tent, side by side. The rain beat down. She could smell his shampoo and his wet skin. It was awkward in a magical way.

She was too embarrassed to consider the tantalizing possibilities that lay before them if she were to let her mind go free. Really, what she most wanted to do was to reassure him. She didn't pose a threat. She didn't. She wanted to prove it to him.

She turned so she was lying on her back looking up. He did the same.

She cleared her throat. 'Tell me about Kaya,' Bridget said. 'What's she like?'

Eric didn't answer right away.

'I bet she's beautiful.'

He let out a long breath. 'Yeah. She is.' He sounded a little guarded. He was private about these kinds of things.

'Light hair or dark?'

'Dark. She's actually half Mexican, too.'

'That's cool.' Bridget, absurdly, wished she could find some way of being half Mexican. 'Does she go to Columbia?'

'She just graduated.'

To Bridget, it sounded so old and sophisticated and totally winning to be half Mexican and have just graduated from Columbia. She felt herself developing an inferiority complex as she lay there stupidly in her sleeping bag, shrinking into her underage, non-Mexican skin.

190

She didn't even want to say anything else, for fear of measuring up even stupider and more juvenile next to his dazzling girlfriend.

Why had Bridget invited Eric's girlfriend into their little orange tent?

He turned on his side, facing her, and propped his head on his hand. Talking a little, even about this, had made things easier between them. 'Hey. I want to hear about *your* friends.'

This was bait she could not resist. And so she spent her nervousness on chirping and blabbing and yammering away, just as stupid and juvenile as could be.

Lena's next hurdle was a big one. It was Valia. Lena had been avoiding her grandmother so scrupulously for so many months, it was almost terrifying to look right at her.

Lena half hoped Valia would refuse to pose, but she didn't. She sat behind the desk in the den and looked at Lena straight on.

'You can work at the computer, if you want. I could draw you that way,' Lena offered.

Valia shrugged. 'I am done vith the computer today.'

Lena calculated it was already late in Greece; that was probably the reason.

'You could watch TV, if that would be more comfortable.'

'No. I vill just sit here,' Valia said.

Lena had to stiffen her spine. She was looking for a way out, and Valia was looking right at her. Lena made herself be brave.

It was rough at first. Lena had been avoiding Valia's obvious pain, and her own associated troubles. Seeing Valia's face, she couldn't ignore that pain. Drawing Valia meant not only seeing it but going in after it. Lena felt that her only hope was to try in stages.

How much her grandma had aged in the past year. Valia's skin was so wrinkled it looked like it might fall off her bones. Her once-dark eyes were watery and faded, with a bluish tinge around the irises. They looked out from the folds of skin as if from inside two grottoes.

Bapi had loved Valia. Lena imagined that even when they were old, Bapi had seen Valia as the young, beautiful woman she had been. Now there was no one to see her that way, and as a consequence, she had shrivelled up.

Lena suddenly grasped her challenge. She was going to try to see that Valia – Bapi's Valia – in this face, if she could. She wouldn't just find the sorrow, plentiful though it was. She would be like an archaeologist. She would unearth the former Valia; she would rediscover her in the midst of all the ravages.

Now Lena was really looking, and Valia stood up to it. She looked right back. Lena had never done a drawing with her subject gazing directly into her eyes. It was like a staring contest fought to a stalemate.

Lena the archaeologist saw clues in the shape of Valia's eyebrows. She borrowed a little from Effie, who some people thought resembled Valia. She saw her father in Valia's mouth and chin. Lena was drawing what she saw, but she was allowing the past to inform the way she interpreted it, if that was possible. She could see the beauty if she really tried.

Valia's usual aggressive frown was slowly sifting out of her features. The parts and places that made up her face took on new, more natural shapes. Lena realized that Valia liked being looked at. And that made Lena consider, sadly, how little anybody had looked at her. They were all afraid of her. They kept their eyes averted from her. Who needed another tragedy in their day? They politely ignored or submitted to her complaints just to make them go away. They all basically wished *she* would go away. Or at least, they wished her anger, her suffering, her loneliness, her discontent and all of her complaining would go away. The rest they would be OK with.

It was no wonder Valia was angry. Her son had brought her here by near force and now spent the entire time wishing she weren't here. And Valia really *wanted* to go away, that was the thing. They wanted her gone; she wanted herself gone. What a mess.

Lena drew and drew. Valia was an exceptional model. Far better than the professionals at school, who got paid fifteen bucks an hour. For seventy minutes, Valia stood stock-still without a single sigh or moan or wriggle.

After a while, Lena felt tears in her eyes, but she didn't stop for them. How lonely Valia was! How much she loved being seen, finally. What a tragedy for all of them that they had starved her so.

When Lena finished, she got up and kissed Valia on the head. They hadn't touched each other in months. Valia seemed shaken by it.

Shyly Lena offered Valia the picture. *I've seen you. I think I finally have*, Lena said silently.

Valia looked at it for a long time. She didn't say anything. She nodded brusquely, but Lena believed that on this strange Saturday afternoon, they had seen each other.

The next morning at breakfast, Valia was back to her usual tricks.

'Who made this coffee?' she demanded, acting as though she might very well spit it on the table.

'I did,' Lena shot back. 'Don't you like it?'

'It's the vorst,' Valia said heartily.

Lena clapped her eyes on Valia's and wouldn't let them go. 'So don't drink it, then.'

Her entire family stared at her in astonishment, and Lena felt quite pleased with herself.

'Hi, Carmen? I hope this is the right Carmen. If this is the right Carmen, then this is Win. If not, it's . . . it's still Win and sorry to bother you. Even if this is the right Carmen, I might be bothering you and I'm sorry if I am. I found your number on the . . . well, never mind. I'm not like a stalker or anything. I swear to God. I've never called somebody up out of the blue like this. But I have to admit I've been thinking about you, and . . .'
Beeeeeeep.

Somewhere in the middle of the night, Bridget felt a tiny tickle of hair against her arm. She opened her eyes without moving a single other muscle. In sleep, Eric had rolled towards her. His head had come so close as to graze her shoulder. She felt breathless. Their bodies were curled in the same direction, hers distantly cupping his. The bottoms of their sleeping bags almost touched.

What little sleep she had had that night was light and full of surface dreams. She couldn't go under any deeper, being this close to him. She wondered if he noticed at all how close their bodies were, how their breath mixed. Or was his sleep innocent and sound?

Gingerly, glacially, she moved her foot. She held her breath until, through her sleeping bag, she could feel, ever so lightly with her big toe, the shape of his heel. She prayed he wouldn't notice or stir. He didn't. He slept.

She withdrew her foot, feeling sorry.

She would have given anything for him to want her again. But she would have given even more for him to trust her.

D on't ask me any

questions right now. I'm

grumpy and I'll probably

make fun of you.

– Effie Kaligaris

Tibby was standing at the front of the theatre, waiting for the one o'clock show to end. She'd stopped watching the movies altogether. These days she preferred to stand by the front windows and look out. One afternoon the box office lady was sick, and Tibby got to take over in the tiny room. That was fun – safe, contained, predictable.

Tibby wondered, once again, about the wisdom of her career choice. She wondered if maybe NYU had any openings in accounting. Or maybe they offered a programme for future tollbooth attendants. Or cashiers. She pictured herself enjoying a career in one of those liquor stores in bad neighbourhoods where you sat behind a thick sheet of bulletproof Plexiglas and people paid for their stuff through a slot in the window. That sounded about right.

She spotted a little group across the street, and she experienced that split second of objectivity when you see someone you know before you realize you know them. The tall one, of course, was Brian. Tibby constantly had to relearn what he looked like now. When he had been the lowliest of dorks, his unkempt hair – longish, unbrushed, needing a cut – had played a role in the vicious circle that had been Brian's appearance. Now it looked conspicuously cool, neglected in exactly the right manner. She bought his clothes for him at Old Navy a couple times a year, so there were no pitfalls there. He had learned to like taking showers of his own accord. That helped too.

The little figure with the giant, lolling, hockey-player head was Katherine, of course. Every time Tibby saw that hockey helmet, she felt her guts constrict. Her facial muscles pulled into a grimace, even when she fought against it. The sight of it made her feel angry and it made her want to cry.

Nicky was holding Katherine's other hand. Even he had become more protective of her.

They crossed the street and approached the doors of the theatre. Katherine caught sight of Tibby in the plate-glass windows. She waved so fervently her helmet slid to the side, the chinstrap bending her ear in half. Tibby opened the doors for them.

'We're going to see a movie at *your* theatre!' Katherine shouted.

Tibby straightened the helmet. She was always doing that.

'Hey, look.' Katherine pointed to her head.

'What?' Tibby said.

'Stickers!' Katherine was exultant. 'Nicky helped me do it.'

The hockey helmet was indeed plastered with stickers, every superhero and cartoon character in the history of cheap merchandising.

'Wow. Nice,' Tibby said.

'Now I might never want to take it off,' Katherine declared triumphantly.

199

Tibby felt her breath catch. There was some torture in this she couldn't even identify. God bless, Katherine. How could she be how she was? How could Tibby be so different? Why was she so pained when Katherine really was OK? Tibby wasn't the one who fell out the window. Her concern for Katherine had become a waste; Katherine didn't need it. Who was it really for?

Forgetting about what had happened for a moment, Tibby looked instinctively at Brian. And Brian touched her tenderly on the hand, enveloping her in a look of support that didn't have anything to do with whether he wanted to kiss her or not.

Carmen had saved Win's telephone message and replayed it fourteen times in one hour. So why was she in the hospital – the very place where he worked – hunkered over a book in a corner, wearing sunglasses and a hat? It was Wednesday afternoon and Valia had her usual physical therapy session. Carmen knew where to find Win. Win might even be looking for her.

Instead, she picked the most remote spot she could find, which happened to be a deserted hallway in labour and delivery. It was nice and quiet for a while, but suddenly there was a virtual gaggle of pregnant women waddling towards her. She bent her head and tried to read a few more pages, but she was distracted. So much for her solitude. There was nowhere to run in this place.

All the women and their spouses were piling into a room. Carmen was imagining what it could mean – a big, wild rave for the pregnant folks? – when something began to dawn on her. She looked at her watch.

For the most part, she meanly ignored anything her mother said that contained the words *labour, birth, pregnancy* or *baby*. But vaguely in the back of her mind she knew her mom and David were coming to a child-birth class at this very hospital.

Could it be? Could it?

Oh, man.

She tried to get back into her book, but she couldn't. For pages and pages, Jane Austen's elegant banter went into her eyes and stopped short of her brain. Carmen was curious now. Once she framed a question, it was so hard for her not to answer it. She put her book in her bag and walked down the hall. She stopped at the room where the pregnant women had gone. It had a frosted-glass window, fairly convenient for snooping. She saw the couples sitting on the floor. The men had their legs spread out with their rotund wives between them. It looked pretty peculiar, frankly. The teacher stood behind a table at the front.

Carmen had come to the conclusion that her mother wasn't, in fact, part of this strange class when she peered farther in to the back and saw the familiar angle of dark hair. Christina was easy to miss because even with her big round belly, she seemed to be shrinking against the wall.

Everybody was a couple and Christina was alone. Why was that? The current exercise involved the men massaging their wives' shoulders, and Christina just sat there.

Where was David? Carmen watched in puzzlement until Christina reached up her arms to massage her own

201

shoulders. That was all Carmen needed. The ache in her chest caught her by surprise and propelled her straight through the door and into the room.

'Can I help you?' the instructor asked her.

'Hold on just a sec,' Carmen said. She went to her mother. 'What's going on? Where's David?'

Christina's eyes were pinkish. 'There was a big emergency on his case. He had to fly to St Louis,' she whispered. To her immense credit, there was lots of sadness in the way she said it, but no blame. 'What are you doing here, *nena*?'

'Valia has physical therapy,' Carmen explained.

Christina nodded.

The instructor appeared in front of them. 'Are you registered for this class . . . ?' she asked Carmen. She didn't say it in a snotty way, but she obviously preferred complete order.

Carmen looked from the instructor to her mother and back again. She pointed to her mother. 'I'm her partner.'

The instructor looked surprised. Politically, it was her responsibility to be open to all kinds of couples. 'Fine. That's fine. We're starting with some labour massage techniques. Just follow the rest of the class to get started.'

Carmen situated her mother between her knees and began massaging her tense shoulders. Carmen had strong hands. She felt like she was good at this. She heard a little hitch in her mother's breathing, and she knew Christina was crying.

But she knew Christina was crying because she was

happy, and that gave Carmen her own feeling of happiness unlike anything she'd felt in a long time.

Hey, you beautiful girls!

My dad just sent me a pile of stuff from Brown.

My room-mate's name is Aisha Lennox. Doesn't that sound cool?

I'm gonna live with her. We're gonna know her. How weird is that?

Bee

Lena thought the drawing of Effie would be the easy one. She didn't dread it. She didn't overprepare. She sauntered in. Lena was not a saunterer, and for good reason, she decided. She always ended up regretting it.

'Where do you want to be?' Lena asked. 'Your room? Your bed? Someplace else?'

'Um.' Effie was painting her toenails. 'Can you just do it here?' She was sitting on the floor in front of the TV in the den. Some reality show was blaring. Effie had her chin resting on her knee and was giving full attention to her toenail, as though it were one of the more demanding things she'd ever grappled with.

'I guess,' Lena said. 'Do you mind if I turn the TV off?'

'Leave it on,' Effie said. 'I won't watch.'

Lena didn't question this. She had an instinct that bossing your model around was no way to get her to loosen up. No matter how stupid she was being.

Lena settled on a profile. Effie's knees bent, her chin down, her toes flexed. She started sketching.

Effie was no Valia. She moved around as though modelling for Lena's picture wasn't even on her to-do list.

'Sheesh, Ef. Can you hold still?'

Effie flashed her a look. She went back to her toenails.

Lena tried. She really did. It was hard to draw a moving hand. Lena let it blur. It was hard to draw someone's character when they kept their face turned away. She tried to suggest the resistance in Effie's pose. It was the only thing that felt true.

And then Lena had to ask herself, why was Effie resisting so hard? It was true they'd been missing each other this summer. They'd both gotten jobs early. They'd both spent as much time away from the house as possible. Was her relationship with Effie another casualty of the Valia debacle?

Had it gone more wrong than Lena knew?

'Effie?'

'What?' Effie snapped, still not turning her head.

Lena's mouth seemed to work a little better with a charcoal in her hand. She opened it. 'Ef, I feel like you don't want this to work. Like you're mad at me.'

Effie rolled her eyes. She made a show of blowing dry the shiny pink polish on her big toe. 'Why do you think that?'

'Because you won't look at me. You won't sit still.'

If Effie had been Lena and Lena had been Effie, this could have taken all day. But luckily, Effie was Effie. When she finally turned, her face was full of expression.

'Maybe I don't want you to go to art school.'

Lena put down her pad. 'Why not?' She couldn't help showing her astonishment. She always just assumed that Effie sided with her in any struggle against her parents, just as she always sided with Effie, even when Effie was wrong. Did Effie actually agree with her parents this time? Did she resent that Lena was causing more turbulence in their already turbulent home?

Effie's eyes were full of tears. At long last she capped her polish and tossed it aside. 'Why do you think?' she demanded.

Lena felt her own eyes pulling wide open. 'Ef. I don't know. Please tell me.'

Effie put her face in her hands. 'I don't want you to go. I don't want you to leave me here . . . with all of them.'

On her knees, Lena made her way the few feet to her sister. She put her arms around Effie. 'I'm so sorry,' Lena said honestly. 'I don't want to leave you.' She felt Effie's tears against her shoulder and she held her tighter. 'I hate to even think about leaving you.'

The beautiful thing about getting someone to tell you what was wrong was that you could tell them something to make it a little better. Lena made a mental note that she should try it more often.

In the lobby a while later, Carmen was hugging her mom goodbye when she saw Win. He smiled eagerly, doubling his pace to get to her, like he was afraid she might slip away.

'Carmen!'

'Hey, Win,' she said. She couldn't help smiling at him. He was too sweet not to. Win and Christina were looking at each other. Win was probably wondering which distant relative of which distant acquaintance Carmen would be accompanying to the hospital now.

'This is my mom, Christina,' Carmen said. 'Mom, this is Win.'

'Nice to meet you, Win,' Christina said.

Carmen saw him through her mother's eyes and was again struck by his exceeding gorgeousness. Carmen found most guys who looked that good intimidating, but Win was different. He was not arrogant or scary. He had a self-deprecating smile and a shuffling posture totally at odds with the usual 'I'm gorgeous' swagger.

'Nice to meet you, too,' he said earnestly. 'I thought you must be related. You're beautiful like Carmen.'

If Carmen had just heard about this statement rather than actually listening to it in person, she would have groaned and rolled her eyes and told Mr Slick to get out of town. But hearing him say it and seeing the look on his face as he did, she believed it was the most innocent and sincere compliment she'd ever gotten. And so did her mother, apparently.

Christina flushed with pleasure. 'Thank you. I like to think I look like her.'

Carmen felt unbalanced, buffeted as she was by all the goodness. She had no idea what to say.

'Carmen saved me today,' Christina volunteered to Win, emotion all through her voice. 'My husband couldn't make it to childbirth class, and Carmen came to my rescue. She's my partner and coach. Can you imagine?' Christina was laughing, but her eyes were full of tears. Carmen had heard about pregnant women being extra emotional, but jeez, this was a bit much.

Win stared at Christina with rapt attention. And then he turned to look at Carmen. She'd wished many times for a boy like Win to look at her this way. But now it was wrong. The stuff her mom was saying made it all worse.

She opened her mouth to say something. And then she realized. 'Oh, my God! I have to get Valia! I'm gonna be late for her.' Oh, God. She could practically hear the bone-splintering howl from the eighth floor.

'I'll come,' Christina said, running after her to the bank of elevators.

'Bye, Win,' Carmen shouted over her shoulder.

He looked a little sad as she waved to him through the narrowing gap of the elevator door. As soon as it closed, Christina burst. '*Nena*, who is he?' She was obviously excited. 'He is . . . he is just *adorable*! And the way he looked at you.'

Carmen's face was hot. 'He does seem . . . nice.' She didn't want her mother to see her flustered smile. She wished she could get her mouth into a normal shape.

'Nice! He's more than nice! How do you know him?'

Carmen shrugged. 'I don't really know him. Or I guess I do kind of know him.' She chewed the inside of her lip. 'But he doesn't know me.'

To the man who only

has a hammer in the

toolkit, every problem

looks like a nail.

– Abraham Maslow

It took four evenings for Tibby to pounce on the garbage bags and take them out to the alley before Margaret could get there first. Margaret was so experienced at her job, having worked at this very Pavilion Theatre for well over twenty years, and so dedicated to it, that it was nearly impossible for Tibby to manage to do her co-worker even this one small favour.

'Tibby, thanks!' Margaret said brightly when she saw the empty cans. 'You're jis sweet.'

'I'm returning a favour,' Tibby said.

Tibby watched as Margaret put her sweater in her employee locker (no pictures pinned up inside, Tibby noticed) and collected her purse, in exactly the same manner she did every evening. Tibby knew Margaret would take the bus on Wisconsin Avenue to her home, which was somewhere north of here. She couldn't exactly guess what Margaret did with her free time, but she felt almost sure Margaret did it alone.

Suddenly Tibby felt inspired. 'Hey, Margaret?'

Margaret turned, her purse dangling neatly from the crook of her elbow.

'Do you want to get some dinner with me?'

Margaret looked utterly bewildered.

'We could just get something quick, if you want. We

210

could go right around the corner to that Italian place.'

Why not spend some time with a gravely lonely person? Tibby thought, silently applauding herself. Wasn't that a worthy thing to do? Tibby felt sure it was something a good person would do.

Margaret looked around, as though to see if perhaps Tibby was talking to someone else. The muscles around her mouth twitched a little. She cleared her throat. 'Excuse me?'

'Do you want to have dinner?'

Margaret looked a bit frightened. 'You and me?'

'Yes.' Tibby was beginning to wonder if she had overstepped.

'Will, uh, OK. I giss I could.'

'Great.'

Tibby led the way around the corner. She had never seen Margaret outside the movie theatre. It was kind of strange. She wondered how many times Margaret had *been* out of the movie theatre – other than when she was home. In her pale pink cardigan, with her white vinyl purse with gold buckles and her bewildered expression, Margaret looked like an innocent victim of some time-travel mishap.

'Is this place OK?' Tibby asked, holding open the door to the restaurant.

'Yes,' Margaret agreed in a slightly quavering voice.

Tibby had been to this restaurant before and it had seemed perfectly normal. But now, with Margaret at her side, the place struck her as raucous, dark, nightmarishly noisy and totally wrong.

The hostess showed them to a table. Margaret

211

perched on the very front of her chair, her backbone stiff, as though ready to flee at a second's notice.

'They have good pizza,' Tibby said feebly.

Did Margaret eat pizza? Did she eat anything? Margaret was terribly thin, nearly as small as a child. There were certain clues to her age: the loose skin of her neck, the texture of her blonde ponytail. Tibby knew she had to be in her mid-forties. But in almost all other respects, Margaret looked just shy of puberty.

What had happened to her to make her like this? Tibby wondered. Had there been a tragedy? A loss? Was there some terrible thing that had caused her to step off the conveyor belt of life around the age of fourteen?

Or, more insidiously, had she just taken the cautious route time and time again? Had she cut off more and more potential branches of life until it had narrowed to just one?

Was Margaret scared of love? Could that be it? Had she left the building just around the time everybody else started hooking up?

Tibby looked at Margaret beseechingly. She wanted to say or do something to make Margaret feel comfortable, but she could not figure out for the life of her what that might be.

'Do you like pasta?' Tibby asked. 'I've heard it's pretty good here.'

Margaret looked at her menu as though it were a devilishly tricky test. 'I'm not sure,' she said faintly.

'You could just get a salad,' Tibby suggested. 'Or if you don't like this kind of food, I totally understand.'

Margaret nodded. 'Maybe a salad . . .'

Tibby felt a stab of sadness, because she knew Margaret wanted to please her, too. Margaret was desperately uncomfortable, but she didn't want to let Tibby down.

Who was doing whom the favour in this exercise?

Slowly the hot air of righteousness leaked out of Tibby, and she realized what an idiot she was. She had dragged poor Margaret far out of her comfort zone, congratulating herself on doing Margaret this great charity. But Tibby wasn't giving solace to a lonely woman; she was basically torturing her. What had she been thinking?

'Maybe I don't feel like Italian food,' Tibby said brightly, wanting only to offer Margaret some salvation. 'Why don't we walk back by the theatre and grab some ice cream and then I'll walk you to the bus stop?'

Margaret look colossally relieved, and that gave Tibby a small piece of happiness. 'Sure thing.'

As they walked, Tibby remembered how her uncle Fred had this line he brought out on the occasion of nearly all family birthdays. Her parents would moan about their children growing older, and he'd say, 'Growing up is crap, but it's better than the alternative.'

Well, for the first time Tibby realized there was an alternative. It was walking right next to Tibby, licking her orange Creamsicle and breaking Tibby's heart.

'He caught me again,' Carmen told Lena, sipping her iced cappuccino and enjoying the air conditioning at the Starbucks on Connecticut Avenue.

'What do you mean?' Lena asked. She wasn't eating

her cookie, and Carmen really wanted it.

'Win caught me in another random act of kindness at the hospital.'

Lena laughed. 'Busted.'

'I feel like I was shoplifting or something. I didn't know what to say to explain myself.'

'Did you tell him it was an accident? You didn't mean it? You'll never do it again as long as you live, so help you God?'

Carmen laughed too. 'Good Carmen strikes again. What are we going to do with that girl?'

'Tie her up in the bathroom.'

'Good idea.'

Lena was squinting at her in thought. 'Maybe you actually *are* Good Carmen. Have you ever thought of that?'

Carmen considered the way she'd knowingly polished off her mother's last coveted pint of Ben & Jerry's the night before. 'Nah.'

Lena still wasn't eating her cookie, so Carmen broke off a piece of it and ate it. 'So guess who's sleeping on my couch tomorrow night?' Carmen asked.

'Who?'

'Paul Rodman. He's driving up from South Carolina and I convinced him to crash here. I haven't seen him in months.'

Lena shifted uncomfortably in her chair.

'He asked about you.'

Lena nodded timidly.

'He always does. It's the part of the conversation he actually initiates.'

Lena looked down at her large feet in their large cork-bottomed flip-flops. 'How's his dad?' she asked.

Carmen stopped chewing. She had been corresponding with Paul by e-mail. She got more words out of him that way. 'He's not good. Paul drives hours to see him every week. It's so sad.'

Lena was nodding as Carmen's cell phone rang. Carmen scratched around in the bottom reaches of her bag until she found it.

'Hey?'

'Carmen, hi. It's David.'

'What's up?' Most of the warmth in her voice evaporated.

'I just wanted to thank you. The way you took care of your mother yesterday. You don't know how much it meant to her. And to me, too. I wanted to be there so bad myself and I really just can't tell you how—'

'It's fine,' Carmen interrupted. 'No problem.'

'Really, Carmen. I really—'

'OK.' She didn't want him to keep going on about this. 'Are you still in St Louis?'

'No, I'm home,' he said heavily.

Why was she annoyed at him? It wasn't his fault he worked like a dog. He had a family to provide for now. He took his responsibilities seriously. Blah blah blah.

'So I'll see you later,' she said.

'Oh, Carmen – one other thing?'

'Yeah?'

'I left my phone recharger in the hotel in St Louis. Could I borrow yours?' It was well known that they had

215

the exact same cell phone. Sometimes it seemed like the only conversation piece between them. He had the ring that sounded like a polka. He thought it was hugely entertaining.

'Sure. It's in the outlet by my night table,' she said.

'The hotel said they'd send mine back. I told them I'm going to need it.'

Why were their conversations always so stilted? 'Yep. You are,' Carmen said. 'Well, bye.'

'Bye.'

She hung up. When she put her phone back in her bag, she realized the recharger was coiled in the bottom of it. Oh. Oops.

Lena was squinting, trying to figure out whom Carmen was talking to. 'David?' she finally guessed.

'Yeah.'

'I knew it wasn't anybody you liked very much.'

'I like him all right,' Carmen said, the slightest petulance creeping into her voice. She sighed. 'I should be nicer, shouldn't I?'

'I'm not answering that.'

Carmen got a mischievous smile on her face. 'I know what to do. I'll invite Win to have dinner with my mom and me and David.' She laughed. 'That'll set him straight.'

Tibby:
Beach equipment + tunes.
No techno crap, as per discussion.

216

Bee and Me:
Food. A lot. Mostly high-calorie snacks with
extra trans fats. (I think I like those. What
are they, anyway?).

Lena:
Other household goods.
(kleenex in addition to toilet paper, missy)

Please make your donations ($60, and I mean
cash money) to the Rehoboth Beach First Annual
Precollege Dream Weekend Fund, aka Carmen's
wallet.

And I mean soon, dang it.

Since Lena had heard about Paul's being in town overnight, she'd been thinking of him. Finally she got up the nerve to call him at Carmen's, and she asked him to come over. He wasn't in her family, obviously, but she felt a pressing urge to draw his picture.

She didn't want to avoid him any more.

That afternoon, charcoal in hand, she met him at the door. She hugged him stiffly. She felt her heart jump a little at the way he looked. Older, sadder, even more handsome.

Somewhat mutely, he followed her to the kitchen.

You two are way too much alike, Carmen said about Lena and Paul and their combined inability to carry on a conversation. Carmen had had high hopes for them once.

'Do you want anything to drink?' she asked him.

He looked nervous. 'No, thank you.'

She gestured for him to sit down across from her at the kitchen table. She ran a hand through her hair. She'd brushed it for this occasion. 'I have kind of a weird favour to ask of you,' she said.

Now he really looked scared. But not unwilling. 'OK.'

'Would it be all right if I drew a picture of you? It would take around an hour or an hour and a half. Just a sketch of you from here up.' She indicated at her collarbone, lest he run from her house in panic. 'You see, I'm making a portfolio of drawings of people, because I'm trying to win this scholarship to RISD. Otherwise, I can't go to art school, and I really want to. Do you think that would be OK?' She had never said so much to him all at one time.

He nodded. 'I'd like that,' he said.

She had an idea. 'Maybe we'll go outside.'

He followed her out to the backyard. She didn't picture him on a lounge chair by the pool or anything. She surveyed the possibilities. There was a tree stump in the far corner, by the fence. It had been a giant, beautiful oak that had grown old and gotten a disease, so her parents had had it cut down before it got the chance to fall on their house. It was strong and sturdy, suitable for Paul. She steered him to it, then ran to fetch herself a chair and her drawing board.

'You ready?' she asked.

He sat squarely. The stump was the perfect height for him. Lena's feet would have been dangling, but his

218

rested solidly on the soil. He put his hands on his knees. This could have looked stiff for another person, but for Paul it looked right. She noticed he wore a large gold class ring on the pinky of his left hand. It was the one thing that didn't fit.

She backed up a bit. She wanted to draw more of him. 'Do you mind if I do a three-quarters?'

'That's fine,' he said.

She clipped her paper to her board. He watched her carefully. This caused her to clip her knuckle. It hurt, so she sucked on it for a second. She put her hair back in a ponytail. She poised the charcoal over her paper.

'Should I look at you?' he asked.

'Um. Yes,' she said. Paul was always remarkably direct in his gaze, so this felt right for him. On the other hand, she felt the pressure building as their eyes met for long moments. She didn't feel about Paul the way she did about other people.

The lines of Paul's face gave the impression of being straight and square. Strong, square jaw; square forehead; squared-off cheekbones. But when she looked harder and longer, she saw many unexpectedly round things. His eyes, for instance. They were large and circular, innocent and almost childlike. But at the outside corners she saw he had faint, fanning creases, proto-laugh lines that she suspected didn't come from laughing. And at the inside corners, the thin skin where his eyes met his nose was blue and slightly bruised-looking.

His mouth was surprisingly full and curvaceous. It was a lovely mouth. She lost herself in the very tiny up-and-down lines at each corner that separated his lips from his cheeks. You wouldn't expect such a sensitive mouth on so large and strong a person. She felt a little manic, looking at it boldly and for a long time. And then she felt guilty for taking advantage of this drawing opportunity in such a way.

She drew his shoulders and arms in big, loose gestures. When she got to his hands, she tightened up a little.

Her hand hesitated over the ring. She made herself open her mouth. 'Can I ask you about the ring?' she said.

The fingers on his other hand instantly enclosed it. He looked down. It was the first time he'd broken the pose, even minutely, in almost forty minutes. 'Sorry,' he said, realizing this.

'That's OK. Don't worry,' she said in a rush. She suddenly felt protective of him. 'You can take a break. You deserve one.'

'No. That's OK.' He was looking down now. His neck arched gracefully and sadly. The tilt of his neck spoke so eloquently that her fingers itched to start another drawing.

It was a miracle how when you looked hard enough, when you really sought out information, there was so much to see, even in a person's tiniest gesture. There was so much feeling, such a dazzling array of things that your words, at least Lena's words, could never say. There were thousands of images and memories and ideas, if you just let them come. There was the whole history of human experience somewhere contained in each of the bits, the most universal in the most specific, if you could only see it. It was like poetry. Well, she had never really found poetry in poetry, to be truthful. But she imagined this was what poetry might be like for someone who understood it and loved it.

Either it was like poetry or it was like getting really, really stoned.

The ring was off and Paul had it cradled in his palm now. He looked at her again. 'This is my father's. He went to Penn, too, so he wants me to have it.'

Lena stared at him solemnly. She wondered if the swelling compassion she felt for him was finding its way out of her eyes. 'He's sick. Carmen told me.'

Paul nodded.

'I'm so sorry.'

He was still nodding, slowing it down. 'It's rough. You know?'

'I do,' she said with feeling. 'I mean, I don't. I do and I don't. I don't exactly, but I feel like I do. My bapi— my grandfather died last summer.' Suddenly she felt a horror at her words. 'Not that it's like that!' she practically shouted. 'Not that that is what is going to happen!' Lena really hated herself sometimes.

Paul's expression was undeservedly kind. It was all sweet forgiveness. And even gratitude to top it off. 'I know you do, Lena. I can tell you understand.'

They just stared at each other, but for the first time the silence didn't feel shamefully insufficient. It felt OK.

'Do you want to take a break?' she asked him again.

'OK,' he agreed this time.

The stump was big enough for two. She sat next to him cross-legged. She leaned into him a little, and he let her. The sun shone down on them benevolently.

The corners of her drawing, where she left it in the grass, flapped gently in the breeze.

She wanted to finish it, but she didn't feel rushed. She realized she'd begun the drawing so she could tell Paul she was sorry.

Jiggle it a little it'll

open.

– Pinky and the Brain

It was another day in the rut.

Valia had used up most of her energy IM-ing her friends back home. It was the one time of the day she looked alive. Now they sat in the darkened den, Carmen preparing to wage another war of attrition, with the TV as the prize.

She hadn't gotten her Ryan Hennessey fix in days. She tried to picture him. For some reason she couldn't picture him. She stood up. 'Valia, we're festering. We have to get out of here.'

'Ve do?'

'We do. It's a beautiful day. We need a walk.'

Valia looked sleepy and cranky. 'I'm vatching a show. I don't vant to valk.'

'Please?' Carmen suddenly felt so desperate she didn't care about their standoff of sullenness. Let Valia win this round. 'I'll do all the work. You just sit in your chair.'

Valia considered. She liked being pled with. She liked her obvious power over Carmen. She shrugged. 'It's too hot.'

'It's not so hot today. Please?'

Valia wouldn't give Carmen the satisfaction of saying yes outright, but she looked at her wheelchair with resignation.

Carmen took the opening. Gently she heaved Valia's skinny body into her wheelchair. 'OK.' Carmen checked for her keys and her money and wheeled Valia right out the door.

The sky was perfectly blue. Though it was August, the swampy deep-summer haze had momentarily lifted. It was so good to be out. Carmen walked aimlessly, letting her mind wander. She tried to look at the world through Valia's eyes, to imagine how each suburban vista looked through the eyes of an old woman who had spent her life on an Aegean island. Not so good, obviously. But when Carmen looked up and saw the sky, she knew it was the same sky. She wondered if Valia saw this lovely, azure sky and knew it was her same sky.

For some reason, a picture pushed into Carmen's mind of a restaurant she'd been to with her mom a few times. She didn't remember the name of it, but she knew exactly where it was. She pointed them in the direction of it and walked. She felt hungry all of a sudden.

At the restaurant, Carmen was pleased to see they still had tables with large white umbrellas set up outside. Red geraniums flowed from wooden boxes along the white-washed walls of the little terrace. Carmen had never been to Greece, but she imagined that if you just looked at a small patch of the wall or looked up at the white umbrella against the sky, maybe it would look a little like this.

She set Valia up at a table. There were no other diners.

'Vhy are ve here?' Valia demanded.

225

'I need a rest and I'm also kind of hungry. Do you mind?'

Valia looked annoyed but martyred. 'Does it matter if I mind?'

'I'll be right back,' Carmen promised.

They didn't have waiter service at the café tables, so she went to order from the counter inside. It was after lunch and before dinner, so the place was pretty deserted. She felt a bit illicit as she studied the menu. It wasn't Greek food precisely, but it was Mediterranean. She recognized a lot of the dishes from things she'd had at Lena's house. She knew the Kaligarises weren't cooking that stuff at the moment. Lena explained that her dad thought it made Valia homesick. He tried to steer her away from everything that might make her homesick. He didn't want Valia cooking, even though it was what she had done her whole life.

Carmen ordered stuffed grape leaves and something hot that strongly resembled spanakopita. She ordered an eggplant dish, a Greek salad, a few squares of baklava, and two large lemonades. She paid up and carried it all to the table, setting all the dishes between her and Valia. 'I bought us a snack. I hope that's OK.'

Valia gazed at it all disdainfully.

Carmen put a steaming spinach pastry on a little paper plate and handed it to Valia with a fork. 'Here, try some.'

Valia just sat there with it, smelling it, completely still.

Immediately, Carmen regretted her impulse, just as she ended up regretting almost all of her impulses.

Valia didn't want to be here. She was going to hate

the inauthentic food. She could already hear Valia's litany of complaints.

You call this food?

Vhat is the green mess? This is not spinach.

As the moments passed, Carmen felt worse and worse. Why did she have such stupid ideas? More than that, why did she actually carry them out?

Valia held the plate up close to her face. She looked like she was going to take a bite, and then she stopped. Carmen watched in wonderment as Valia put it down on the table and bent her head.

Valia just sat like that with her head bent for many long moments, and then Carmen saw the tears. Lines of tears bumped down Valia's wrinkly face. Carmen felt her own throat constricting. She watched as Valia's face slowly collapsed into pure sorrow.

Carmen was up and out of her chair. Without thinking, she went to Valia and put her arms around the old lady.

Valia was stiff in Carmen's arms. Carmen waited to be pushed away, or for some other signal of Valia not wanting to be hugged any more, especially not by Carmen.

But instead, Valia's head got heavier as it sank into Carmen's neck. Carmen felt the soft, saggy skin against her collarbone. She hugged a little harder. She felt Valia's tears, damp on her neck. She realized, sort of distantly, that Valia's hand had made its way to her wrist.

How sad it was, Carmen thought, that you acted awful when you were desperately sad and hurt and wanted to be loved. How tragic then, the way everyone avoided you and tiptoed around you when you really

227

needed them. Carmen knew this vicious predicament as well as anyone in the world. How bitter it felt when you acted badly to everyone and ended up hating yourself the most.

Carmen tenderly patted Valia's hair, surprised that for once that it wasn't she who was acting awful. It wasn't Carmen who was being needy, but rather feeling needed.

She thought about Mr Kaligaris and all of his theories about protecting his mother. Yes, smelling Greek food made Valia sad. He was right about that. And being held by another human seemed to make her sad too. But sometimes, Carmen knew, being sad was what you had to do.

'I vant to go home,' Valia croaked into Carmen's ear.

'I know,' Carmen whispered back, and she understood that Valia wasn't talking about 1303 Highland Street, Bethesda, Maryland.

'Have fun with Michael.' Bridget lifted her eyebrows suggestively. 'But not too much fun.'

As she helped Diana put her duffel bag into her car, Bridget felt a strange rolling sensation under her eyeballs. Her head was aching and she was tired. She was happy for Diana that she was going back to Philadelphia to spend the weekend with her boyfriend, and she was sorry for herself that she was staying here.

She decided against stopping in the dining hall. Friday night dinner was one of the better meals, involving an ice-cream sundae buffet where she was always happy to return for seconds and thirds. But tonight she wasn't hungry. 'I gotta go to bed,' she muttered to herself, trudging through the parking lot and past the equipment sheds.

The camp felt strangely empty. It was middle week-end, so the vast majority of campers went home. Only about a quarter of the staff remained to keep an eye on things.

As she pulled off her clothes and crawled under her covers, Bridget was grateful that her cabin was quiet for once. She bundled herself up as tight as she could. It was at least eighty degrees outside; why was she so cold? The tighter she bundled, the colder she felt. She was shaking. Her teeth were chattering. The more she focused on it and tried to stop, the more they chattered and clacked. Her cheeks burned.

She was getting a fever, she concluded. She meant to do something about this. Maybe she could steal a couple of Advil from Katie. She kept imagining herself doing this, without actually doing it. She passed, gradually, into a state between awake and asleep. She imagined getting another blanket. She imagined drinking a glass of water. She could not figure out whether she was doing it or not. She puzzled and tortured her brain trying to figure out what was and wasn't real. She must have drifted like that for a long time, because it was dark when she was startled by the presence of somebody next to her.

'Bee?'

She tried to orient herself. It was Eric's face, floating near hers.

'Hi,' she said softly. She didn't want to pull the

229

blankets from around her chin, because she hated the idea of a draught reaching her hot skin.

'Are you OK?'

'I'm OK,' she said. Her teeth were chattering again.

He looked worried. He pressed his hand to her forehead. 'God, you're hot.'

She meant to laugh and make a joke about this, but she couldn't summon it. She was too tired. 'I think I got the flu.'

'You got something.' Tenderly, almost automatically, he pushed her hair back from her forehead. It was so nice, how he did it. She felt strangely cosy and happy inside her fever.

He moved his hand to touch her flushed cheek. His hand felt remarkably cold. 'Do you want to take something? Should I see if the nurse is around?' His eyes were fixed on her, full of concern.

'Don't worry, it's not a big deal.' Her fatigue made her talk extra slow. 'I always run high fevers. My mom used to say' – she had to take a break to work her energy back up – 'I'd get to a hundred and six degrees with just a little cold.' She didn't mean to sound tragic when she said this, but she must've, because Eric looked distraught. He knew about her mother. She had told him almost the first time they'd met.

'I'm not sure if the nurse is here, but I'm going to get you something. Do you take Tylenol or Motrin or something like that?'

'Anything,' she said.

'I'll be right back. Don't go anywhere, OK? Promise?'

She coughed up a tiny laugh. 'That I can promise.'

★ ★ ★

'You have to let Valia go home,' Carmen said to Ari, following her into the Kaligarises' kitchen.

First she'd had to get Lena's blessing. Then it had taken Carmen two days to get Ari alone in a room, but Carmen was nothing if she wasn't dogged.

Ari put the mail down on the kitchen counter and turned to Carmen in surprise. 'I'm sorry?' Ari's eyes were large and lovely like Lena's, but dark and indefinable, where Lena's were fair, green and fragile.

'I know it's none of my business,' Carmen backtracked, 'and I know you and Mr Kaligaris probably don't want to hear my opinion.' Carmen always called Ari Ari and she always called Mr Kaligaris Mr Kaligaris. She couldn't remember a time when it was different.

Ari nodded slightly, inviting her to pursue that unwanted opinion.

'I really think that you and Mr Kaligaris should let Valia go back to Greece.' Tears welled in Carmen's eyes, and she felt so annoyed by her ready-to-wear emotions. 'She's dying here.'

Ari sighed heavily and rubbed her eyes with the backs of her hands. At least this wasn't entirely news to her. 'How can Valia take care of herself? Especially now, with her knee? Who is going to look out for her if not us?' She didn't sound like she was voicing her own conviction, but more like she was reciting somebody else's.

'Her friends? She has her friends, and they are like her family. I can understand that. The only time I've ever seen her look happy is when she's IM-ing Rena.' Carmen kneaded her hands, sort of amazed to hear herself take on

Ari like another adult. 'Valia is too depressed to get herself a glass of water, but I swear she could have programmed the computer herself if it meant making a connection to home.'

Ari looked at her, pained and tired, but with tenderness, too.

Couldn't Ari see that Valia wasn't the only one suffering? Carmen had never seen Ari so tense, and Mr Kaligaris hadn't always been as angry and rigid as he was now. Couldn't Ari see the toll it took not only on her, but also on her daughters?

Carmen knew she wouldn't have been able to have this conversation if Mr Kaligaris were here. But she trusted Ari to love her. Ultimately she trusted Ari to read her good intentions and, hopefully, the truth.

'Carmen, sweetheart, I'm not saying you aren't right. I appreciate what you're trying to do. But it's complicated. Really, how can Valia go back to that house she shared with Bapi for fifty-seven years? How could she tolerate the pain of living there without him? Sometimes change is the right thing.'

Carmen couldn't help looking sour. She was no friend of change. 'I know that. I know being back in her house on the island will make her sad. Of course she'll be sad. But that's her home. That's her life. She can handle being sad. I'm sure of that. What she can't handle is being here.'

There was that law of life, so cruel and so just, that one must grow or else pay more for remaining the same.

– Norman Mailer

Tibby couldn't fall asleep. She sat in her bed and looked out the window at the hazardous apple tree. The apples were growing plump and red now. How had she never even tried one?

She associated them with having fallen, that was part of it. She could viscerally recall the smell of the over-sweet, rotting, fermenting apples from seasons past that fell without ever being picked. That smell and the sight of the marauding worms and beetles nauseated her. She loathed the apples wounded on the ground, but she had never thought to pick one from a branch.

The tree seemed to be considering her just as she considered it. She felt its judgement. It wasn't judging her for leaving the window open. That wasn't her crime. Her crimes were deeper and more numerous: she wasn't big enough to love Katherine as Katherine deserved. She wasn't brave enough to love Brian as he deserved. She wasn't strong enough to keep the things she loved alive (Bailey, Mimi), nor was she wise enough to grasp the meaning of their deaths.

Tibby was good at hiding. It was the one thing she knew how to do. She was good at sealing herself in a little box and waiting it out. But waiting for what? What was she waiting for?

She thought she'd learned a lesson from Katherine's fall out the window. The lesson was: don't open, don't climb, don't reach, and you will not fall. But it was the wrong lesson! She had learned the wrong lesson!

The real lesson embodied in Katherine's three-year-old frame was the opposite: try, reach, want, and you may fall. But even if you do, you might be OK anyway.

Flexing her feet under the covers, Tibby thought of a corollary to this lesson: if you don't try, you save nothing, because you might as well be dead.

Time passed for Bridget in the strangest way, a little forward, a little back. She was vaguely aware of Katie and Allison returning to the cabin. They probably assumed she was asleep, but that didn't stop them from flipping on the light and gabbing noisily and turning on music. She suspected they'd been partying with the other remaining staff. They smelled like it, anyway.

Sometime after that, Eric returned. He sized up the situation with Katie and Allison. He was furious. 'Can't you see that Bee is sick? Why are you making all this noise? What the hell's wrong with you?'

Even through her haze, Bridget could tell this was not a side of Eric she'd seen before.

'Dude. Back off,' Katie snapped. 'Why are you barging into our cabin and telling us what to do?' She was too drunk to yield her ground, even if Bee was sick.

Eric knelt next to Bridget. He put his hand on her forehead again. He bent down close to her ear. 'I don't really want to leave you in here with the two of them.

You want to come back with me? My cabin is empty this weekend. You can sleep.'

She nodded gratefully. She was only wondering how she was going to get from here to there without freezing to death. She wasn't wearing anything but her underwear under the blankets.

He had an idea for that, too. He put his arms under her and scooped her up, still tucked inside her blankets. He carried her out of the cabin and into the night, with Katie and Allison watching his back in surprise and indignation.

She felt light in his arms. She rested her burning face against his neck. She was shivering again. He pulled the blankets closer around her and rested his chin lightly on the top of her head.

She was trying her hardest to remember each of these things he did, to mark them in her brain permanently, because they were immeasurably sweet. Maybe they were the sweetest things that had ever happened to her or ever would. She kept hoping that this, unlike all those blankets she imagined getting and glasses of water she imagined drinking, that this was real. *Please let it be real*, she thought wistfully. *And if it's not, let me just stay here anyway.*

He pushed open the door of his cabin with his back and put her very gently into a bed – his bed, she hoped. She wanted to smell his smell. He was careful to tuck her blankets around her snugly. She tried to stop shivering.

'I'd put another blanket on you, but I don't want you to get overheated, you know?'

She nodded. She noticed he'd been carrying a bag

236

also, looped around his wrist. 'Here.' He unloaded a bottle of Advil, a bottle of aspirin, a bottle of water, a bottle of orange juice, a thermometer and a paper cup. 'The nurse isn't back till Sunday, but I got into the infirmary in case we need anything else.'

She fluttered her eyes, trying to focus on his solemn face. 'It was unlocked?'

He shrugged. 'Now it is.'

He filled the cup with water and poured two pills into his palm. 'Ready?' He helped her to sit up in bed.

She tried to figure out how to get her hand out without letting any cold air in. She stuck her hand out up by her neck, keeping the rest of the blanket tight around her. She thirstily drank the water and another cup and another with her little T. rex arm.

'Poor thing. You were thirsty,' he said.

She took the pills, wincing as they went down. Her throat felt swollen.

'Thank you,' she said, lying back down. She felt tears fill her eyes at the extravagance of his kindness to her.

He put his cool hand on her cheek again. 'I am worried about you,' he said quietly. And looking at his face, she could never again question whether they had really become friends.

He took the thermometer out of its case. 'Open up.'

'Are you sure you want to know?' she asked. She knew she was hot.

He nodded, so she opened her mouth. He waited for the mercury to settle. It didn't take very long. He studied it with his eyebrows furrowed. 'God, it's 104.7. Is that safe?'

237

'I've been there before,' she said faintly. Why did she have to do everything in such dramatic fashion?

'Should I call a doctor?' he asked.

'I think I'm going to be OK,' she answered truthfully. 'I'm not scared or anything.'

He lay on the bed opposite her, propped on his side, watching her carefully.

'I'm going to call your dad,' he announced, sitting up. He got his cell phone from the top drawer of his bureau.

'Don't call my dad,' she said softly. 'He's not . . . there.'

'It's midnight. Where would he be?'

'No. I mean.' She took a break. 'He's just not there. In that way.' She was too tired to explain any better.

He looked at her, the corners of his mouth turned down. He looked deeply troubled about that.

He lay down across from her again.

The more she wanted to stop shivering, the more she shivered. She didn't want him to worry about her.

He couldn't stand to watch her shake. He got up and came over to her. He picked her up inside her ball of covers and moved her over on the bed. To her great astonishment and joy, he lay down alongside her. He put his arms around her and tucked her face into his neck, and she felt as though her fevered heart might burst.

He held her as though he thought he could absorb her fever and her sickness and her sadness at not having a mother or even a father she could count on. He stroked her hair and lay with her like that for hours.

And maybe he did absorb her ache, because in his arms she finally fell asleep.

★ ★ ★

By four a.m., daylight was beginning to haunt the sky. Tibby did not want the sun to rise without some real measure of awakening.

After all these hours she felt as though she knew the tree in a new way and the tree knew her. It wasn't an unfriendly tree, but it did pose a challenge to her.

Somewhere around two o'clock, Tibby had remembered she had the Travelling Pants. They had been sitting for a shameful number of days under her bed. She'd been hiding from them. Somewhere around three, she put them on.

She hoisted up the window sash and sat with her elbows on the sill, resting her chin in her hands. The tree waved. Katherine had thought she could reach it from the window but, in fact, she couldn't. Tibby could reach it but thought she couldn't. Tibby's mother's ovaries seemed to produce a heartier strain of egg as they got older.

Tibby put one foot out the window and then the other. She sat on the sill. She looked down. It was far. She would feel incredibly stupid if she fell. She and Katherine could wear matching hockey helmets. Tibby smiled in spite of herself, knowing what a huge kick that would give Katherine. She wondered if Nicky would be similarly willing to help with the stickers.

Tibby caught a sturdy branch with two hands and held it tight. She knew just where she needed to put her feet. She tried to figure out how to do it so that her weight would not at any time be up for grabs. Then she remembered that this was kind of the point.

When she hoisted herself off the window, she would have to transfer her weight completely to her hands for a second or two until she could place her feet. She would just have to do that.

OK.

Yes.

Like, now.

Tibby looked at the ground. She could already see a couple of wormy apples languishing in the dark grass. The ground was psyching her out, so she looked at the sky.

She lifted; she swung. She actually screamed in that moment. But before her scream had gotten all the way out of her mouth, her feet were on the lower branch. She was balanced. She was safe.

She passed herself down slowly, branch by branch. She had a bit of the monkey in her after all. She hung from a low branch by both hands, skimming above the ground with her feet. Then she let go.

The fall was small, but it was grand. Her hands hurt like crazy. Her whole body was shaking with nervousness and pleasure. Her chest was so full she could barely fit a breath into it. She felt like she was living someone else's life.

She crept around the house to let herself in the front door. Before she even turned the knob, she realized it would be locked. And so would the back door. And so would the side door. She was locked out of her house.

This struck her as so unbearably funny that she rolled around on the grass and laughed until she cried.

★ ★ ★

Sometime towards morning, Bridget's fever broke. As dramatically as it had gone up, it came down. She was hardly aware of what was happening when the air around her suddenly turned from bone-cold to sweltering hot. The sweat seemed to pour from every inch of her skin. When she awoke with a start, she realized she had thrown off all her covers in her sleep. More alarmingly, she was lying in her underwear, still circled in the arms of Eric's sleeping body. Now she was afraid to move. Whether Bee was sick or not, this would not look good to Kaya, for example. She didn't want Eric to wake up and see how it was.

She thought she could very carefully untangle the sheet from the bottom of the bed and cover herself with it before he woke up. She was feeling remarkably lucid as she grasped the edge of the sheet between the first and second toes of her left foot. Moving as slowly and smoothly as she could, she pulled her foot towards her.

How funny and strange that she and Eric had slept in the same space twice in less than two weeks. And not for having chosen it. Not for having wanted to sleep together at all. (Well, maybe she did . . . but no longer at his expense.)

In a way it was a tragic waste, and in a more profound way it was the most romantic thing she had ever experienced. Two years before, they had slept together in the figurative sense; this summer, in the literal one. The former had split her in two. And the latter made her feel whole. The first summer had made her feel abandoned. This made her feel loved.

Sex could be a blissful communion. But it could also

241

be a weapon, and its absence, sometimes, was required for the establishment of peace.

Eric shifted and she halted her foot abruptly. Still asleep, he pulled her closer, so her whole self was pressed against him, his arms and chest against her bare skin. He sighed. He probably dreamed she was Kaya. She also dreamed she was Kaya, the one he truly loved.

Bridget wanted to enjoy this, but she couldn't. She couldn't bear to think of him waking up and feeling embarrassed and compromised after he had cared for her with such perfect kindness. She wanted to protect him from that.

She waited until his breathing sank into a rhythm again, and she started back up with the sheet. Morning was almost fully upon them, and the sun was streaming through the window, illuminating their twined bodies. *Don't wake up yet*, she begged him.

She had gotten the sheet almost up to her thighs when he awoke. *Oh*.

For a moment, in that transition, he clung to her hard. And then, in stages, he seemed to recognize the yellow hair spread over his arms and to realize who it was he held like that. Confused, he looked at her full on, at the two of them together, and then he looked away.

'I'm sorry,' he muttered, pulling his arms from her.

How she missed them. She pulled the sheet up over herself. The bedding under her was soaked with sweat. 'Please don't say that,' she said.

Bridget had always believed that the night was more dangerous than the day. But in the preceding twelve

242

hours, her conviction had reversed itself. The night protected her and the morning laid her bare.

'I didn't mean—' he began, flustered.

'I know,' she said quickly.

He couldn't look at her any more. 'Are you feeling . . . ?'

'So much better,' she supplied.

He was up on his feet, turned away from her. 'I . . . uh, I'll let you get dressed. Grab anything you want of mine. T-shirt or whatever.' He pulled a pair of shorts over his boxers.

There were so many things she wanted to say to him. So many shades of the words *thank you*. So many routes to get to an apprehension of love. Not *that* kind of love. This kind of love. Any kind of love, really.

She wanted to say these things to him, to make him understand her feelings and also to make him know that though this thing between them was fragile and strange (she knew, she really knew it was!), he was safe.

But it was too late. He was already gone.

This 'telephone' has too many shortcomings to be seriously considered as a means of communication. The device is inherently of no value to us.
– Western Union internal memo, 1876

'Mom?' Carmen strode into her mother's room and towards the closed door of her bathroom. 'Hey, are you OK in there?'

Carmen was nervous to begin with because her mom had stayed home from work, explaining she was a little under the weather. Carmen had made her scrambled eggs for breakfast and Christina had only picked at them.

Christina had been in there a long time. Carmen heard a moan and then nothing.

'Mama?' She knocked on the bathroom door. 'Is everything all right?' She felt her heart pounding. When her mother opened the door a moment later, her face was white.

'Mama! What's going on?'

Even Christina's lips were white. 'I think . . . I'm not sure . . .' She put her hand on the door frame to steady herself. 'I think my waters broke.'

'You . . . you . . . you do?' Carmen felt like she'd been transported to one of those old-fashioned movies where the wife goes into labour, only in this version, Carmen was the bumbling husband.

'I think so.'

'Does that mean . . . ?'

Christina transferred both hands to her spherical

stomach. 'I don't know. I don't feel like I'm in labour.'

'It's too early!' Carmen shouted at her mother's stomach, as though the baby should know better. 'The baby isn't due for four more weeks!'

'*Nena*, sweetie, I know.'

'Should I call the hospital?'

'I'll call my midwife,' Christina said. She walked slowly towards the phone.

'Do you . . . feel OK?' Carmen asked, watching her mother call.

'I feel like I'm . . . leaking.' Christina pushed a button and waited. She waited longer while the receptionist paged her midwife.

Carmen paced while Christina alternately talked and listened. When she hung up she looked scared, and that pushed Carmen's heart from a trot to a canter. 'What?'

Christina's eyes were teary. 'I have to go to the hospital to get checked. If my waters really broke, I have twelve hours to go into labour naturally and after that they induce. The fear of me getting an infection is bigger than worrying about the baby being early.'

'So the baby is coming . . .'

'Yes. Soon,' Christina said faintly.

'Where is David?' Carmen asked. It was obviously the thing Christina was thinking about.

'He's, uh . . . he's . . .' Christina put her hands over her face. She was trying not to cry, and that made Carmen feel worse. 'I'm trying to think . . . He's been away so much. I think he's in Trenton, New Jersey. Maybe he's in Philadelphia now. I'm not sure.'

'We'll find him!' Carmen shouted, further alarming them both. 'We'll call him!'

'First we'll go to the hospital, OK? The midwife said go right over.'

Carmen's hands were clammy and she raced around ineffectively. 'Have you got your bag? I'll drive.'

Once in the car, Carmen watched her mother intently.

'*Nena,* honey, keep your eyes on the road. I'm OK.'

'Are you having . . .' Carmen wasn't sure what the right terminology was, having diligently tuned it out most of the summer. '. . . labour?'

Christina kept her hands on her stomach, her eyes vague, as though she were feeling for some message tapped in Morse code from within. 'No. I don't think so.'

'Does anything hurt?' Carmen asked.

'Not really. My back is cramping, but it's just un-comfortable. Not really painful.'

Once they were at the hospital and Carmen had landed her mother with a resident to get checked out in an examining room on the labour and delivery floor, she called David's cell phone. It went right to his voice mail without even ringing. That wasn't a great sign. She left a message for him. She meant to sound calm, mature and informative, but as soon as she hung up she knew she sounded more like semi-hysterical.

She shot up at the sight of her mother's face, at the door of the waiting room.

'What?' Carmen said softy, inwardly screaming at her-self to be calm.

'My waters did break,' Christina said. She looked overwhelmed. Her voice was quiet and she was clearly scared.

'OK.'

'I'm not in labour, though.'

'That's good, right?'

'Yes.'

'So now what? We go home?'

'I have to stay here,' Christina said. 'They want to keep an eye on me until eight tonight. Then they'll induce.'

'Induce means like . . .'

'They give you chemicals to make you go into labour.'

Carmen nodded solemnly.

'But I told them we can't do it until . . . I can't have the baby unti . . .' Carmen watched in agony as the tears brewed in Christina's eyes. 'I can't do it until David gets here.' The tears spilled over, and Carmen pulled her mother into her arms. Christina let herself cry for real, and Carmen wondered if this had ever happened before in her whole life.

Christina always took her mothering so seriously, she hardly ever let herself cry or act scared in front of Carmen. Carmen felt scared too, but at the same time she felt grown-up. She felt proud that her mother was letting Carmen take care of her this time.

Holding her mother, Carmen wanted, really wanted, to be brave this time.

'I'm going to go get David,' Carmen promised her. 'I'm going to get him and bring him home so you can have the baby together, OK?'

* * *

Carmen sat in the hospital lobby trying to calculate. The timing was bad on almost every front. Grandma Carmen, Christina's mother, was still in Puerto Rico with her aunt. Everybody, David included, was getting travel engagements out of the way in time for when the baby arrived. But the baby apparently had little consideration for anyone else's plans. Carmen was beginning to wonder if this baby was going to have a few things in common with its big sister.

Carmen couldn't leave her mother alone while she got David. It could take a while. Her mother was not yet in labour, true, but who wanted to sit in the hospital without someone who loved you?

The thing to do was call one of the people Carmen trusted most in the world. Of those three, Bee was out of town, and Carmen had misgivings about Tibby and hospitals. She called Lena. Lena didn't answer her regular phone or her cell. Not surprising, since she often didn't carry the cell. Carmen didn't feel like leaving another crazy-girl message. She called Tibby. By some act of fate, Tibby picked up after the first ring.

'Can you come to the hospital?' Carmen begged, her voice runny with tears. 'My mom's waters broke, and David is out of town, and I have to find him before my mom's doctor gives her medicine to get the labour going. Can you keep her company until I get back?'

'Yes,' Tibby said instantly. 'I'll be there in a minute.'

'Keep your cell with you, OK? I'll call.'

'OK.'

They both hung up.

250

★ ★ ★

Carmen's call came not long after Tibby woke up. It had been a long night. It was tiring, after all, staying up till dawn watching a tree, climbing down that tree, and then getting locked out of your house for a few hours and not getting into bed until after seven in the morning. It was. Ask anybody.

And it was surreal sitting in a chair next to Carmen's mother on a bed in a labour room at the hospital listening to the foetal monitor bleep. It was made even more so on three and a half hours of sleep.

Tibby wondered at the mountain that was Christina's belly. She remembered pretty well her own mother's pregnancies with Nicky and then Katherine. She was thirteen for the first and almost fifteen for the second. She hadn't found the whole thing at all amusing at the time.

But fear not, she reminded herself and, silently, Christina. *We at the Tibby Corporation have a new policy towards younger siblings and even babies generally. We like them and like for them to be safe. We even admit that we love them, though not more often than is necessary.*

'How are you feeling?' Tibby asked. She somehow felt that, much as she cared about Christina, she wasn't the best person for this job.

'Just fine,' Christina said, through a mouth that was tense. Her eyes were distracted.

'Are you sure?' Suddenly Christina was doubled over.

'I think so,' Christina said grittily, clenching her jaw.

Tibby was on her feet and fluttering nervously. 'Should I . . . get the midwife, do you think?'

'I – I don't . . .'

Christina couldn't talk, which said to Tibby she should get the midwife.

The midwife – Lauren was her name – was filling out papers at the nurses' station. 'Uh, Lauren? I think Christina is maybe having some trouble.'

Lauren looked up. 'What kind of trouble?'

Tibby raised her palms skyward. She was not a doctor. She was not a nurse. She wasn't a mother or anybody's husband. She couldn't even vote yet. 'I don't know,' she said.

Lauren followed her into Christina's room. 'Are you having contractions?' she asked Christina.

Christina sat up holding her stomach. 'I'm not sure.'

Lauren looked at the paper spooling out of the monitor. 'You, my dear, are having contractions.'

'But I'm not in labour.' Christina said it half as a statement and half as a question.

'I would say you are in labour.'

'But it's too early,' Christina said. Her eyes weren't focusing quite right. 'I thought tonight—'

'Tonight we'd induce if you didn't go into labour naturally. You are going into labor naturally from what I can see.'

'But David and . . .' Christina closed her eyes and put her chin to her chest.

'Another one, right?' Lauren said. 'You're getting into a pattern – every seven minutes or so. Let me check your cervix, OK? Lie back and open your legs.'

Tibby did not like the sound of this. She floated towards the door.

Lauren was one of those plain-faced, plain-spoken people who liked to say and do embarrassing things as flatly and as often as possible. Like Tibby's eighth-grade health science teacher, who said the words *breast* and *anus* so often you'd think she'd never heard of pronouns.

Tibby loitered in the hallway until Lauren appeared at the door. 'She's at three centimetres,' Lauren announced.

'I don't know what that means,' Tibby said.

'It means her cervix is opening. That's what happens when you're in labour. When her cervix is all the way open – that's ten centimetres – she'll be ready to push the baby out.'

Tibby had one more question and Lauren couldn't very well answer it for her: *How did I get here?*

'How long will that take?' Tibby asked.

'Hard to say for sure, but it's still early labour. It'll probably be a few hours at least.'

Tibby hoped, really and truly hoped, that Carmen and David would be back by then.

Lauren was looking at Tibby seriously. She actually had very pretty brown eyes. Her no-nonsense look was countered by a streak of dark purple liner under her eyelashes.

'Tibby, you need to get in there with her. She's a little freaked out. She could use some support.' Lauren turned to go.

'Um, excuse me,' Tibby said politely, 'but I am, uh, Christina's daughter's friend, if you see what I mean?'

Lauren shrugged. 'Yeah. But you're who she's got right now.'

★ ★ ★

Frantically Carmen called David's cell phone again and got his voice mail again. She paced up and down the sidewalk at the entrance to the hospital. She called Irene, David's secretary, and got *her* voice mail. Why did important things have to happen at lunch time? She called the family number at Lena's house and barked out a message that she couldn't come for Valia today. Somewhat hopelessly, she called David's cell phone again and hung up on his voice mail. She threw her bag on the sidewalk.

'Carmen?'

She turned round and saw Win. Of course it was him. He took in her general dishevelment and her teary eyes. 'Are you OK?'

'My mom's about to have a baby and I can't find her husband,' Carmen burst forth. 'Her waters broke and the baby isn't supposed to be born for a month. But now they want her to have the baby tonight so she doesn't get some kind of an infection.'

Carmen couldn't quite believe she was talking particulars about her mother's amniotic fluid with a boy on whom she had a crush. But she was scared and she wanted to do the right thing and she didn't even know how to do it. Win's concern was so apparent it was heart-rending. 'I promised her I'd find David.'

'Her husband?'

'Yeah.'

'Do you have any idea where he is?' Win asked.

'He's been travelling a lot for work,' Carmen explained balefully. She was walking in a tighter and tighter circle until she was basically spinning on the side-walk. 'We weren't on high alert yet, because the baby wasn't due yet. I have to find him right now!' Her voice was climbing, tinged with hysteria.

'OK. OK. Does he have a cell phone?'

'It's not even ringing! He might be on a plane or something.' Or it might have run out of batteries, and someone who offered to lend him her recharger might not have done so, she added miserably to herself.

'You tried his office?' Carmen appreciated how much he wanted to help her. He was a good person.

'His secretary was at lunch. I'm going to drive over there,' Carmen muttered. 'What else can I do?'

'Can I come?' Win looked intent.

'You want to?'

'Yeah.'

She was now running towards her car and he was following her, stride for stride. 'Can you get out of work?'

'I'm on lunch break. I'm done with paediatrics for today and the old folks can do without my antics and my pocket change for one afternoon.'

'You're sure?'

He looked at her as seriously as if she'd asked him to plunge to the bottom of the Atlantic Ocean with her. 'I'm sure. I'm sure I'm sure.'

Carmen drove. She felt like Starsky and Hutch as they pulled up to the kerb and leaped out of the car. He followed her to the elevator and then to the reception desk.

Mrs Barrie greeted Carmen warmly, and Carmen

explained where she was going without breaking her gait. Christina had worked at this same law firm since Carmen was a toddler. Carmen knew her way around the place.

Carmen and Win staked out Irene's desk, and thankfully, she returned from lunch ten minutes later. 'What can I do for you, Carmen?' Irene asked, looking confused. Carmen wore a bandana on her head, do-rag style, and her feet were in flip-flops.

'We need to find David.' Carmen's intensity was such that Irene seemed to shrink back from her own cubicle. 'I think my mom's gonna have the baby soon,' Carmen explained, 'but don't tell anybody anything yet.'

Irene, good soul that she was, got right with the programme. 'Oh, my.' Briskly she pulled up the calendar on her computer. Her long fingernails clickety-clicked on the keys until she got to the right day. 'Your poor mother. We'll find him.'

Carmen sometimes got the feeling that everybody rooted for her mother. She was probably like a poster girl for legal secretaries. She'd won the respect and ardour of a handsome young lawyer without even meaning to.

'He has a meeting in Trenton this afternoon. He's renting a car there and driving to Philadelphia. He's supposed to stay in a hotel in Philly tonight. He has a meeting scheduled there tomorrow morning and then he comes home. And wait.' She studied her notes a little more closely. 'He told me he was hoping to stop off and visit his mother in Downingtown on his way to Philly.'

Carmen was thinking. 'Do you know the number of the meeting place in Trenton?'

'Yes.' Irene looked it up and called it. She went through several people and several bits and pieces of conversation before she hung up. 'He left already.'

'Oh.' Carmen chewed her thumbnail. 'How about the car rental place?'

'Yes.' Irene called them, too. She listened for a bit and put her hand over the receiver. 'He rented the car and left about twenty-five minutes ago.'

'Shit,' Carmen mumbled. She walked in a small circle. She realized Win was watching her carefully. But she was too preoccupied to be self-conscious or even to consider all the ways in which she was diverging from Good Carmen.

'Do you have David's mother's number?'

Irene winced. 'I don't think I do.' She riffled through her Rolodex and then scrolled through her computerized version. 'No, I'm sorry.'

'The address?' Carmen asked without much hope.

Irene shook her head. 'I don't know David's stepfather's name, do you?'

Carmen should have known it. She had certainly heard it before. But in her efforts to tune out most of the things David said, she'd tuned out this potentially helpful bit of information.

'We should leave a message at the hotel in Philadelphia just in case,' Win suggested.

Irene nodded and did it. 'He hasn't checked in yet, but they'll have him call as soon as he does.'

Carmen's brain was working fast. 'Can you call the

257

rental car company again?' she asked.

Irene did it without asking questions. Carmen held out her hand for the phone. 'Can I talk?'

'Sure.' Irene handed it over.

Carmen talked to a representative for a few minutes. As soon as she hung up she looked at Win and Irene brightly. 'I have something. They can't get hold of David in his car, but they can tell us where the car is.'

'Really?' Win looked impressed.

'Yeah. And like I always say, thank the Lord for satellite systems.' She laughed at herself. 'I don't really go around saying that.'

Win smiled at her, also clearly relieved that they had a lead. 'How far is Downingtown?' he asked.

Irene shrugged. 'I think about an hour and a half.'

Win and Carmen looked at each other. 'So let's go,' Win said.

'You think so?' Carmen asked, suddenly nervous about the extent to which she'd embroiled an innocent guy in her drama. 'You sure you want to come with me?'

His eyes told her she should take this for granted. 'I'm sure I want to come with you.'

Of course she found it in the last place she looked. If she hadn't found it, she'd still be looking.

– Susannah Brown

Lena walked into her father's study with expectations so low, she would have been happily surprised if he'd taken a paperweight from his desk and thrown it at her.

He was thumbing through a stack of papers on his desk. He was listening to Paul Simon. It was one of about three CDs he ever listened to, and he always struck Lena as slightly tin-eared and immigrant in his appreciation. The song was perky and polished, something about a camera that took bright colour pictures. To Lena the song was like an A-plus paper, a maths problem where you showed your work, a form fully filled out. But it didn't sound to her like music. She liked her colours dingier.

Her father looked up at her over his half-glasses. He turned the music off.

'Do you mind if I make a drawing of you?' Lena had practised saying this in her head so many times, the words had long ago lost their ordinary feel and had begun to taste funny in her mouth.

He waved her to the empty seat across from his desk. He was prepared for this. Lena's mother had no doubt warned and mollified him.

Lena's paper was already clipped to her drawing board and her charcoal was squeezed into her clammy hand.

She hadn't come in willing to take no for an answer. She sat down. 'You don't need to do anything special.' She'd practised saying that, too.

He nodded absently. He didn't need to be asked twice. He was already back to his papers. But she noticed he kept his face angled straighter now, only his eyes cast down. The lenses of his glasses glinted, but his eyes within them appeared shut from where she sat.

She watched him for a long time before she began to draw. She made herself do this. She didn't care if it made him uncomfortable.

For a while she saw what she expected. She could have drawn his angry face with not only his eyes closed but with hers closed too. This was how she pictured him, and this is how he looked. She saw what she felt, and what she felt was his anger. She had certainly suffered for it. Why else was she here?

She knew what she felt. But what did she see?

She began to wonder. With drawing, you were always pitting your feelings and expectations against what the cold light offered your optic nerves. Like the first time you tried to mix colours to paint water. You thought you'd be using a lot of blue and maybe green. But if you made yourself see, you ended up with a lot more grey and brown and white, and even weird unexpected colours like yellow and red. And if you tried to paint it again, it would all be different. You couldn't paint the same water twice.

She remembered once standing with her mother on a street corner in Georgetown and watching a painter at work. Her mother let her watch for a long time, and as they were walking away, Lena remembered asking how come he used so much brown.

As a child, you were taught to see the world in geometric shapes and primary colours. It was as if the adults needed to equip you with more accomplishments. ('Lena already knows her colours!') Then you had to spend the rest of your life unlearning them. That was life, as near as Lena could tell. Making everything simple for the first ten years, which in turn made everything way more complicated for the subsequent seventy.

And now her feelings about her father made a mask over his actual features. She had thought that her challenge would be to paint his anger, to confront it. But now she knew that wasn't the challenging thing. The challenging thing was to see past it.

She stared at him without blinking until her eyeballs dried and her vision blurred. She wished she could turn her father upside down. Sometimes you could see things more truly when you forfeited your normal visual relationship with them. Sometimes your pre-existing ideas were so powerful they clubbed the truth dead before you could realize it was there. Sometimes you had to let the truth catch you by surprise.

Lena looked away and closed her eyes. She opened them and looked back at her father's face, but only for a second. It could catch you by surprise, or maybe, if you were bold, you could catch it.

She turned away, and then turned back for a little longer. She was seeing more now. She was holding onto something. She took a deep breath, carefully keeping herself in this other visual dimension. This place where she saw but didn't feel.

Her hand was finally connecting charcoal to paper. She let it fly. She didn't want to bog it down with thinking.

Her father's face was no more to her than a topographical map. The mouth was a series of shapes, nothing more. The downturned eyes were shadings of darkness and light. She stayed there a good, long time. She was careful not to blink too hard or too long for fear that this new way of seeing would abandon her.

She wasn't afraid of him any more. The scared part of her was waiting out by the mouth of the cave; the rest of her had gone in.

She saw something in her father's mouth. A little tick. Another tick, and then a sag.

She wasn't scared any more, but was he?

The trick of drawing was leaving your feelings out, giving them the brutal boot. The deeper trick of drawing was inviting them back in, making nice with them at exactly the right moment, after you were sure your eyes really were working. Fighting and making up.

And so her feelings were coming back in, but they were a different kind this time. They were guided by her eyes, rather than the other way around. Tentatively, she let them come. A good drawing was a record of your visual experience, but a beautiful drawing was a record of your feelings about that visual experience. You had to let them come back.

She saw her father's fear, and it so surprised her, she could barely contemplate it. What was he afraid of?

263

She could imagine if she tried. He was afraid of her disobedience. He was afraid of her independence. He was afraid of her growing up and not being the kind of girl he could feel proud of – or the kind of girl Bapi would be proud of. He was afraid of being old and powerless. He was afraid she would see his vulnerability. But also, she suspected, he wanted her to see it.

She felt her fingers softening around the charcoal. Her lines got looser. She felt sad and moved by these things she saw in his face. She didn't want to make it hard for him to love her. But at the same time, she couldn't deny who she was to make it easy.

Her fingers were flying. The muscles in her father's neck quivered slightly with the great effort of holding still for her. He was trying. He really was.

That moved her too.

After almost two hours she set him free. 'Thank you,' she said earnestly.

He pretended he didn't notice so much.

She held the drawing board facing out as she left, so he could peek at the results if he wanted to. He didn't peek.

But later that night, when she was going to bed, she tiptoed past the kitchen, where she'd left her drawing of him propped on a chair. He stood alone in the quiet room. And even though she just saw his back, she knew he was looking.

Win offered to take the wheel so Carmen could work the phone. Half an hour into the drive they had to stop for gas. He bought two Cokes and a bag of Corn Nuts. Carmen had never had Corn Nuts before, and she loved them. They could barely hear each other over the crunching, so they found themselves shouting, which they both thought was incredibly funny once they realized it. The laughter made Carmen's eyes start running again, and the salt made her lips burn.

She was tired and punchy and worried and also happy that they were driving towards David and doing everything they could.

By her calculation they had four hours to find David and get back to her mom. He was only an hour away now. It would work. It had to work. She felt confident that Tibby could keep her mom company for the waiting part, and David and Carmen would be there in time for the inducing part, when the real drama started.

Win was a good driver. He was confident and sharp about it, and yet effortless too. For some reason, the look of his hands on the wheel (at ten and two – Valia would have approved) struck her as masculine and even sexy.

Furthermore, he had an excellent profile. Not a Ryan Hennessey profile exactly – Win's nose was a tiny bit crooked, and his upper lip went out a little farther than his bottom one. But on him, it worked. It was fun how you could get away with watching someone when they drove. He concentrated on the road, and she braved a full look at him.

They barely knew each other, and yet they always had a project together. It was the opposite of most of her romantic relationships, which were all form and no content. Carmen was infamous for writing out talking points to use with the boys she dated. She never searched for things to say to Win.

'You're close to your mother, huh?' he asked her thoughtfully.

'Yes.' It was the Good Carmen answer instead of the Whole Carmen answer. 'What about you?'

'I'm close to both my parents,' he said. 'I'm the only one, so it gets intense sometimes.'

'Me too,' Carmen chimed in. Then she remembered. 'Until today, I guess.'

'Pretty strange, becoming a sister at the age of . . . how old are you?'

'Seventeen,' Carmen said.

'Seventeen,' he echoed.

'Almost eighteen. And you?' she asked. These were questions they could have gotten out of the way on an awkward date two months ago, but somehow they hadn't.

'Nineteen.'

'And yeah, it is strange. Stranger than I can say.'

'I had a sibling for a short while.' He tried to say it lightly and conversationally, but it didn't come out that way.

'What do you mean?' Carmen wanted to know, but she didn't want to demand anything. 'I mean, if you want to tell me.'

'I had a little brother. He was born when I was five and he died just before I turned six.'

'Oh.' Carmen's tears were so near the surface these days, even a fourteen-year-old tragedy concerning a person she didn't really know called them up. 'I'm so sorry.'

'It was a long time ago. But he is part of my identity, you know?'

She didn't know, but she could try to guess. She nodded.

'I still think about him sometimes. I dream about him too. I try to remember what he looked like. It's hard to remember, though, either because of time or because of strong feelings. I sometimes think the stronger you feel about someone, the harder it is to picture their face when you are away from them.'

Carmen's tears were falling now, and she tried to hide them from Win. He would interpret her tears as belonging to Good Carmen. He would think she was crying selflessly, for him and his family's pain. Whereas Bad Carmen was crying because Win had spent a lifetime missing a baby who'd been lost, and she'd spent a summer resenting a baby who hadn't yet come.

Tibby was learning something about her future. She was learning that it would not include having children. Not unless she adopted some.

Christina was in hell, and Tibby could barely watch it. With each contraction – and they seemed like they were coming all the time now – Christina seemed to lose some of herself. When she came down she was less focused, less coherent, less recognizable. Tibby glanced at the printout. One line followed the baby's heartbeat and the other followed the quaking of Christina's uterus. It reminded Tibby of a seismogram. Christina had gone from a five on the Richter scale to about a twenty. If Christina's stomach were California, then California would be under the ocean by now.

Tibby tried calling her mother again, but there was no

answer. Alice would know all about this stuff. She would know how to help. She was dialling in Carmen's cell number when a nurse appeared in her face.

'You have to put that away,' she snapped, pointing at Tibby's cell phone. 'It interferes with the equipment. You could get thrown out of here.'

Tibby considered that possibility with a certain amount of longing.

'Can you give her some medicine or something?' Tibby asked Lauren when she popped her head in. Tibby was afraid of this much pain. She didn't know how to get close to it.

Lauren came over and put her hands on Christina's shoulders. 'You doing OK, honey?'

Christina tried to focus. It didn't look like the question made any sense to her. The answer was so profoundly *no* that the question hardly applied.

'In her birth plan she specified natural childbirth. That means, basically, no drugs,' Lauren explained to Tibby. 'That's partly why she's working with me instead of an OB. Midwives don't prescribe the heavy stuff.'

It didn't seem a good sign that they were talking about Christina rather than to her. 'An OB is . . . a doctor?' Tibby asked, wondering for a moment if a doctor wouldn't be a good idea right now. If she were Christina she would want the heavy stuff. She would want the heaviest stuff, and every bit of it they had. She would want them to knock her out so completely that she wouldn't wake up for a week.

'It seems like you should make that plan when you're actually giving birth. Then at least you know what it feels like,' Tibby opined, but Lauren wasn't listening.

Lauren was now studying the printout with some degree of interest. 'Christina, let me check you again, hon. These contractions are coming fast and furious.'

Christina was shaking her head. 'No. I don't want to.' Her legs were clamped shut.

'We'll wait until this contraction is over.' Lauren stroked Christina's shoulders in a way that was meant to be soothing, but Christina was not soothed. She was writhing. She pushed Lauren away. 'I can't. I'm not ready.' Christina's voice was breaking up into sobs.

Lauren cast a look at Tibby that seemed to say she was certainly the most horrendous labour partner any pregnant woman had ever been saddled with. Tibby did feel bad. Not because of Lauren – she didn't really care what Lauren thought – but because of Christina. Christina was alone here. She didn't have her husband or her sister or her daughter or her mother. She had Tibby.

Tibby's instinct was to get on the bed with Christina, but her muscles were fighting with her. They were remembering Bailey, and more recently, Katherine. Tibby did not have happy associations with beds in hospitals. Who did?

Christina was in a ball. She was crying quietly. Tibby suffered a deep ache in her chest, climbing up to her throat.

'I need to check you, Christina. I need to see where you are,' Lauren said.

She's right there! Tibby felt like screaming. *Leave her alone!*

269

'I'm not ready,' Christina said, weeping.

Lauren tried to uncurl Christina, but Christina fought her off.

Tibby couldn't stand it any more. She got on the bed with Christina. She grabbed her hands and squeezed them hard. That seemed to get her attention.

Lauren still pulled at Christina's legs.

'She said she's not ready!' Tibby roared.

Lauren looked taken aback, like Tibby had smacked her. Then, to Tibby's utter astonishment, Lauren put her face to the side of Tibby's head. She kissed her temple.

As if this day could get any stranger.

'That a girl,' Lauren whispered. 'Fight for her. She needs you.'

Tibby pulled Christina up by her hands. She looked into her eyes. 'Christina, I'm here. Look at me, OK? Hold my hands. Squeeze them as hard as it hurts.' That was something Alice used to say to Tibby when she had to get a shot.

Christina was coming down from a contraction. She looked lost, but slowly she zeroed in on Tibby.

Tibby knelt by her. 'I'm here. You're OK. Show me how much it hurts.'

The pain mounted again in Christina's face. She squeezed Tibby's hands so hard, Tibby saw them turning white. She tried her hardest not to flinch. The pressure mounted until Tibby half expected to see her ten severed fingers lying on the mattress.

'That's good!' Tibby shouted. 'I feel it! That's so great!'

Christina's eyes were tracking hers now. Tibby felt, on some level, that that was the right thing.

'I need to check her. I think this is happening,' Lauren said to Tibby under her breath. 'Help me, OK?'

Tibby did not know what *happening* meant. She did not want to know what *happening* meant. She straddled Christina's legs, so she was practically sitting on her, though carrying her own weight. 'Tina, Lauren's gonna do her thing. Stick with me, OK. With my eyes. Are you watching?'

Christina nodded.

'Squeeze my hands. Can you do it?'

Christina allowed Lauren to examine her cervix, though she was desperately uncomfortable. Tibby's hands were mottled white and purple.

'My goodness,' Lauren said breathlessly. 'This is fast. Christina, you are ten centimetres and ready to go.'

Tibby stared at Lauren, dumbfounded. Wasn't Lauren supposed to do this kind of thing every day? Why did she allow herself to get surprised? She said this was going to take hours. As in several. Not as in one. Did Lauren have any idea what she was doing?

Tibby hadn't even gotten hold of Carmen. She hadn't wanted to scare her. She'd thought they had *hours*. She'd thought Carmen would still have enough time to get back. Now what? What were they supposed to do now?

Christina started crying again. There was a whole lot of blood on the bed, under Christina's legs.

Tibby didn't want to show her fast-rising fear. If she panicked, where would that leave Christina? She needed to get them focused again.

Christina was in a new kind of pain, making a new

271

kind of noise. Tibby tried not to be alarmed. It wouldn't help.

'You need to push, hon,' Lauren said. 'You're feeling the pressure and that means you need to push. You're almost there!'

'No!' Christina was suddenly livid. 'I'm not ready! I can't do this! David isn't here! Where is he? Where is Carmen? We took the classes! This baby is not due for *four weeks*!' In her anger, Christina had tuned herself right back in. She let go of Tibby's hands, rolled back onto her side and curled into her ball.

Tibby could see from her body that Christina was fighting a ferocious urge.

'She needs to push. I can see it,' Lauren said. 'Don't fight it, Christina. It's time to have this baby. You gotta let go!' She was trying unsuccessfully to get Christina's attention.

Tibby tried pulling her up again, but Christina wouldn't budge. 'Tina, will you look at me? Do you see me? You can do this! I know it!'

Christina wouldn't look. 'I can't.'

We are born believing.

A man bears beliefs, as

a tree bears apples.

– Ralph Waldo Emerson

Roughly twenty minutes south of Downingtown, Carmen realized there was another sizeable topic she and Win hadn't considered.

'Are you going away to school next year?' he asked her without looking at her. He was bearing down on a slow Nissan in the fast lane.

'Um.' She licked her lips. 'Yes.'

This was the obvious moment to say where she was going. It suddenly struck her how badly she wanted to say she was going to Williams. She wanted Win to think she was smart.

She tapped her bare toes against the dashboard. But she wasn't going to Williams. She was going to Maryland, and she didn't want to lie to him any more. She liked him too much to keep doing that.

'I'm going to Maryland,' she said. She quelled the urge to spout her near-perfect grades and her academic honours. She left it at the truth. If he didn't like the truth, well . . . then that was a good thing to know.

'Oh.'

Did he find her disappointing?

'What about you?' she asked. It was strange that she didn't know. Carmen was a great student. She cared about that kind of thing. Most boys she assessed almost like a brand, and where they went to college added or subtracted from their cachet. Win was different. She'd gotten to know him from the inside, it seemed.

'I go to Tufts. In Boston.' He smiled a little and tipped his head towards her. 'I was kind of hoping you were going somewhere up around there.'

I was! she felt like shouting at him. *I could have! I almost did!*

But she stayed quiet, which was good in a way, because when her cell phone started ringing she heard it right away and snapped it open.

It was Tibby, trying to be calm.

'Oh, my God! Oh, no! Tell me you are kidding,' Carmen roared into the phone.

Tibby wasn't kidding.

'We'll be there as fast as we can,' Carmen said helplessly.

'What happened?' Win asked.

'She's in heavy labour,' Carmen said, a little sob getting past her. 'It's going fast. She's asking for David and for me.'

'Man,' Win muttered. He took his foot off the gas pedal. 'What do you want to do? Keep going or turn round now?'

'Turn round,' she answered. As soon as he flicked the blinker she thought better of it. 'No, keep going. It's David's baby, too. We have to tell him. He'll be heartbroken if he doesn't even know.'

Win seemed to think that was a good answer. He got back into the left lane of the highway and pushed the speed. He was going eighty-five and Carmen wasn't complaining.

The news shook her and sent her mind back to Bethesda to be with her mother. Carmen knew Christina was scared. She was probably in a lot of pain. 'I was her labour coach,' Carmen murmured.

She *was* close to her mother. Underneath everything was that. It wasn't just the good answer, it was true. How else could you explain how powerfully she felt her mother's distress?

Her mother told her once that when you feel someone else's pain and joy as powerfully as if it were your own, then you knew you really loved them. Right now Carmen knew she had the pain part right. The joy . . . well, she still had work to do on that.

Win expertly took the exit for Downingtown. Carmen focused her energies on the map. She was a good map reader. They had the cross streets and the car make and the licence plate number. That would be enough information, they both hoped. God forbid David had parked in an underground garage or something.

The co-ordinates led them to a housing development. Carmen screamed when she saw the green Mercury. She screamed out the letters and numbers of the licence plate. Win was laughing and yelling too. The two of them stormed the front door of the recently built clapboard house. Carmen fidgeted, trying to restrain herself from ringing the doorbell more than twice.

A woman appeared at the door. Carmen saw David behind her and immediately started waving and yelling.

It was all a flurry after that. Carmen couldn't remember who said what, but five minutes later, Carmen, Win and David were speeding south towards Bethesda, Maryland.

'I forgot my rental car,' David muttered from the back seat, still whitish grey in the face.

'It's OK. Somebody can take it back for you,' Carmen reassured him. She looked from Win, in the driver's seat, to David. 'By the way, David Breckman, this is Win—'

Was it possible that she didn't know his last name? Here they'd run the gauntlet of emotions, he'd experienced everything with her from Valia's friable ligaments to Katherine's hockey helmet to her mother's unexpected labour, and she really didn't know even that? 'Uh, what's your last name?'

'Sawyer.'

'Win Sawyer,' she murmured.

'Thanks for your help, Win,' David said robotically. He was trying to call the hospital on Carmen's cell phone. Her battery was almost gone.

'What's yours?' Win asked her. They were in their own world.

'Lowell.'

'How do you do, Carmen Lowell?'

She smiled at him gratefully. 'Ask me later.'

By Baltimore, they were flying down 95 at just as many miles per hour. Carmen was incensed when a siren started blaring behind them. Win groaned.

'Oh, you're joking,' Carmen said.

Win pulled onto the shoulder. Carmen opened her door.

'Carmen, no!' Both Win and David were yelling at her. 'You're not supposed to get out of the car!'

Suddenly a policeman was yelling at her over his bullhorn. It made her angrier. She slammed the door and crossed her arms over her chest.

'My mother is in the hospital about to have a baby without her husband, and you are holding us up!' she practically exploded.

After an impassioned chat with the policeman, Carmen got back in the car.

Win looked a bit shell-shocked. He and David both looked defeated, as though expecting tickets and fines of hundreds of dollars and also to go to jail.

'He said he was sorry,' Carmen reported instead. 'Go ahead.'

'*What?*' both Win and David yelled at her.

'Win, go!' she said. And Win obliged. 'He offered us an escort but I said no,' Carmen continued once they'd gotten back up to speed. 'I told him no, but please radio ahead to his fellow cops and tell them to leave us alone.'

Win was trying to hold back his smile. Carmen couldn't think about whether she was being Good Carmen or not. She couldn't keep track any more.

David was shaking his head. 'Win, this girl is a force of nature.'

Win cast a sideways look at Carmen. 'I'm getting that impression.'

'We need some help here.' Lauren and Minerva, the labour and delivery nurse, had pulled Tibby aside. 'I'm

278

not getting through to her,' Lauren added. Like Tibby didn't know that.

Aren't you the professionals? Tibby felt like screaming at them. *Aren't you supposed to know how this goes? I'm seventeen! I'm not even supposed to be here!*

Minerva cleared her throat. She was a stocky Filipina. 'This isn't a medical issue. It's an emotional issue. Do you know what I'm saying?'

'You mean Christina is freaking because her husband isn't here?' Tibby asked impatiently. She was tired. She was scared.

'Yes,' Lauren said. 'And she doesn't want to let the baby go. She's gotta release it, she's gotta make the leap. We need to help her so she feels safe.'

Tibby knew a thing or two about leaps. She turned and strode back to Christina. She felt like a soldier going back into battle. She'd already done the sensible thing of putting a pair of hospital scrubs over the Travelling Pants, which she still wore from the night before. She prayed they would bring Christina some of their magic by association, but she wasn't crazy enough to leave unwashable Pants uncovered in such a circumstance.

Christina was fighting. And all in a rush, she reminded Tibby powerfully of her daughter. Like Carmen, Christina was a fighter, all right, and also like her daughter, she was fighting to total destruction.

Tibby got on the bed. She held Christina by her shoulders. Inside herself, Tibby made Christina a promise. *If you leap, I will. We'll do it together.*

Tibby could be a fighter too. At least, she could try.

She propped Christina up on her pillows. She held Christina's face between her hands.

'Tina. I know it's hard. You don't want to let go. I know how it feels. I mean, not having a baby. Obviously I haven't had a baby, but—' OK, she was getting off track.

To her amazement, she saw a look of mirth flit through Christina's eyes. Here and then gone. If Christina could even consider laughing at Tibby, then maybe they were in business.

'David and Carmen are coming. And they want to see this baby so bad. And the baby wants to come out, so you gotta do it.' Tibby figured she would just talk. Christina was listening to her now. Her body was shaking from head to toe, but she was listening.

Lauren and Minerva had their latex gloves on. They were positioning themselves at the foot of the bed for the main attraction. Christina allowed them to pull her onto her back. Her knees were bent. She was in position.

Christina let out a whimper. She was bearing down, crumpling up her face.

'Let go! You can do it! I know you can. You're Carmen's mom, right? You can do anything! Right?'

'Tell her to push,' Lauren muttered. 'She needs to push or we're all in trouble here.'

'Tina, push!' Tibby said it so loud she felt her eyeballs rattling. 'You can do it! Get that baby out of there, would you?' Tibby didn't even care what she was saying, because Christina was listening.

Christina was clinging to Tibby now, holding her

tight around her neck, looking for strength. It made Tibby feel strong. 'You know how much we love you! You know how happy David is going to be to see this baby! Just picture Carmen's face!'

Tibby was just as hysterical as Christina, but Christina was pushing now, and both Lauren and Minerva looked nearly delirious with relief.

'Tibby, I'm pushing!' Christina whimpered.

'You are! You are unbelievable! You are a star! You are the hero! You are the bomb!' Tibby was shouting; she was beyond herself. Somewhere back there was self-consciousness, and here, right up here, was she.

'Tibby!' Christina cried. She was getting some control now.

Tibby kept right on yelling and screaming, the dumbest, silliest things. She wasn't even listening to herself any more.

Contractions came, and with each came a push. Minerva and Lauren were shouting their encouragement too, but the world had shrunken to just the two of them – Tibby and Christina, a funny pairing most every other day of the year.

Christina kept her eyes fixed on Tibby's, on Tibby's very pupils, and Tibby did not blink. As long as she could keep Christina right there with her, she could make a difference.

'I see the baby's head! I feel it!' Lauren shouted.

'Oh, my God. Did you hear that!' Tibby thundered. 'She can feel the baby's head!'

Christina smiled a real honest-to-God smile.

'The baby is right there. *Right there!*' Tibby was beside

herself. She had Christina's shoulders in her hands, then her face. 'You got it! You know that?'

'I got it!' Christina cried. She was coming to life.

'I feel it,' Lauren said. 'I feel the hair.'

'Tina, your baby has hair!' Tibby screamed. 'Can you believe it?'

Christina looked like she liked the idea of a baby with hair. 'Carmen had hair,' she said faintly, 'when she was born.'

'Well, lucky thing, that is. I love hair. Hair is great!' Tibby was giddy now. She pushed long, sweaty strands of Christina's hair off of her neck.

'One more push, and this head is out,' Lauren said. She left Tibby to her own insane translation.

'Tina, one more big one! Biggie. Big big big push. Don't you want to meet your baby?'

Christina went all out. She screamed bloody murder. Her face turned dark purple.

'And . . . it's . . . a . . . baby!' Lauren shouted.

One more gigantic push and the rest of the baby followed the head. Tibby was afraid to look down, because it was all pretty damn gory. But Lauren raised this wriggling, slimy, purple little body up.

Tibby could barely breathe. The baby waved its hands and let out a cry. It was a very tiny person, a real person, who had hands to wave and a cry to cry.

Lauren landed the purple body on Christina's chest and Christina sobbed. She held her baby and cried. Tibby watched in wonder and cried too.

The professionals did their professional stuff between Christina's legs. Then they cut the cord, weighed the baby, and did a few other medical things. Then the baby, now more pink than purple, arrived back in Christina's arms.

Christina held the baby to her breast, and Tibby knew it was done. Christina's little world remained at two, but the second one wasn't Tibby any more. That was as it should be, sad and happy at once.

Slowly Tibby unfolded her limbs and climbed off the bed. She wanted to leave quietly, to let Christina have her unadulterated joy.

But before she did, she planted a kiss on Christina's head. 'You kicked ass,' she whispered. It wasn't quite the wording of a Hallmark card, but it did express her true feelings.

Near the door, she bumped into Lauren, bustling about. Lauren paused. 'Tibby, you have an unorthodox coaching style, but it is very effective. Would you be available for future labours?' Lauren was half laughing, but Tibby could see she'd been crying too. She was wiped out.

'No way.' Tibby stopped. She needed to know something. It felt important, like her future suddenly hung on the answer. 'Hey, Lauren?'

'Yeah?'

'Don't you get used to this? I mean, haven't you done it hundreds of times?'

Lauren pushed her hair behind her ears. Her purple liner was smudged. Her face was shiny with sweat. 'Yes.' She looked at her hands. 'But no. It's a miracle. It's different every single time.'

To love another person

is to see the face of

God.

— Victor Hugo

The three of them, Carmen, David and Win, crashed into labour and delivery with such speed and force you would have thought they were each having a baby of their own.

Tibby's was the first familiar face they saw. She was wearing hospital scrubs with a lot of scary-looking stains, standing in the hall with a bewildered expression. As soon as she saw Carmen she burst into tears. 'You have a baby!' she screamed.

'We do?'

'Oh, my God.'

David was darting around, trying to find Christina.

'Over here!' Tibby grabbed him by the shirt and pulled him into a room.

It was a hospital room and, of course, it featured a bed. The bed featured a flushed woman in a pale pink gown, and she in turn featured a tiny, blanket-wadded bundle topped by a knit hat the size of a tennis sock.

Carmen was surrounded by shouts and yells and exclamations of surprise and joy, so many and so voluble that she couldn't tell which one came from whom – not even if it came from her own throat. She let David beat her to the bed, but she was a fast second. With expansive arms she pressed herself on her mother and this baby and even David. Christina was laughing and sobbing, and Carmen felt her own breaths coming out in those same general types of contortions.

'We have a baby!' David pulled away a few inches to try to get a grasp on the situation. 'Right?'

Christina was the madonna now, calm and wise. She laughed at his tortured face. 'Yes, this one is ours.'

Tears were coursing down David's face. He needed to make sure of Christina before he grappled with the idea of this baby of his. 'Christina, I am so sorry – I don't know how—'

Christina pressed her hand to his face. 'Don't say anything else about that. I had Tibby. We have a beautiful, healthy baby.' She looked at Carmen. 'You too, *nena*. Right now I have everything on the earth that I want.'

With trepidation Carmen and David both peered at the tiny thing.

'Do you want to know what it is?' Christina asked.

Carmen was so overwhelmed, she'd forgotten about that whole issue. That had mattered to her once, hadn't it?

'It's a boy,' Christina said joyfully.

'Oh!' Carmen let out another scream, but she thoughtfully directed it away from her mother's ear. 'We have a boy!'

David cried some more.

Carmen looked over her shoulder at the door of the room. She wanted to share this deep pleasure with Tibby and Win, but both of them had gone.

Carmen realized she needed to find them. She also

needed to give her mother and David and their baby a moment together.

She backed up a little, seeing the three of them framed in a triangle. Her mother's face radiated such relief and joy that Carmen felt her own face pressing itself into that same shape, without even thinking. Her connection was so overpowering, she felt like her mother's face was her own, her mother's heart was beating with hers, her feelings were the same.

And she remembered the thing about being able to feel someone else's joy and knowing that you loved them.

Good and Great Carmen,

This is a day for miracles. Put on the Pants, and take one for your very own.

All my love,

Tibby

When Carmen found the Travelling Pants neatly folded with the note right outside the door to her mother's hospital room, she raced into the bathroom and pulled them on.

Then she took the elevator up to geriatrics. Win stood by the vending machines. He was searching his pockets for change. It so happened that neither of them had eaten anything but Corn Nuts in many hours.

Her impulse was to hug him, and she didn't give herself the time to chicken out. She just threw her arms around him. 'Thank you so much, Win!' she exclaimed with a full throat. 'Thank you for everything.'

'I'm sorry we didn't get to her in time,' Win said into her hair. His arms had made their way around her, too.

'I think it's OK. I think everything is OK now.'

'Hey, I didn't mean to disappear before. I just didn't want to get in the way of your family and everything,' he explained.

'I know, but I needed to see you.' She pulled away a little, to give him some room.

He didn't seem to want to take it. He put his face back into her hair, pressing his cheek against her ear. 'I need to see you, too,' he murmured.

He held her closer. She let her body relax into his, feeling his breathing. She felt his backbone under her palms. Her heart was beating only a few inches from his.

'I need to say something to you,' she said over his shoulder.

He lifted his head. He let her back up from him a little. He had a look on his face that said it was girding for disappointment.

'There's this thing I've been worrying about, and I have to set it straight.'

His look of apprehension grew.

She breathed out. 'I think you might think I'm a good person, and I wanted to let you know that I'm not. I am mean and selfish most of the time.'

He tipped his head, confused.

'You are too good for me,' she explained.

'That's impossible.'

'No, seriously, Win. You are a good person, and I'm only pretending to be one. I've given you this false impression that I'm selfless and kind. And I'm not.'

Win raised his eyebrows. 'God, that's a relief. You may think I'm good, but I was starting to feel pretty intimidated.'

'Really?'

'Oh, yeah.'

'I got eight fifty an hour to babysit Valia.' She figured she might as well go for full disclosure.

'Man, you deserved a hundred.'

She laughed. 'Funny thing was, I ended up really caring about her. That part was free,' she added.

He studied her for a long moment, a quizzical look in his eyes, before he opened his mouth. 'I used to be fat.'

Carmen felt her eyebrows floating upwards. 'Excuse me?'

'I used to be fat.' Win shrugged. 'I was the fat kid. Since we're uncovering our inner selves, I might as well throw that in.'

She couldn't help glancing over his body in case there was a hundred pounds she had forgotten to notice. There wasn't.

'The summer I was thirteen my parents sent me to fat camp. The next summer I grew six inches and got serious about swimming. But still, a fat kid lives inside me.'

Carmen tried to fit this piece into the puzzle of Win. It did fit, in a funny way.

He cleared his throat. 'So as I see it, I'm the pretender. You're too good for me.'

'That's impossible,' she said.

He moved closer again. He looked in her eyes for a

290

long time. Then he tugged, most intimately, on a belt loop of the Pants. 'If you're too good for me and I'm too good for you, what does that mean?'

'We're just right?'

He smiled. 'Can I?' He wanted to put his arms around her again.

'Please.'

In front of the candy machine, under the glare of fluorescent hallway lights, surrounded by the smell of old people, he put his lips on hers. He kissed her soft and slow at first, and then deeper.

He buried his head in her neck. He pushed her hair aside and kissed her there. She let out a small sigh.

'I've wanted to do this for so long,' he murmured into her ear.

'Mmmm,' she said. She found his lips again with hers. With abandon, she kissed him. Perhaps for the first time ever, she kissed without a single thought about how it was or what it was or what it meant. She kissed from the inside.

An old lady wheeled out of her room and caught them in the act. 'Can you two lovebirds take that somewhere else?' she clucked.

Carmen and Win both started laughing, running for the elevators. They held hands as they descended and as they strode through the lobby.

Carmen walked, and squeezed his hand, and suddenly she had the strangest impression that Good Carmen walked before her, a few feet in front of her, like a ghost, a glistening spirit.

This was a day for miracles. Carmen overtook that

291

spirit. She walked right into Good Carmen and absorbed her into her soul. Let her fight it out with Bad Carmen if she needed to.

And, thus, the hospital doors opened and Whole Carmen emerged, newly born, into the world.

My shoe is off

My foot is cold

I have a bird

I like to hold.

– Dr Seuss

Tibby wasn't done leaping yet.

Dazed in the fading light, she stumbled down Connecticut Avenue. Cars rushed by; people went around. Tibby felt like she'd been sucked into a wormhole of heightened experience and then spat back out into the regular world. The world was regular, but she wasn't regular any more.

The wormhole happened to be pretty messy. Back at the hospital she'd washed her hands and face and shed her stained gown. She'd taken off the Pants and made away with just the pair of scrub pants on her legs. She hoped she wouldn't get arrested for it. Still, she felt sticky. She didn't want to think about that too much.

She needed to find Brian. She didn't want to get comfortable with the ground yet.

She knew he'd be at home. At her home. She pointed herself in the right direction.

A block from her house she saw him walking towards her. She didn't question that. It was one of those days.

They didn't run into each other's arms or anything. He walked towards her and when he reached her, she turned 180 degrees so they were walking in the same direction. They walked like that for a while. She reached for his hand. He held on.

'I have an idea,' she said.

'OK,' he said. He didn't ask what it was. He was willing to go along.

They walked blocks and blocks and then up a long hill up to Rockwood pool. Then they step-jumped over moving water. And then ascended that long staircase. By the time they got to the fence, it was dark. And they were good and high. A high place was what you needed for a leap.

'Here's where it's good to climb up.' She pointed to the break in the barbed wire.

Brian seemed to think that made sense. She led the way; he followed. For such a chicken she really was a pretty good climber. She jumped the last five or so feet to get herself in the right spirit. He appeared gracefully by her side.

'You ready?' she asked.

'I think so,' he said faithfully, even though he didn't know what she was talking about.

She began unbuttoning her shirt and his eyes widened slightly. She cast it off. She was wearing a pretty bra. That was nice. She saw her skin glowing in the warm evening air. She pulled off the aqua green scrubs. This was new. She slipped them off and folded them carefully. Her underpants were pink and not embarrassing.

Brian's eyes glanced off her and then back on. They were careful, surprised, hopeful. And longing. There was that, too. He was looking for permission to let his eyes stay on her. And with her eyes, she gave it.

'Now you,' she said.

He took off his own shirt and jeans in a matter of

seconds. He left them in a pile. His skin glowed just as brightly above and below the boxers that she herself had picked out for him, three pairs for nine dollars at Old Navy. She hadn't realized she'd be seeing them again in this context. She drew in a sharp little breath. She had pictured him in her mind many times before. This was better.

She held his hand again. They let their eyes run over each other unchecked. What was there to hide any more? She didn't want to hide anything.

She led him to the edge. She picked the deep end on purpose.

They stood side by side, their toes curled over the edge. She looked at him, right in his eyes and he looked in hers. This was going to be fun.

One. Two. Three.

And so they jumped together.

Bridget's body felt better. Dramatically ill, dramatically better, that was her all over.

Learning about the birth of Carmen's baby brother gave her great joy. The news came like a dash of cold, fresh water on her soul. She spent almost a week's pay sending flowers and balloons to Christina.

But, still, her heart hurt. She wanted to see Eric. She needed to see him. She craved his presence. But he was gone. Saturday he disappeared without a trace.

He wasn't in his cabin. He wasn't in the dining hall for three meals in a row. Finally she sucked it up and went to Joe. 'I seem to have lost my partner,' she said, trying to sound casual.

'You like him now, do you?' Joe said smugly.

She felt like smacking him. 'Do you know where he went?' She couldn't bring herself to say Eric's name.

'No idea,' said Joe.

She tapped her bare foot against the floor planks of the main office. 'Do you know when he'll be back?'

'He better be back by Monday,' he said. 'We've got a tournament starting.'

She hated Joe at this moment, San José Earthquakes or no. He was a guy who rode his own agenda hard, and he didn't care about yours. 'Did he say anything to you?'

'He said he had to take off for a couple days. That was it.'

Bridget stalked away angrily. She practically screamed when a chunk of the pine floor dug itself deep into her big toe. Why didn't she wear goddamn shoes? What was the matter with her?

Where had Eric gone? Why? Did he need to get away from her? What had happened between them?

That evening she tried running, but she felt weak. She couldn't eat. She called Lena, Carmen and Tibby on the common phone in the staff lounge and left messages for all of them. That made her feel panicky. Why couldn't she find them? She felt terribly alone.

She thought to call Greta, but she didn't know how to get her feelings up and over the transom. How could she explain? Eric wasn't her boyfriend. He wasn't her anything. Why did she feel like she needed him so desperately?

She sat on the dock at the lake and watched the clouds thicken. She wished it would rain hard and long and clear everything away. Rain never came when you asked for it.

She couldn't sit. She paced. She kicked a soccer ball around an empty field. The lightning in the distance wasn't the real thing. It was empty, dissipated and fake: heat lightning. It brought no rain.

As much as she prided herself on making this summer with Eric different from the one before, it was beginning to seem eerily similar.

Like before, she was laid open by a glimpse of intimacy, and when she tried to find it again, there was no one and nothing there. Eric offered, whether he meant to or not, some giant idea of love. But she only grasped it long enough to know her poverty. He pushed her to destroy herself. He made her want and then gave her no satisfaction.

Why did he do this to her? Why did she let him? How could she give herself away like this, even after she'd already learned such a bitter lesson?

She wished he hadn't found her in that feverish, vulnerable state. She wished he hadn't worried over her and taken care of her and held her all night. Having it was ecstasy, but its sudden, inexplicable loss was too painful to bear. She'd rather go through her life doubting such a thing was possible than knowing it was real and she couldn't have it.

What a pitiful waste she was. She was willing to give away, to throw away, the very best she had. For what? It was one thing to sacrifice yourself for a great cause. It was another to destroy yourself for a person who didn't even want you. It was an act of self-immolation, a sacrifice nobody wanted, that did nobody any good. What could be more tragic than that?

She thought she was independent and strong, but she got one small taste of love and she was hungrier than anyone. She was ravenous.

All the drawings had been difficult, but Lena saved the hardest for last.

She'd procrastinated. She'd gotten a manicure and pedicure with Effie. She'd spent mornings shopping and cooking for Carmen's household, wanting to help out with the new baby. She and Carmen had spent happy evenings together on the floor talking about drawing and Win and the beach, simply watching the baby breathe.

But now the time had come. Her portfolio had to be postmarked by the following day; she couldn't put it off any longer. When the house was quiet and the light was good, she pulled on the Travelling Pants and sat herself in front of the mirror in her bedroom, and got to work.

It was one thing looking at other people's troubles. It was another looking at your own. If feelings and expectations made it difficult to see a loved one's face, how blind were you to your own face?

But one surprising thing, Lena found as she looked at her face in the mirror, was that it wasn't as familiar to her as some. Yes, she had looked at herself plenty over the years. But her face wasn't as rutted in her brain as her mother's or her father's.

Lena had a funny relationship with her face. She wanted it to be beautiful, and she also didn't. She looked at it with the desire to find some overriding flaw that would kick her from one category (beautiful) into another (not). And she also looked at it with the fear that she'd succeed. Either way, she usually didn't find it.

It was like what Tolstoy said in *Anna Karenina* about all happy families being alike. Lena felt that all pretty faces were alike – straight, even, regular. It was the ugliness, the sadness that set them apart. Lena couldn't find that much objective ugliness in hers. But the sadness was apparent.

As she began to draw the outer edge of her cheek, she realized she had the look of a person who was waiting. Not impatient, not tortured, not frustrated. Just waiting. What was she waiting for?

The eight-thousand-pound elephant in the middle of her room snorted in irritation. Kostos, of course. The one who was always there while she studiously avoided him.

She was still waiting for him to come back to her, even though he wasn't going to. She was still holding out for something that wasn't going to happen. She was good at waiting. That seemed like a sad thing to be good at.

Release me, she begged, silently, of her elephant.

She needed to be free of him. She needed to get on with her life. Maybe even to fall in love again. She had a candidate in mind.

It was easy to wish to let go of the torture and the heartbreak and the missing Kostos. It seemed easy, at least. But there was a catch. To let go of the pain, she had to give up the other parts too: the feeling of being loved. The feeling of being wanted and even needed. The way Kostos looked at her and touched her. The way her name sounded when he said it. The number of times he'd written *I love you* at the end of his third to last letter. (Seventeen – once for each year of her life.) And yes, she did still read those letters. Time for a full confession: She did.

It wasn't the suffering she wilfully clung to. It was the precious stuff. But the precious stuff attached her, irrevocably, to the pain.

She waited for Kostos to come for her. She waited for him to release her. She lived quietly, passively, at the margins of other people's bigger lives: her father's, Kostos's. She took up the space they left for her.

She couldn't wait for Kostos any more. That was the thing she learned from the face she saw in the mirror and on her paper. There was one person who could release Lena, and Lena was looking right at her.

Beezy,
    Call me, would you? These are for you, and they are full strength, so wear them well. (And carefully! I had to say that, Bee. I'm worried about you.) I am here. I can be there in a flash. Call me.
        Love,
            Len

I just need your star

for a day.

– Nick Drake

Bridget didn't see Eric until late Monday morning. She felt like the universe could have exploded and cooled and spat out a few new galaxies in the time that had passed.

He didn't look at her and she didn't look at him. Or she didn't let him see her looking at him, anyway. He was an avoider, wasn't he? She hated avoiders. She hated being one. How could a person transform from her hero to her destroyer in so short a time?

The intercamp tournament began Monday. Because it was tournament week, she and Eric got off lake duty. This was the time of the summer when everybody lived and breathed only soccer. Eric and Bridget stopped needing to see each other.

By Tuesday afternoon, Bridget's team had already taken their first two games. Usually she drove her players hard, but she was fun. Now she drove them harder and she wasn't fun. She was vicious.

Eric's team had also won two of two games. As angry as she was, Bridget had to grant that Eric was probably the best of the coaches. He was patient and he was intuitive, and he already had three years of Division 1 soccer under his belt. Bridget was considered by the other staff to be talented but unpredictable and inexperienced. And she had a few real cases on her hands. Everybody agreed Eric's was the team to beat. So Bridget determined to beat them.

Maybe it wasn't the most mature way to deal with her anger. But she had a lot of dangerous energy, and it was better used in soccer than in, say, operating heavy machinery.

So she knew her team and Eric's would meet in the final on Friday. She spent every moment until then working on her line-up and her strategy. She had a few really fine players: Karl Lundgren, Aiden Cross, Russell Chen. She knew exactly what to do with them. It was a player like Naughton who required some thought. She scouted Eric's team. She scheduled surreptitious meetings of her own team by flashlight in the woods after dinner. She took them on early-morning runs. She had to hold herself back from setting a crushing pace.

Three or four times in those days that passed, Eric looked up at her and waved or tried to catch her eye. She kept her head down. She wasn't going to hope any more.

Thursday night, she found the Travelling Pants bundled up inside a Jiffy bag in her mail cubby with a note from Lena. She was in business.

Friday morning she got up at five. She was too preoccupied to sleep. She put on her team's blue jersey. She brushed her hair and wore it down. As an afterthought she applied mascara and a little blue eye shadow. The colour matched her eyes, her Pants, her mood and her jersey. Team spirit and all.

She went outside to consult her notebook in the

streams of first sunlight that crept across the ground. She was still stuck on Naughton. Everybody deserved a chance. Everybody had something to give.

In a fit of inspiration, she went to his cabin and woke him up. 'Get dressed and meet me at the south field,' she told him. He had a hopeful look about him, which she suspected related to something other than soccer. '*Naughty*. Nothing like that. I need to figure out what to do with you.' He knew he was an unconventional player. If he didn't, he should have.

When he got out on the field she ordered him into the goal. In one way, Eric had been right. Naughty's deficits made him a terrible choice for goalie. But on the other hand, there was something about him . . .

'Ready?' she called, lining up with the ball fifteen or so yards out from the goal. She kicked one straight at him, hard but not very hard. He moved away from it and fumbled the ball with his hands, allowing it into the box. His big feet weren't good and his hands were worse. She wondered why he'd stuck with soccer since first grade, as he'd proudly told her that he had.

'Let's try another one.' He threw her the ball and she stopped it neatly with her foot. She tried several more straight shots on goal. He couldn't just stand there and catch a ball coming right at him. He felt the need to move. He screwed it up almost every time.

She decided to try out her theory. She stood farther back and gave herself a little room to run. She kicked the ball hard, sent it sailing right into the top left corner of the goal. She watched in amazement and also satisfaction as his body took off in the direction of the ball. He leaped high, and with arms outstretched, he caught it. 'Wow. Nice,' she called out.

Inside she was screaming, but she didn't want to make a big deal.

She sent him several more hard, angled shots and he pulled each of them down. He couldn't tend goal when it meant just standing there. He couldn't be given any time to think, or his mind sabotaged him completely. But he could move. He had a remarkable, almost spooky sense for where the ball was going to be, and the faster it came, the farther away it was, the more impressive his ability.

On her final shots, she actually challenged herself to get one past him. Only her last and finest shot made it into the goal.

She went over to him and shook his hand. She smacked him hard on the back. 'Naughty, you have something. I don't know what it is, but it is something.'

'You look amazing,' Tibby said, sitting across from Christina at the small table in their kitchen. Christina bowed her head modestly. She peeked proudly at her baby. It would appear that she felt amazing too.

'I am lucky, is what it is,' Christina said, hiking the baby up a little in her arms. 'But Tibby, listen.' Christina cast her eyes at the closed door. 'I wanted it to be just the two of us' – she paused and glanced at the baby – 'well, the three of us – for a few minutes, because I wanted to ask you something. It's kind of serious, and you don't need to say yes and you don't even need to answer right away.'

'OK.' Tibby couldn't help feeling a little nervous. 'You aren't going to ask me to be your labour coach again, are you?'

Christina snorted so loud in her laughter that the baby startled. 'No. I promise.'

Tibby laughed too.

'Not that you weren't everything I needed,' Christina said more seriously. 'You were.' Her eyes looked perilously shiny, and Tibby felt her own eyes getting like that too.

'I wanted to ask if you would be the baby's godmother.'

Tibby's eyes widened.

'I know it sounds heavy, but it doesn't need to be. You played a special role in his life already. I want to acknowledge that. I'd love to think you would continue to share your life with him a little.'

Tibby didn't need to think. 'I'd love to.'

'Seriously?'

'Absolutely,' she said.

'Great.'

'Do I need to offer religious guidance?' Tibby asked with some trepidation.

Christina shook her head. 'No, no. Teach him film-making. Or teach him about cars. Take him to movies I won't let him see.'

Tibby nodded. She liked this idea. 'God, wait till I tell my parents,' she said joyfully. 'I'm a teenage single mother.'

Christina's laughter came out in a snort again, but the baby didn't notice this time.

308

Carmen appeared at the door. She was wearing a tangerine sundress and her skin was tanned and glossy.

'So what did she say?' Carmen demanded.

Christina beamed. 'She said yes.'

'Congratulations to all three of you,' Carmen said.

'Thanks. And where are you going, Miss Gorgeous?' Tibby asked.

'She's going out with Win.' Christina looked as happy as if it had been her own date. 'Have you met him yet?'

Tibby shook her head. 'I can't wait to. So what's he like?' she asked.

Carmen pointed to her pink, wrinkly little spud of a brother. 'Well, he's no Ryan Breckman . . .'

The championship game was a long, fierce defensive grind. By late in the second half, both teams were exhausted. It was soccer's version of the rope-a-dope. Bridget put her best and brightest on defence. She did virtually nothing on offence. Even Naughty got some playing time at centre forward. She kept Mikey Rosen in the goal. He was balanced and competent. On regular and even on good shots, he didn't mess up. And anyway, her defence was so strong and so psyched up, she didn't think his job would be all-important.

The thing was, she wasn't coaching her team for the win. Not yet. That made her strategy simpler. She was going for a tie of the 0–0 variety. Her team did not grasp exactly why this was so, but they trusted her.

'Defence,' she said to her subs. 'Defence,' she said to every player every time she opened her mouth. 'Defence!' she screamed at the top of her lungs when any ball passed centrefield. She was single-minded. '*Non passerat*,' she muttered to them. Sometimes it was easier to concentrate fully and completely on one clear objective.

She paced her sideline and Eric paced his. He saw what she was doing, but he couldn't figure out why. She liked him confused. He needed to change his strategy to fit hers, and it put his team a little off their game, just as she had hoped it would.

The final whistle passed the verdict she'd hoped for: tied at zero. Now they just had to gut it out through the overtime, to prevent the Golden Goal.

The entire camp had gathered on the sidelines by this point. They were screaming for blood. It was frustrating to watch this long without a single goal. Without even a particularly thrilling attempt on goal.

She pulled her team close around her. All eyes stayed locked on hers. As a coach, this was just what she wanted: to feel totally attached and in sync with each of her players. Her intensity was catching. She didn't need to make a big speech. She just held their eyes. 'Zero,' she said in a whisper. 'Can you do it?'

They shouted and yelled and spilled back onto the field.

Amid all the yelling and bullying from the fans, her team stayed the course throughout the extra time. No heroics. They played hard, gritty defence. They made their coach proud.

Another whistle signalled the end of the game and the beginning of the shoot-out to determine the winner.

The ref tossed the coin and Bridget's team won the

first kick. This was just how she wanted it to go. She nodded to Russell Chen. He wasn't as great an all-around player as Lundgren, but he was a sublime kicker, and having held back all game, he was ready to explode.

Her heart pounded as Eric's goalie took his position and the other team members clustered in the centre circle. The refs took their positions and Russell set up at the penalty mark. She watched the ballet of guesswork between kicker and goalie, and then Chen made his shot. Bridget's heart soared as the ball fired straight into the top of the goal. Eric's goalie guessed wrong. He didn't get a finger on it.

Her entire team and roughly half the fans erupted in cheers. Telepathically she warned them not to lose focus yet, and being in sync as they were, they seemed to receive the message.

Now Eric's team got their turn.

There was no question whom he'd choose to kick. Jerome Lewis was probably the best player in the camp. He walked out to the penalty mark.

Bridget's team watched her breathlessly. They knew she had something up her sleeve. She poked Naughton in the shoulder. 'Go get 'em,' she said.

He looked surprised, like he didn't think she actually meant it.

'Go!' she yelled.

He went. Slowly. Everybody was whispering and chattering as they watched his slow march to the goal. Even the refs looked back at her as if to say, 'Are you sure this is what you mean?' She waited until Naughton was in position before she nodded to the ref.

For once Eric was staring directly at her. He was competitive, sure, but now he looked more concerned for her sanity. His players were smiling at each other smugly in the centre circle.

Bridget put her eyes on Naughton and kept them there. He needed to know she believed in him.

According to camp rules, this was sudden death over-time. If Lewis made the shot, the shoot-out would continue to the next round. If he missed it, the game was over.

The ref blew his whistle. Usually, as the opposing coach, you hoped for the kicker to blunder it. In the strange case of Naughton, it was the opposite. *Please let this guy get a good shot off*, Bridget thought.

Lewis launched a magnificent shot. The entire camp was perfectly silent as they watched the ball stab through the air towards the goal. Naughton seemed to jump the very instant the ball left Lewis's foot. That was one thing, Bridget decided. Naughton had incredible eyes.

The ball flew, Naughton leaped, and the two came together at the very uppermost corner of the goal. Naughton pulled the ball out of the air and landed with it in his hands. He looked so surprised at his accomplishment that he stumbled and let the ball dribble from his grasp. Luckily it dribbled out of the goal rather than into it.

Stunned, the crowd burst into cheers. Bridget watched with pleasure and pride as her team rushed the goal and carried Naughton out on their shoulders. They carried him to his coach, placing him at her feet. Amid the cheering, she hugged him and planted a fat kiss on his cheek. He seemed to like that.

She graciously allowed them to dump the icy contents of the water cooler on her head. Then it was time to shake hands with their opponents. They lined up, Bridget at the back, and slapped or shook hands. The last two to come face to face were the coaches.

'You win. Of course,' Eric said gallantly, bowing to her like she was a Japanese businessman and not a girl who loved him to oblivion.

She couldn't help locking on his eyes for a moment. *I didn't, though, did I?*

'Lenny. Hey. It's Bee. I'm fine. I really am. Stop worrying right now! But I do want to talk to you. I'm ready to come home. I miss you so bad. Hey! I heard the baby's name! I love it! Was it Carmen's idea? She must have laughed for an hour. Call me . . . no, never mind. It's impossible to call me here. I'll call you. And don't worry! OK? I miss you.' *Beeeeep.*

I have

Immortal longings in

me.

– William Shakespeare

Lena thrust her portfolio at Annik. She was girding herself for a long wait, and suddenly feeling strangely impatient. But it wasn't like that. Annik put down her pencil, put on her glasses and began flipping through right away.

Not three minutes later she closed it and looked up.

'It doesn't matter if you get the scholarship,' she said.

Lena cocked her head in confusion. 'It matters to me,' she said.

'You will get it,' Annik said, almost dismissively. 'Unless the committee guys are blind or completely idiotic.' She smiled at Lena. 'The reason it doesn't matter is because you've done it. Whatever happens after is a little of this or a little of that. A little car wreck. A little dread disease. A little heartbreak. Now you are an artist.'

Annik said the word *artist* like it was the best possible thing you could say of someone. Better than being a superhero or an immortal.

'Thank you. I think.'

'It's not like it's a gift I'm giving you. You did it yourself.'

'You helped.'

'I hope so. You've done more and better than I imagined.'

316

'I'm getting there. I'm really beginning to think so.'

'You are. I can see it. I can feel it.'

Lena smiled at the thought of all the seeing and feeling that went on in this room. 'Hey, can I ask you something?'

'Sure,' Annik said.

'I've been wondering for a long time. I feel like I should probably just ask.'

Annik nodded encouragingly, almost like she knew what Lena was going to say.

'Why are you in a wheelchair?'

Annik clapped her on the back in her Incredible Hulk way. 'God, I thought you'd never ask me.'

Win was waiting outside her apartment building with the car running. Carmen had never imagined there would be a boy with whom she would want go to Target to shop for school stuff. It was yet another project they had together, more light-hearted than some.

Carmen burst through the front door to collect her shopping list and her debit card. She'd forgotten to bring them when a bunch of them had met for breakfast – Tibby, Brian, Lena, Effie and Win – at the Tastee Diner a couple of hours before.

Carmen slowed to a pause in the living room. She was struck by how different the apartment felt to her in these days since Win, since the baby. The walls felt closer in and yet the floor seemed slightly farther away. It was quiet. For once the air conditioners were mute. The tiniest hint of autumn blew in the open window. Maybe that was why the air felt new to her.

317

She was in a hurry; she had things to do. This apartment waited for her nonetheless. It always waited.

She knew that when she turned the corner of the hallway she would find her mother in her room with the baby. And there she was. She and baby Ryan were curled up in the bed.

They spent their mornings nursing and sleeping. Carmen often visited them in her free moments, kissing the baby's fists and swaddling him like a burrito before he kicked his way out again. Now Christina was sleeping, and Ryan was starting to wriggle. Carmen put her hand on his miniature back, admiring the efforts of her small brother.

She felt so different about him than she had expected. He was hers, and she ached at his fragility and his temper and the shape of his ears, already just like hers. But she also respected that he was Christina and David's.

She had expected, before he was born, that he would be part of her old world, vying for her space and all that she claimed. But he wasn't. He belonged to the new world. They both did, together.

Bridget's victory wasn't so sweet. Well, except for her players. It was sweet for them. They strode around the camp like superheroes for the rest of the week, clucking and retelling the major points of the game (there weren't many). She was happy for them. She had grown to love them.

She'd had a blessed, one-day return home to Bethesda, and seeing her friends made her feel like life made sense again. When she came back to camp, she hung out with Diana and slept and ate, building up her strength again. She knew she could withstand her injured heart, but it took work, and in some moments, a lot of faith.

She realized she wasn't completely finished with Eric. She could keep her sadness to herself and wonder for ever what had really happened. Two summers before, she had been mute. She had taken it all upon herself and let it churn and spoil inside of her. But she didn't feel like doing that any more.

She waited until the camp was mostly quiet and went searching for him in his cabin. It brought back memories of a certain other experience long ago, fetching him from his bed. That time she went in after him. This time she was prim as a pilgrim. She knocked politely and waited.

He came to the door and opened it. Did he look slightly afraid of her, or did she imagine that?

'Would you mind taking a walk with me?' she asked. She was going to say something to reassure him that she wouldn't jump him or anything, but was that really necessary? Hadn't she proven her good intentions? Hadn't they earned her anything? Or could you never live something like that down? Could a girl ever really repair her reputation in the ways that counted?

He nodded. He disappeared for a few seconds and returned wearing a T-shirt and shoes along with his shorts.

They just walked for a while. She had her hair bunched up in an elastic. She wore a beat-up football jersey over the Pants. She'd tried wearing shoes for a week, but now she was back to bare feet. She'd decided she could accept a splinter every now and then as the cost of foot freedom.

Without thinking they wandered down towards the lake and ambled onto the dock. She sat down and he sat next to her. If they had a place, this was it.

The moon was full, and bright enough to make shadows of them on the quiet water. She liked their watery selves.

'I'm just going to talk for a while and you listen. OK?' Why had she added the OK? She didn't mean to ask him for permission.

He nodded.

'I may talk about stuff you don't like,' she warned him.

He nodded again. He looked tired, she realized. Even in this frail light she could see the bluish half-circles under his eyes. He looked as though he hadn't shaved in a while.

'I thought we became friends this summer,' she said. 'I didn't know if it would be possible after what we did – I did – two summers ago, but then it happened. I was happy. I loved being your friend. I admit I may have had some other thoughts too, but they didn't matter to me nearly as much as being your friend. I was happy to be close to you on any terms.' Bridget needed to be honest tonight. That was the reason she was here.

He looked down, fiddling with the worn leather watchband around his wrist.

'I wasn't trying to be your girlfriend. I know you have one. I accept that. I didn't want to get in the way of it.

320

I am happy for you if you are happy with her. I'm not saying it wasn't hard for me, but I meant it . . . I mean, I mean it. I wanted you to trust me.'

Still looking down, he appeared to nod.

'And we spent time together and we did stuff and we had fun. At least, I had fun. And I thought you had fun.' Her voice was getting a little wobbly, but she pushed ahead. 'And then when I got sick you took care of me. You took care of me as nicely as anyone ever did in my life. Even if our whole lives pass and we don't see each other or talk to each other again, I will never forget it.' She paused so that the tears wouldn't drown her words. She wanted to keep them in her eyes if she possibly could.

'I trusted you. I thought you cared about me. Not like a girlfriend. I'm not talking about that. I trusted you to be my friend. And then you just disappeared. I couldn't figure out what happened. I felt so close to you and then you were gone. You made me believe in you and then you let me down. Is that how it is with you? Do you let people get close just so you can disappoint them?' She brushed the tears out of her eyes before they could fall.

Eric was looking up now, his eyes serious and shiny like hers. 'Bee. *No*. That's not how it is with me.'

Her chin quivered, though she wished it would not. 'Then how is it?'

He sat up a bit straighter. He studied his knuckles. He opened his hands and shut them again. 'I'm just going to talk for a while, and you listen, OK?'

'OK.'

'The reason I don't like to talk about what happened

two summers ago is because I hate myself for it. I'm not saying you didn't do your part; you did. But I could have resisted. That would have been the right thing to do. But I didn't because I wanted the same thing you wanted, and that was wrong. You think it was just you, but I wanted it just as much. You should know that.'

She could hardly move. She watched his face and listened.

'The reason I disappeared after you got sick is because I needed to go to New York and it couldn't wait. I drove up there and saw Kaya because I needed to tell her that I couldn't be with her any more.'

Bridget sucked in a little breath.

He looked sad. 'I thought I loved her. Two months ago, I told her I loved her. I couldn't let that stand. It seemed wrong.'

Bridget wanted terribly to ask him questions, but she also wanted to do her fair share of being quiet. She pressed her lips shut.

He opened his hands and put them together like he was going to pray. 'And the reason it was wrong is because I knew I couldn't really love her if I felt something so much bigger for somebody else.'

Bridget was frozen. She was scared to think through what he meant in case he didn't mean what she thought he meant.

'And the reason I've been mostly staying out of sight is because when I'm near you my thoughts don't go straight. I need to get them straightened out before I do anything else stupid.'

Bridget grabbed a look at him. Hope was filling

her chest even as she tried to push it back out.

'When I was in New York, all I wanted was to rush back to you. But what would that mean? That I dumped Kaya so I could be with you? That I was a guy who'd forget a girl he thought he loved in five hours or less?' He was shaking his head. 'And anyway, I didn't want you to feel responsible for breaking us up. I know you weren't pulling for that. All summer you were selfless enough to respect the thing with Kaya, and I wasn't. That sucks. I didn't feel like I deserved to come running back to you. I felt ashamed.'

Bridget couldn't follow all these thoughts at once. She couldn't figure out which way they led.

'There is one thing I feel sure of, and I know it is right. All these days I keep coming back to this one thing. We spent that night together, me holding you, and I felt something stronger than I ever felt for anybody else, and stronger than I even thought it was possible to feel. It blew me away. On theory alone, that made me know I couldn't be with Kaya any more.'

He shook his head again. He looked sort of disgusted with himself, but tempted to laugh too. 'I've been wanting to be rational, to believe my decision about Kaya is theoretical and not just driven by my insane, out-of-my-head attraction for you.'

'Is it,' she asked breathlessly '. . . theoretical?'

He looked at her face very closely. 'Not at all.'

You guys!
  6-½ days! Ahhhhhh! Yahhhhhhh! Wahhhhhhh!
                                           Carma

323

The letter came to Lena postmarked from Providence, Rhode Island, at almost the last moment it could have before the end-of-the-summer beach trip. Lena's heart throbbed as she opened it, but she knew it wouldn't determine her fate, even if the answer was no.

Because Annik was right. She was an artist. She would find her way no matter who said what. Her fate didn't belong to anyone else any more.

The letter didn't say no; it said yes. Lena closed her eyes and allowed the pleasure to seep through her. She was strict with herself about feeling joy, but this moment she had earned.

She went into the kitchen and literally sat on the letter, thinking about it for a long time. She would go and she could go. She didn't need her parents' money and she didn't need their permission. She thought about that, too. She didn't need it, but she wanted it. That's what she realized.

She put on a neat navy skirt and a pretty linen blouse. She brushed her hair smooth and put pearl earrings in her ears. She borrowed her mother's car to drive to her father's office.

Mrs Jeffords, her father's secretary, sent Lena in without announcing her.

Her father looked surprised to see her in the doorway. Indeed, he was so surprised, he appeared genuinely happy at the sight of her, like he'd forgotten everything that had happened in the preceding two months and returned instinctively to his old tenderness.

'Come in,' he urged, standing up.

She was still holding the letter when she sat down

across from him. 'I heard from art school about the scholarship,' she said.

'You got it,' he said evenly.

'How did you know?' she asked.

He looked placid, almost philosophical. 'Because I saw your drawings. When I saw them I knew you would get it.'

This was one of the less direct compliments she had ever received. If it even was one.

'Daddy, I don't want to upset or disappoint you. But I really do want to go. I want you and Mom to want it with me.'

He sighed. He put his elbow on his desk and rested his cheek in his palm in a boyish way. 'Lena, I'm afraid I'm the one who's upset and disappointed you.'

She didn't hurry up and nod, but she wasn't going to argue, either.

'You should go to art school. You proved it to me with those drawings just as you proved it to the scholarship people.'

She kept her expression in check. She didn't trust him yet. 'So it's OK with you, then?'

He thought about this for a while. 'I'm honoured that you're asking me when you earned the right not to have to.'

Her chest ached. 'I want to ask you,' she said. 'It matters to me what you say.'

'The answer is yes.'

'Thanks.'

She got up to go.

'Lena?'

'Yes?'

'When I began to realize, with your mother's help, the depth of my recent mistakes' – he cleared his throat – 'I felt proud of you for not going along with them.'

'You didn't make it easy,' she told him honestly.

Valia123: God help me, Rena dear, I am coming home. George has finally seen the sense in it. Effie will fly home with me in one week. Please make arrangements with Pina, if you can spare her, to air out my house?

RenaDounas: Dearest Valia, I cry as I read this. How happy we will be to have you home where you belong!

I have tried in my way

to be free.

– Leonard Cohen

'Hi, Dad.'

'Carmen? Hi, bun! How are you?'

She felt slightly sheepish, but she couldn't let this wait any longer. 'I'm fine.'

'How's the baby?'

'He's great. He kicks like a black belt.'

Albert laughed appreciatively, even though it was the baby of his ex-wife and her new husband they were talking about.

'How's your mom?' He asked it in a genuine way.

'She's great, too. She says it's all coming back to her, even eighteen years later.'

'I'm sure it is,' her dad said a little wistfully.

'So, Dad?'

'Yeah?'

'I've been thinking.'

He waited patiently, though she sort of wished he would interrupt.

'Do you think . . . um . . .' She pulled her heavy hair off of her sweaty neck. 'Do you think Williams might consider taking me back again?'

'Do you think you want to go there?'

Carmen didn't want to seem like she was making her

decisions rashly, so she didn't belt out her answer, but rather, paused. 'I do.'

'What about Maryland?'

Carmen chewed her lip. 'I was thinking I might board there, you know, get the college experience and still be close to home. But then I realized I really, *really* want to go to Williams. Do you think they'll take me back? God, I mean, what are the chances they would keep a spot?' Her voice ended squeaky and she didn't sound calm any more.

'I'll tell you what,' her dad said. 'Let me call.'

Carmen made attempts to clean her room while she waited. In truth, she did that spasmodic, surface rearranging, like putting the random AA battery into her sock drawer to get it out of sight, that would only make the job bigger when she got down to real cleaning.

Less than ten minutes later, the phone rang. She pounced at half a ring. So much for calm.

'Hi?'

'Hi.' It was her dad again.

'Did you talk to them?' she blurted out.

'I did. And Williams College says you're good to go.'

'They'll take me?'

'Yep.'

'Just like that?'

'Yep.'

'You're kidding.'

'Nope.'

'Seriously?' Carmen was afraid to let herself be happy quite so soon.

'I'm happy for you, bun,' her dad said. 'I can hear in your voice that it's really what you want.'

'It's really what I want,' she echoed.

She shook her head, feeling the nerves sizzle and zing all over her body. 'I can't believe it's that easy.'

He didn't respond. 'You better start packing,' he said instead. 'And you have fun at the beach with your friends this weekend.'

'I will. Thanks.'

After she told him she loved him and hung up the phone, she got another sneaking suspicion. Could this have been a case of parental collusion again? Maybe even deceitful parental intervention?

Had her dad ever called Williams and told them she wasn't coming? Had he ever gotten his deposit back? Was this another case of her parents knowing her better than she knew herself?

It was really annoying, in a way. But then, it was good to be loved.

Carmabelle: Will you pack the green tube top, so I can be extremely tricky and steal it the first minute you turn away?

Tibberon: Sure. But how am I going to figure out who took it?

Carmabelle: I'm excited.

Tibberon: I'm excited too.

For three long days, Bridget left Eric alone so his thoughts would go straight. And at the end of the third day, just when she thought she couldn't stand it any more, his head, thoughts and all, appeared by her bed, where she lay.

'Would you mind taking a walk with me?' he whispered.

She jumped out of bed. She followed him out of her cabin in her T-shirt and boxers. Suddenly she remembered something Carmen had said at the beginning of the summer. 'Can you wait for me for one second?'

She left him outside and went back into the cabin. She found her white halter dress from the senior party still balled up in the bottom of her duffel bag. She hadn't thought she would be wearing it. She shed her clothes and pulled the dress over her head. Luckily, the silky material didn't hold its wrinkles.

The Pants would have been her first choice, of course, but she'd had to send them back to Lena. And besides, she didn't want to be greedy. She'd already gotten what she needed from them.

'OK,' she said, reappearing beside him in the darkness. Her feet were still bare and her hair was loose.

He blinked and took a step back to get a better look at her. 'God, Bee,' he murmured. She wasn't sure what that meant, but she wasn't going to press him on it.

They walked side by side down towards the lake. She tried not to bounce on her feet, but she couldn't really help it. She was happy. Her hand collided with his briefly and it set her nerves singing. After all they had been through together, all the things they'd felt and now spoken, they didn't even know how to touch each other.

They took their usual spots at the dock. Bridget could practically see the warmth they'd left on the weathered planks from last time. She swung her legs over the water, loving the empty air under her bare toes. Their bodies made no shadows tonight; they were fully contained.

Eric pulled a little closer. His expression was wistful. 'You know what?'

'What?'

'When I saw your name on that list of coaches before the summer started, I had a premonition. I knew you were going to turn my life inside out again.' He didn't sound so sorry about it.

'If I had seen that list, I wonder if I would have come,' Bridget mused.

He let out a breath. 'Did you dislike me so much?'

'Uhhhh. Dislike?' She smiled a little. 'No. That's not the word. I was afraid of you. I didn't want to feel like that again.'

'It was hard, wasn't it?' He was sorry, she knew.

'I was a little out of control.'

'You've grown up since then.'

'Some. I like to think so.'

'You have. You are different. And also not.'

She shrugged. That sounded about right.

'I'm sorry I disappeared,' he said sorrowfully. 'I didn't mean to hurt you. I didn't know if you felt what I felt. I was worried it was just me.'

'It wasn't.'

'Now I know.'

They considered these things.

'I'm glad I didn't read the coach list. I'm glad I did come,' she said after a while.

'Me too. We had to find each other eventually.'

'Really?'

'Yeah. We were meant to be.'

She loved that idea. 'You think?'

'I do.'

'Is that what your thoughts told you? When they went straight?' she asked. Her heart was swelling inside her ribs.

He smiled, but he looked serious too. 'Yeah. It is. Maybe that doesn't sound so straight. Maybe that's not what I was expecting them to tell me. But they did. So there you go.'

'How did they know?'

'Because when I lay with you in my bed, there was a moment when I could feel everything you had been through, and I had this idea that if I could make you happy, then I would be happy, too.'

Bridget was too full to talk. She leaned her head against him. He put his arms around her, and she put hers around him. He'd said them simply, but these were words enough for a lifetime. He could make her happy. He had.

Last time they had started at the end. This time they started at the beginning. You couldn't erase the past. You couldn't even change it. But sometimes life offered you the opportunity to put it right.

Maybe tomorrow they would kiss. Maybe in the next weeks and months they would figure out how to touch each other, to translate their feelings into gestures of every kind. Someday, she hoped, they would make love.

But for now, all she wanted was this.

Following the light of

the sun, we left the Old

World.

– Christopher Columbus

The Morgans' beach house had sandy carpets. The fridge was empty but for one half-loaf of mouldy Wonder bread. The pots and pans looked as though they had been washed most recently by Joe, their almost-two-year-old.

It was also staggeringly beautiful, pitched on the sea grass in a low field of dunes set just eighty yards or so back from the Atlantic Ocean.

The first thing they did when they got there was to tear off their clothes (by previous agreement they'd all worn bathing suits under them) and run yelling and screaming straight into the ocean.

The surf was big and rough. It clubbed, tackled and upended them. It might have seemed scary, Tibby thought, except that they were all holding hands in a chain so the undertow couldn't drag them down the beach. And that, in addition to all the hollering and taunting and shrieking, made it fun.

The second thing they did was collapse on the warm sand. The afternoon sun dried their backs as they lay there, shoulder to shoulder. Tibby's heart still pounded from the thrill of the water. She had pebbles in her bathing suit. She loved the feeling of the sand under her cheek. She felt happy.

She wanted to let this happiness be her guide. She wouldn't look forward with trepidation. She wouldn't rev her brain like that.

There would be the inescapable goodbyes. The nitty-gritty ones. Like when she would watch Lena and Bee drive away to Providence in the U-Haul on Thursday. She could picture Bee laying on the horn for the first five miles away from home. Then there would be the moment on Friday when she'd kiss Carmen and watch her roll off to Massachusetts with her dad and all fifty million of her suitcases. There would be the goodbyes at the train station on Saturday morning when she and her mom would board the Metroliner for New York City. Her father would clap her on the back and Katherine's chin would tremble and Nicky would shuffle and not kiss her back. Tibby could picture it if she tried. And the goodbye to Brian. She knew that one wouldn't stick for long. Brian was supposed to go to Maryland, because it was almost free, and yet she suspected he hadn't gotten an 800 on his maths SAT for nothing. He would find his way to her. She knew he would. It was a good thing she had scored a single room.

But this moment was for the Septembers and for them alone. This was their weekend out of time. She would live in the happiness of each one of these moments, no matter how finite. Together, the Septembers could just be.

They all showered (the hot water ran out after Carmen's and before Lena's) and made a late lunch of grilled cheese sandwiches and brownies, feeling sun-tired and extra hungry, the way the ocean makes you feel.

The first cell phone rang just after lunch.

'Really? How great!' Carmen was laughing into the phone. She moved it a few inches from her mouth. 'Win saw Katherine in the kids' lounge at the hospital today,' she explained to Tibby. 'The hockey helmet is off!'

'I know. She misses it.' Tibby smiled appreciatively. She liked Win. She gave Win the big thumbs-up. But she found herself wishing that he weren't joining them just now.

The second call came from Valia. Valia apparently couldn't find the photocopy of the drawing Lena had made of her, and wanted urgently to bring it back to Greece. Valia had new life in her – and she was putting it all into packing. Valia then insisted on getting Carmen on the phone so she could tell her something about the new soap opera she had adopted, the same dumb show Carmen was always watching.

The third call was for Bee. Tibby watched Bee melt into the phone and she knew it was Eric. She could never begrudge Bee – or anyone she loved, for that matter – a voice that could give her so pure a look of happiness.

Tibby sat on the kitchen counter and considered the sheer number of voices that had joined their lives.

Then Brian called on Tibby's cell phone. He wanted to talk to her, and she wanted to talk to him – just for a few minutes, at least.

As soon as Tibby hung up, two other phones started ringing simultaneously. Lena caught Tibby's glance.

'What's going on here?' she said. 'It's like a joke.'

Tibby nodded. 'Only I can't figure out if it's funny or not.'

Dinner was a chaotic affair, what with the phones ringing and Carmen almost burning down the house when she forgot about the rice. There wasn't much peace. It was sort of wonderful in the sense that it reassured Tibby how rich and funny and interconnected her world was. It was sort of sad in the sense that she'd imagined that world would stop for this one weekend, so that they could just exist together in solitude. But the world hadn't stopped for them. If anything, it had sped up.

Hours later, midnight had come and gone and Tibby couldn't sleep. She sat on the floor of the small, sandy bedroom and couldn't help feeling a little bleak. It wasn't that their night hadn't been fun; it had been. After the kitchen fire was brought under control, they decided to abandon the stove altogether and had milkshakes and peanut butter fudge for dinner instead. They ate so much of it they had all lain groaning and exhausted on the living-room floor.

There were so many things to talk about, so many new people to process, so much future bearing down on them, they had barely gotten started. They had listened to music and fallen into sugar-induced slumber and crawled off to their various bedrooms.

Tonight, for the first time, the world had felt too big to contain and digest within their small circle of friendship. Was this the way the future was going to go?

They were growing up. It was inevitable, and Tibby

had learned enough this summer not to stand in its way. There were boyfriends and families and big plans burning just ahead of them.

But please, God, she couldn't do it if it was a trade-in. She couldn't strike the bargain if growing up meant drowning out the friendship that stood at the very centre of her life, the thing that gave her strength and balance.

Darkness closed her in the house and the black waves beat against the shore for all to hear. All of a sudden Tibby felt claustrophobic. Perhaps for the first time in memory, she felt more afraid of a small, confining space than the big, infinite one. Without thinking, she tiptoed out of the bedroom, down the stairs and out into the air.

Tibby felt like she was walking into a dream, a happy dream, when she saw the three distant silhouettes sitting on the sand. She laughed at the sight of those three familiar heads. It was like a dream too, in that she knew more than she really could know. She knew what they were feeling; she knew it was the same thing she was feeling, and in that knowledge she felt the strength of their connection.

As in a dream, it seemed as though they were waiting for her, even though they had no practical reason to know she would come. When Tibby got close enough, Bee reached up for her hand and pulled her down into their little cluster.

'Hi.' Tibby's voice was quiet, but almost giddy.

'This is where the cool kids go,' Bee said, laughing.

Lena shrugged. 'I guess nobody could sleep.'

'We have too much stuff to talk about,' Carmen mused.

A wave washed close to their feet. This didn't give anybody the idea to move.

They tightened their circle, and Carmen set the Pants in the middle, making a circle of their summer as well.

Tibby breathed out, finding inexpressible comfort in her friends' faces. Before her eyes, this night had transformed into a gift of reassurance. This was the future. Life would get busier and more varied, populated both by beautiful things and unfortunate circumstances. If their friendship demanded exclusivity or solitude, it couldn't work. If it required that everything go as planned, it would turn brittle, and ultimately it would break. On the other hand, she knew that if they could be flexible and big, if they could encompass change, then they would make it.

Tibby remembered her dream about taxidermy and understood in a new way the beauty of the Pants. The Pants could move along with them.

'Whatever happens,' Bridget said, 'we will find each other. We always will.'

I'm going back to the

start.

– Coldplay

EPILOGUE

For our last hour at the beach, we exchanged gifts instead of saying goodbye. We didn't plan it that way, exactly. It just kind of fell into place, like us all finding each other on the beach in the middle of the night. We each wanted a few things we could hold onto.

The sun streamed pink and orange behind our heads, and the ocean churned dark. The sand felt softer in the sweet light. The air was warm and comforting.

I can't tell you all that was said and what was felt. I just can't. But I'll tell you what happened and you can imagine it. You'll do better with your imagination than I could with my words.

Carmen got to go first, because she is the least patient. Not about getting, about giving. 'For the walls of our dorm rooms,' she announced, handing them out.

Carmen had found four long, vertical frames and pasted three photographs into each of them. The first photo, on the top, was the one of our mothers, as young, happening, late-eighties moms sitting on a wall, arms around each other's shoulders, wearing jeans. The photo was familiar to us now. A little speckled. A little old. A little heartbreaking to remember Marly, as it always was. The next photo, in the middle, was also old, one I barely remembered ever seeing. It was the four of us as toddlers, our faces peeking over a couch. We looked like a miniature girl band. Carmen looked like the singer. I, small and confused, looked like the one who plugged the instruments into the amplifiers. It made me laugh. The bottom photo was from graduation, the four of us in the same order, the same faces, the same expressions.

The crying started for each of us around then. It was inevitable. It was like that feeling of being outside in a rainfall without a raincoat or umbrella. You fight getting wet for a while and then you just surrender to it and you realize it feels pretty nice. You wonder, why do we fight the things we fight when giving in to them isn't so bad at all?

Bee went next. She passed out tiny jewellery boxes. We pulled the tops off all at once.

On four delicate silver chains dangled four tiny, identical charms. Of pants. They were tiny silver charms in the shape of pants, just like our Pants. Now they *were* our Pants, in a new and different way.

Bee explained how Greta first spotted one in a jewellery kiosk in the middle of the mall in Huntsville, Alabama. And how she and Greta made a joint project of hounding the jeweller, Mr Bosely, until he came up with three more.

We all put them on each other, fiddling with clasps, holding up hair. I pressed the tiny charm flat against my sternum, knowing it would live there now. We couldn't look at each other except in little bits. It was hard to feel so much.

Lena handed hers out next. She had even wrapped them. We tore the paper off with different degrees of care: I folded the wrapping paper for future use, Bee tore at hers savagely and sat on the crumpled paper so it wouldn't blow down the beach.

Lena had made four nearly identical drawings and framed them, one for each. She'd drawn the Travelling Pants twice, front and back. But she'd drawn them upside down and side by side so that together they formed a big W. Next to it Lena added the letter e. The picture said *We*.

I went last. I handed out video cassettes with specially decorated labels. 'We have to go inside for this,' I said.

I had already made sure the Morgans' VCR was in working order. So once we'd scrambled up the beach and into the house, it didn't take me long to get the movie fired up.

It was short. Just ten minutes. Most of it was stuff from my own parents' collection, but I'd managed to get stuff from Tina and Ari too. I'd even given the two of them and my mom a little preview a few nights before in our den, though I made them keep it a secret. The three of them wept while I crowded up all close to the TV and pretended not to. The three moms hugged afterwards. That made me feel happy.

The first part was on old-fashioned Super 8 film, atmospheric and a little jerky, showing us crawling around in Lena's backyard. Well, Lena was timid about crawling, so we mostly nudged and rolled her. I was a stringy baby, bald and purposeless. Bee's hair looked like white feathers adorning her head. She was a fast

346

crawler. Her mother had to pull her away from the side of the pool. Bee's brother, Perry, made a brief appearance. He didn't move much, but he did find a bug in the grass. Carmen had perfect brown ringlets, giant eyes and a very loud voice with which to coax inert baby Lena.

By the time we were two, some parent or other had sprung for a real video camera. The next part showed the four of us girls lined up on four plastic potties. Lena sat patiently, her elbow on her knee, her chin in her palm. I was tiny and seemed to be falling into mine. Carmen was trying to yank a Mary Jane off her foot. Bee finished first. 'I'm done!' She stood up and shouted at someone off camera.

The next bits were fast takes, a catalogue of joint birthday parties, bad haircuts and complex orthodontia. Siblings, parents, grandparents and other relatives filtered through in various fashion mishaps.

The last one was a long shot, taken when we were about seven. I didn't even understand the significance of it when I'd picked it out and smoothed it into the end of the movie.

It was taken at Rehoboth Beach, probably within a mile of this very place. The camera showed the four of us holding hands in the rough surf, jumping waves, shouting and screaming.

It was just like now. Exactly as we had done the afternoon before and early that morning. As I looked at the screen I could feel the cold, salty water covering my hands, linked with Bee's on one side and Lena's on the other. I could hear Carmen's shrieks of joy in my ear.

Different times we lined up in a different order. It didn't matter the order.

The image stayed on the screen and we all watched it, even when it went still.

Back then was exactly the same as now. To brave the undertow, we had learned to hold hands.

THE SISTERHOOD OF THE TRAVELLING PANTS
Ann Brashares

Four best friends, one pair of jeans and a few important rules:

- You must never wash the Pants
- You must never double-cuff the Pants. It's tacky. There will never be a time when this will not be tacky.
- You must never say the word 'phat' while wearing the Pants. You must also never think 'I am fat' while wearing the Pants.
- You must not pick your nose while wearing the Pants. You may, however, scratch casually at your nostril while really kind of picking.
- You must write to your Sisters throughout the summer, no matter how much fun you are having without them.

Quirky, original and heart-warming, *The Sisterhood of the Travelling Pants* is an irresistible celebration of female friendship and self-discovery.

'An outstanding and vivid book that will stay with readers for a long time' *Publishers Weekly*

0 552 54827 8

CORGI BOOKS

THE SECOND SUMMER OF THE SISTERHOOD
Ann Brashares

'This is it,' Carmen breathed. The moment was all around them. She remembered the vow from last summer. They all remembered it.

'To honour the Pants and the Sisterhood
And this moment and this summer and the rest of our lives
Together and apart.'

Spend a long, lush summer with four best friends as they share secrets – and swap a pair of truly magical jeans.

A *New York Times* bestseller – the sequel to
The Sisterhood of the Travelling Pants

0 552 55050 7

CORGI BOOKS

MY DESPERATE LOVE DIARY
Liz Rettig

There's G. Isn't he gorgeous? I think he just looked at me – well, he looked in my direction anyway. Do you think he'd ask me out if I dyed my hair and got breast implants? *Kelly Ann*

I think you need BRAIN implants, Kelly Ann, then maybe you'd see what a complete idiot G is.
Stephanie

Stephanie's right. OK, G's not ugly but he's SO up himself! You'd be much better off with Chris. He's gorgeous and crazy about you, if only you'd open your eyes . . . *Liz*

Don't be stupid! Chris is a good friend but that's it. I'd rather snog my brother (if I had one). Now be serious, how do I get G to notice me? A blonde wig and a Wonderbra? *Kelly Ann*

Navigating her way through teenage embarrassments, sick-filled parties, awful love poetry and green condoms, Kelly Ann is a hilariously endearing character. *My Desperate Love Diary* is Liz Rettig's debut novel.

0 552 55332 8

CORGI BOOKS

HOPE WAS HERE
Joan Bauer

Life's never been a bowl of cherries for Hope but at least with her Aunt Addie around, the food's been good.

Addie and Hope have worked in diners from New York City to Atlanta. Now they're getting ready to transform the tastebuds of Mulhoney, Wisconsin. Butter pecan pie is sure to be a hit but someone in Mulhoney is cooking up something a lot less whole-some. Can Hope find the antidote to the poison at the heart of their small town? It's a tall order, but then again that's her speciality!

When Hope gets released in a place, all kinds of things are possible.

'Hope is as full of optimism as her name and there are lots of fabulous descriptions of food. Heartwarming' *Observer*

'This is a thought-provoking, beautifully written novel' *Waterstone's Books Quarterly*

'Once you pick it up you won't be able to put it down until you get to the end' *Mizz*

0 552 54972 X

CORGI BOOKS